PRAISE FOR JAMES PATTERSON'S ALEX CROSS THRILLERS

HOPE TO DIE

"Action aplenty sends Alex Cross on to the finish, and James Patterson has done it again with his fantastic storytelling gifts. Readers will note that this is very close in action and eeriness to some of the best of the best in the series including *Along Came a Spider* and *Kiss the Girls*..." —*Suspense Magazine*

"HOPE TO DIE is full of surprising revelations, twists and turns, as well as heart-stopping suspense and sharp-edged violence. There is something for nearly everyone here. Those who haven't picked up an Alex Cross book for a while by all means should read *Cross My Heart* and HOPE TO DIE, both of which demonstrate that Patterson, notwithstanding his prolific ways, retains the ability to surprise, excite and scare the heck out of you." —BookReporter.com

CROSS MY HEART

"Twenty years ago, I wrote, '*Along Came a Spider* is the best thriller I've come across in many a year. It deserves to be this season's #1 bestseller and should instantly make James Patterson a household name.' A household name, indeed. CONGRATULATIONS, JIM, ON TWENTY YEARS OF ALEX CROSS AND ON *CROSS MY HEART*, WHICH I AM LOVING. YOU THE MAN." —Nelson DeMille

"TWENTY YEARS AFTER THE FIRST ALEX CROSS STORY, HE HAS BECOME ONE OF THE GREATEST FICTIONAL DETECTIVES OF ALL TIME, A CHARACTER FOR THE AGES. *Cross My Heart* has got to be the most terrifying and shocking Cross thriller to date, full of unexpected twists, savage turns, and electrifying suspense. This is the page-turner to end all page-turners."

—Douglas Preston & Lincoln Child

"PATTERSON HAS NEVER SHIED AWAY FROM MAKING DRAMATIC CHANGES IN CROSS'S LIFE, AND FOR THIS TWENTIETH ANNIVERSARY BOOK, HE PULLS OUT ALL THE STOPS EVEN MORE SO THAN USUAL." —BookReporter.com

"*CROSS MY HEART* IS ONE OF THE BEST BOOKS OF THE SERIES BECAUSE IT IS NAIL-BITING SUSPENSE WITH A SURPRISE TWIST OF AN ENDING… will leave readers wanting more." —WestOrlandoNews.com

MERRY CHRISTMAS, ALEX CROSS

"*MERRY CHRISTMAS, ALEX CROSS* MAY HAVE A HOLIDAY BACKDROP, BUT IT IS A THRILLER NOVEL FOR ALL SEASONS…ONE OF PATTERSON'S BEST BOOKS TO DATE." —BookReporter.com

"JAMMED-PACKED WITH ACTION…WE SEE ALEX BEING PULLED IN ALL DIRECTIONS."

—AlwayswithaBook.blogspot.com

"FANS WILL BE ENTHRALLED." —BookLoons.com

"HIS BRUTAL DESCRIPTION IS SPOT ON AND I CAN HONESTLY SAY HE REALLY MOVED ME IN ONE SCENE...A GREAT ADDITION TO THE SERIES."

—RitualoftheStones.blogspot.com

ALEX CROSS, RUN

"THE MAN IS A MASTER OF THE THRILLER. HE KNOWS HOW TO SELL, WRITE SUSPENSE, AND PLOT HIS TALES WITH PRECISION...*ALEX CROSS, RUN* IS PATTERSON AT THE TOP OF HIS GAME...A HELL OF A READ BY A MASTER STORYTELLER."

—Breitbart.com

"A SHOCKER...PATTERSON SHOWS NO SIGN OF SLOWING DOWN AND GIVES EVERY INDICATION THAT HE HAS NOWHERE NEAR EXHAUSTED HIS SUPPLY OF IDEAS OR, MORE IMPORTANT, UNFORGETTABLE CHARACTERS."

—BookReporter.com

"ENTERTAINING AND EASY TO READ."

—ReadersRefuge.blogspot.com

KILL ALEX CROSS

"A THRILLER WITH FAMILY AT ITS HEART...IT'S PATTERSON AT THE TOP OF HIS GAME."

—Lisa Scottoline, *Washington Post*

"A ROLLER COASTER…CLASSIC PATTERSON."

—*Washington Times*

"NON-STOP ACTION…EXCITING…The ending is a typically great, surprising Patterson ending that you'll want to read more than once to make sure you really got it."

—AlwayswithaBook.blogspot.com

"PATTERSON'S NARRATIVE STYLE PROPELS READERS THROUGH THE BOOK LIKE A LOCOMOTIVE THROUGH TISSUE PAPER…PATTERSON SHOWS NO SIGNS OF SLOWING DOWN ON ANY FRONT."

—BookReporter.com

CROSS FIRE

"FAST-PACED…THE TWISTS AND TURNS WILL KEEP YOU GUESSING WHAT WILL HAPPEN NEXT AND YOU'LL NEVER BELIEVE HOW IT ALL ENDS…another great and addicting tale of murder and mayhem—Alex Cross style! I was hard-pressed to put it down!"

—BibliophilicBookBlog.com

"YOU DON'T WANT TO MISS THIS LIFE-CHANGING BOOK…WILL LEAVE YOU TURNING PAGE AFTER PAGE WITH ENDLESS SUSPENSE."

—BeyondtheBookshelf.com

I, ALEX CROSS

"THE STAKES ARE HIGHER THAN EVER BEFORE… MORE THAN A CRIME THRILLER, IT'S AN ABSORBING FAMILY DRAMA." —NightsandWeekends.com

"A RAW, ENGROSSING THRILLER THAT WILL KEEP YOU CHURNING PAGES LONG INTO THE NIGHT."

—FictionAddict.com

ALEX CROSS'S TRIAL

"A LITTLE BIT OF ATTICUS FROM *TO KILL A MOCKINGBIRD* AND A LOT OF JAMES PATTERSON HEADING IN A NEW DIRECTION."

—TheReviewBroads.com

"A COMPELLING AND UNFORGETTABLE NOVEL…A POWERFUL DRAMA AND A GRIPPING THRILLER—AND THE STORY THAT IT TELLS IS AN IMPORTANT ONE." —NightsandWeekends.com

CROSS COUNTRY

"THE MOST HEART-STOPPING, SPEED-CHARGED, ELECTRIFYING ALEX CROSS THRILLER YET."

—FantasticFiction.com

"INTENSE, SUSPENSEFUL, EMOTIONALLY CHARGED."

—BestsellersWorld.com

DOUBLE CROSS

"THE SUSPENSE, CHILLS, AND THRILLS ARE THERE, AND AN ENDING WHICH I NEVER SAW COMING. ANOTHER GREAT OUTING FROM PATTERSON, AND ONE THAT I SIMPLY LOVED. HIGHLY RECOMMENDED." —NewMysteryReader.com

"EXHILARATING AND INTENSE…FANS WILL BE THRILLED." —NightsandWeekends.com

"VINTAGE PATTERSON…IT IS FAST MOVING AND SUSPENSEFUL AND TAKES THE OCCASIONAL SURPRISE TWIST…Life for a Patterson fan doesn't get much better than this." —1340MagBooks.com

CROSS

"THE STORY WHIPS BY WITH INCREDIBLE SPEED."

—*Booklist*

"ANOTHER GREAT ONE FROM JAMES PATTERSON. HOLD ON TO YOUR SEAT!" —ArmchairInterviews.com

"SMART AND STRAIGHTFORWARD, IT BUILDS INTEREST AND MOMENTUM IN SHORT, TIGHT CHAPTERS THAT CAPTIVATE, CREATING AN ADDICTIVE READ." —TheMysterySite.com

MARY, MARY

"THE THRILLS IN PATTERSON'S LATEST LEAD TO A TRULY UNEXPECTED, ELECTRIFYING CLIMAX."

—*Booklist*

"*MARY, MARY* FLOWS EFFORTLESSLY AND WITH MOUNTING SUSPENSE TO ITS FINAL, SHOCKING TWIST; A FASCINATING PSYCHO WILL CAPTIVATE THE AUTHOR'S MANY FANS." —*Library Journal*

"PATTERSON'S HYPNOTIC THREE-OR-FOUR-PAGES-TO-A-CHAPTER PACE WILL KEEP YOU UP READING FAR INTO THE NIGHT...A GREAT PLOT TWIST." —*Fort Worth Star-Telegram*

LONDON BRIDGES

"EXCITING...A FULL PACKAGE OF SUSPENSE, EMOTION, AND CHARACTERIZATION...THIS THRILLER WORKS SO WELL...ANY THRILLER WRITER, WANNABE OR ACTUAL, WOULD DO WELL TO STUDY [*LONDON BRIDGES*]." —*Publishers Weekly*

"AS WITH THE BEST OF PATTERSON'S WORK, IT IS IMPOSSIBLE TO STOP READING THIS BOOK ONCE STARTED." —BookReporter.com

THE BIG BAD WOLF

"THE BIGGEST, BADDEST ALEX CROSS NOVEL IN YEARS."
—*Library Journal*

"VASTLY ENTERTAINING... THE FINEST CROSS IN YEARS."
—*Publishers Weekly* (starred review)

"POWERFUL... YOUR HEART WILL RACE."
—*Orlando Sentinel*

FOUR BLIND MICE

"THE PACE IS RAPID... ACTION-PACKED." —*People*

"CHILLING." —*New York Times*

"BRISK... SATISFYING." —*San Francisco Chronicle*

VIOLETS ARE BLUE

"PARTICULARLY JUICY... ENJOYABLY SPOOKY... BOTTOM LINE: BLOODY GOOD CREEPFEST."
—*People*

"AS ADDICTIVE AS ALL OF PATTERSON'S BOOKS... YOU HAVE NO CHOICE: YOU MUST READ IT."
—*Denver Rocky Mountain News*

ROSES ARE RED

"THRILLING…SWIFT…A PAGE-TURNER." —*People*

"THERE ARE NO FASTER READS THAN PATTERSON'S ALEX CROSS BOOKS. I CAN'T WAIT FOR THE NEXT ONE." —*Denver Rocky Mountain News*

POP GOES THE WEASEL

"Fast and furious…In the Patterson pantheon of villains, Shafer is quite possibly the worst." —*Chicago Tribune*

"PATTERSON DOES IT AGAIN. THE MAN IS THE MASTER OF THIS GENRE. We fans all have one wish for him: Write even faster." —Larry King, *USA Today*

CAT & MOUSE

"THE PROTOTYPE THRILLER FOR TODAY."

—*San Diego Union-Tribune*

"A RIDE ON A ROLLER COASTER WHOSE BRAKES HAVE GONE OUT." —*Chicago Tribune*

JACK & JILL

"FORTUNATELY, PATTERSON HAS BROUGHT BACK HOMICIDE DETECTIVE ALEX CROSS…He's the kind of multilayered character that makes any plot twist seem believable." —*People*

"CROSS IS ONE OF THE BEST AND MOST LIKABLE CHARACTERS IN THE MODERN THRILLER GENRE."

—*San Francisco Examiner*

KISS THE GIRLS

"TOUGH TO PUT DOWN... TICKS LIKE A TIME BOMB, ALWAYS FULL OF THREAT AND TENSION."

—*Los Angeles Times*

"AS GOOD AS A THRILLER CAN GET."

—*San Francisco Examiner*

ALONG CAME A SPIDER

"James Patterson does everything but stick our finger in a light socket to give us a buzz." —*New York Times*

"When it comes to constructing a harrowing plot, author James Patterson can turn a screw all right... James Patterson is to suspense what Danielle Steel is to romance."

—*New York Daily News*

HOPE TO DIE

ALSO BY JAMES PATTERSON

FEATURING ALEX CROSS

Cross My Heart

Alex Cross, Run

Merry Christmas, Alex Cross

Kill Alex Cross

Cross Fire

I, Alex Cross

Alex Cross's Trial (with Richard DiLallo)

Cross Country

Double Cross

Cross (also published as *Alex Cross*)

Mary, Mary

London Bridges

The Big Bad Wolf

Four Blind Mice

Violets Are Blue

Roses Are Red

Pop Goes the Weasel

Cat & Mouse

Jack & Jill

Kiss the Girls

Along Came a Spider

A complete list of books by James Patterson is at the back of this book. For previews of upcoming books and information about the author, visit JamesPatterson.com or find him on Facebook or at your app store.

HOPE TO DIE

JAMES PATTERSON

GRAND CENTRAL PUBLISHING
NEW YORK BOSTON

This book is a work of fiction. Names, characters, places, and incidents are the product of the author's imagination or are used fictitiously. Any resemblance to actual events, locales, or persons, living or dead, is coincidental.

Grand Central Publishing
Hachette Book Group
1290 Avenue of the Americas
New York, NY 10104

www.HachetteBookGroup.com

Printed in the United States of America

LSC-C

Originally published in hardcover by Hachette Book Group.

First trade edition: May 2015

10 9 8 7 6 5 4

LCCN 2014940686

ISBN 978-1-4555-1582-0 (pbk.)

For the courageous men and women of the
Palm Beach Police Department

HOPE TO DIE

Part One

CHAPTER 1

WHEN MARCUS SUNDAY ARRIVED at Whodunit Books in Philadelphia around seven that evening, the manager told him not to expect much of a crowd. It was the Tuesday after Easter, lots of people were still away on vacation, and it was raining.

But Sunday and the manager were pleasantly surprised when twenty-five people showed up to hear him read and discuss his controversial true-crime book *The Perfect Criminal.*

The manager introduced him, saying, "Marcus Sunday, who has a doctorate in philosophy from Harvard, has hit bestseller lists around the country with this book, a fascinating look at two unsolved mass-murder cases explained by a truly original mind focused on the depths of the criminal soul."

The crowd clapped, and Sunday, a tall, sturdy man who looked to be in his late thirties, stepped to the lectern wearing a black leather jacket, jeans, and a crisp white shirt.

"I appreciate you coming out on a rainy night," he said. "And it's a pleasure to be here at Whodunit Books."

Then he talked about the killings.

Seven years earlier, two nights before Christmas, the five members of the Daley family of suburban Omaha had been slain in their home. Except for the wife, they were all found in their beds. Their throats had been cut with a scalpel or razor. The wife had died similarly, but in the bathroom, and naked. Either the doors had been unlocked, or the killer had had a key. There had been a snowstorm during the night, and any tracks were buried.

Fourteen months later, in the aftermath of a violent thunderstorm, the Monahan family of suburban Fort Worth was discovered in a similar state: A father and four children under the age of thirteen were found in their beds with their throats slit; the wife, also with her throat slit, was found naked on the bathroom floor. Once more, either the doors had been unlocked or the killer had had a key. Again, owing to the storm and the killer's meticulous methods, the police found no usable evidence.

"I became interested because of that lack of evidence, that void," Sunday informed his rapt audience.

Sunday said that the dearth of evidence had confused him at first. He talked to all the investigators working the case, but they were equally baffled. Then his academic training took over, and he began to theorize about the philosophical worldview of such a perfect killer.

"I came to the conclusion that he had to be an existentialist of some twisted sort," he said. "Someone who thinks life is meaningless, absurd, without value. Someone who does not believe in God or laws or any other kind of moral or ethical basis to life."

Sunday went on in this vein for some time, reading from

the book and explaining how the evidence surrounding the murder scenes supported his controversial theories and led to others. The killer's disbelief in concepts like good and evil, for example, "perfected" him as a criminal, made it impossible for him to feel guilty, which was what allowed him to commit such heinous acts with dispassionate precision.

A man raised his hand. "You sound like you admire the killer, sir."

Sunday shook his head. "I tried to describe his worldview accurately and let readers draw their own conclusions."

A woman with dirty-blond hair, more handsome than beautiful, raised her hand, revealing a sleeve tattoo that depicted a panther in a colorful jungle setting.

"I've read your book," she said in a southern accent. "I liked it."

"That's a relief," Sunday said.

Several people in the audience chuckled.

The woman smiled, said, "Can you talk a little about your theory of the perfect criminal's opposite, the perfect detective?"

Sunday hesitated, and then said, "I speculated that the only way the perfect killer would ever get caught was by a detective who was his direct antithesis—someone who believed absolutely in God, someone who was emblematic of the moral, ethical universe and of a meaningful life. The problem is that the perfect detective does not exist, and cannot exist."

"Why is that?" she asked.

"Because detectives are human, not monsters like the perfect killer," he said, seeing some confusion in the audience.

Sunday smiled, said, "Let me put it this way. Can you imagine a real cold-blooded, calculating mass or serial murderer suddenly turning noble, doing the right thing, saving the day?"

Most of the audience shook their heads.

"Exactly," he went on. "The perfect killer is who he is. An animal like that doesn't change."

Sunday paused for effect.

"But how hard is it to imagine a noble detective brought low by the horrors of his job? How hard is it to imagine him abandoning God? How hard is it to imagine him so beaten down by events that he finds life meaningless, valueless, and hopeless to the point that he becomes an existential monster and a perfect killer himself? That's not hard at all to imagine, now, is it?"

CHAPTER 2

AFTER SIGNING TWO DOZEN books, Sunday politely turned down the bookstore manager's offer to take him to dinner, saying that he had a previous engagement with an old friend. The rain had stopped by the time he left the store and started down the sidewalk.

He crossed Twentieth Street and was walking past a Dunkin' Donuts when the woman with the panther tattoo fell in step beside him and said, "That went well."

"Always helps to have the mysterious Acadia Le Duc in the audience."

Acadia laughed, put her arm through his, and asked, "Shall we get something to eat before we drive back to DC?"

"I want to see it leave first," he replied.

"It's fine," she said in a reassuring tone. "I watched you seal it myself. We're good for sixty—no, make that about fifty-eight hours now. Almost seventy hours, if we had to push it."

"I know," he said. "Just call me obsessive."

"All right." Acadia sighed. "And then we're doing Thai food."

"I promise," Sunday said.

They went to a late-model Dodge Durango parked two blocks away, and Sunday drove through the city until they were abreast of the empty Eagles stadium on Darien Street. He turned left into the vast lot at Monti Wholesale Foods opposite the stadium and parked at the far end, up against the iron fence, where they could look beneath the Delaware Expressway and across into the South Philadelphia rail yard.

Sunday picked up a pair of binoculars and found what he was looking for about a hundred yards in: a line of freight cars, and one in particular, a forty-five-foot rust-red container, the top of which was fitted front to back with solar panels. A reefer—a refrigeration and heating unit—stuck out of the front of the container. He lowered the binoculars, checked his watch, and said, "It should be rolling out of here in another fifteen minutes."

Bored, Acadia slouched in her seat, said, "So when is Mulch going to contact Cross?"

"Dr. Alex will get a message loud and clear on Friday morning," he said. "It will be a week. He'll be ready."

"We have to be in St. Louis by five p.m. on Friday at the absolute latest," she said.

Sunday felt irritated. Acadia was the smartest, most unpredictable woman he'd ever known. But she had an annoying habit of constantly reminding him about things of which he was well aware.

Before he could tell her just that, he caught a flash of movement in the rail yard. He raised the binoculars again and saw a young black guy dressed in dark clothing slinking along the freight cars. He was wearing gloves and carrying a small knapsack and a crowbar. He stopped and looked up at the solar panels.

"Shit," Sunday said, watching the man.

"What?"

"Looks like…shit!"

"What?" Acadia said again.

"Some asshole's trying to break into our car," he said.

"No way," she said, sitting forward to peer into the shadows of the rail yard. "How would he—"

"He wouldn't," Sunday said. "It's random, or he saw the solar panels."

"What are we going to do?"

"Only thing we can do," he replied.

Sixty seconds later, Sunday and Acadia were over the fence. They split up beneath the overpass and hurried in opposite directions, both keeping low behind an earthen berm that ran next to the nearest set of tracks. Sunday carried a tire iron and was seventy yards past the rust-red container car before he stopped. The rail yard was lit, not as well as it was to the north, but he'd be visible until he reached the shadows along the freight train.

He had no choice. Sunday clambered over the berm and angled out into the yard, dancing across the tracks, aware of Acadia doing the same to the north, trying not to make noise until he reached the shadows where he'd seen the black guy slinking. The container with the solar panels was six cars ahead. He stood there until he felt his phone buzz, alerting him to a text.

Sunday started forward quickly, keeping his steps light until he was alongside the rust-red car. Hearing metal scraping metal, the sound of the crowbar working that lock, he slowed to a creep and then stopped at the corner.

He waited until he felt his cell phone buzz again, and he gripped the tire iron like a hammer.

"Just what do you think you're doing there, mister?" Acadia said.

She was on the opposite side of the train.

"Fuck, bitch" was all the thief got to say before Sunday sprang around and spotted him up on the turnbuckle, facing Acadia and menacing her with the crowbar.

Sunday's tire iron smashed into the man's knee. He grunted in pain, fell off on Acadia's side. Sunday vaulted up and over the buckle and was on the man before he could do a thing to defend himself.

He aimed for the guy's head this time and connected with a thud that put the thief out cold. The third blow was more considered and caved in his skull.

Breathing hard, Sunday looked at Acadia, whose eyes blazed and whose nostrils flared with the sexual excitement she always displayed after a killing.

"Marcus," she said. "I'm suddenly—"

"Later," he said firmly and pointed to the adjacent line of freight cars ten feet away. "Help me get him underneath that train. If we're lucky, he won't be found till morning. Maybe later."

They grabbed the dead guy under the armpits, dragged him and pushed him over and in between the rails, and put him facedown beneath the line of railcars.

A sudden squealing noise startled them both.

The freight train, including the container car with the solar panels, was moving out, heading west.

CHAPTER 3

"CARTER BILLINGS WAS AMAZING!" Ali yelled in the twilight. "His first at bat!"

My seven-year-old ran up the stairs ahead of us onto the front porch of our house and adopted a funny, exaggerated batting pose while holding the little souvenir bat I had bought him earlier in the day. He waved the bat and swung wildly.

He made a cracking noise and did a decent imitation of Billings's hilarious and passionate run around the bases after the rookie got a pinch-hit, walk-off, grand-slam home run in his very first trip to the plate, winning the opening game for the Nationals.

I had gotten tickets to the game through an old friend, and we'd all seen that miraculous moment along with Ali—my wife, Bree; my older son, Damon; my daughter, Jannie; and my ninety-something grandmother, Nana Mama. As Ali wound down his victory run, we all clapped and crowded through the front door of our home on Fifth in Southeast Washington, DC.

It had been construction time at the Cross household the past few weeks; we were remodeling the kitchen and adding a great room and a new master bedroom suite upstairs. When we left for the game, the project was exactly as the construction crew had left it on Good Friday—exterior walls framed and up, windows in, and the roof on, an empty, dusty shell separated from the main house by plastic sheeting.

But when Nana Mama left the front hallway and looked deeper into our house, she stopped in her tracks and screamed, "Alex!"

I rushed forward, expecting some domestic catastrophe, but my grandmother was beaming with joy. She said, "How did you ever manage it?"

I looked over her shoulder and saw that the addition and the kitchen remodel were done— as in, completely done. The cabinets were up. The Italian tile floor was in. So was the fire-engine-red six-burner industrial stove and the matching fridge and the dishwasher. I could see, beyond the kitchen, that the great room had been filled with new furniture; it looked like some gauzy picture in the Pottery Barn catalog.

"How is this possible, Alex?" Bree asked.

I was as shocked as the rest of my family. It was as if a genie in a lamp had given us a hundred wishes, and they'd all come true. The kids ran through the kitchen and into the great room to test out the couches and the overstuffed chairs while Nana Mama and Bree admired the black granite countertops, stainless-steel sinks, and pewter light fixtures.

My attention, however, was drawn to a piece of legal-size paper that magnets held horizontally to the refrigerator door. At first, I figured it was a letter from our contractors saying they hoped we were pleased with the finished product.

But then I saw that the paper showed copies of five photographs laid side by side. The images were difficult to make out until I stepped right up and took them all in with one slow, horrifying scan.

In each picture there was a member of my family lying on a cement floor, head haloed with blood, blank face and eyes twisted dully toward the camera. Above each left ear and slightly back, there was a wound, an ugly one, the kind that only a close-range shot creates.

Somewhere in the distance, a siren began to wail.

"No!" I screamed.

But when I spun around to assure myself the pictures weren't real, my children, my wife, and my grandmother were gone. Vanished into thin air. All that was left of them were those sickening photographs on the refrigerator.

I am alone, I thought.

Alone.

Pain knifed through my head. Terrified that I was going to have a stroke or a heart attack, I sank to my knees, bowed my head, and raised my hands toward heaven.

"Why, Mulch?" I screamed. "Why?"

CHAPTER 4

I JERKED AWAKE IN the predawn light, felt the dull pounding in my head again. At first I had no idea where I was, but gradually I came to recognize my bedroom in shadows. I was in bed, still dressed for work and soaked through with sweat. Instinctively, I reached over to feel for my wife's sleeping form.

Bree wasn't there, and in one gut-wrenching instant, I knew that I had woken once more into a reality worse than any nightmare.

My wife was gone. They were all gone.

And a madman named Thierry Mulch had them.

Determined not to succumb to his insanity, I rolled over in bed and pressed my face into my wife's pillow, trying to find Bree's smell. I needed it to keep me strong, to renew my faith and hope. I caught a trace of her but desperately wanted more. I got up, went to her closet, and, strange as it sounds, buried my face in her clothes.

For several minutes, Bree's perfect scent intoxicated my

brain so thoroughly that my headache was gone and she was right there with me, this beautiful, smart, laughing woman who danced just beyond the outstretched fingers of my memory. But the sensation of having her there with me ebbed away all too fast, and the smells in her closet changed, some threatening to go stale and others sour.

That petrified me.

Was it the same in the other bedrooms? Were their smells fading too?

Sickened and fearful at what I might find, I had to force myself to open Ali's door. Holding my breath, I went quickly inside and shut the door behind me. I didn't turn on the light, wanting to deaden one sense to heighten another.

When at last I inhaled, Alex Jr.'s little-boy smell was everywhere, and I could suddenly hear his voice and feel how good it was to hold my son, remember how he loved to nestle in my arms when he was tired.

I went to Jannie's room next. The air there left me puzzled and then upset. I guess I had gone in longing for the smells of years gone past. But Jannie was finishing up her freshman year in high school and was already a track star. For a long while I stood there in her pitch-dark bedroom, overwhelmed by the understanding that my little girl had become a woman and then vanished along with everyone else in my family.

I stood outside Nana Mama's room, and my hands shook when I reached for the doorknob and twisted it. Stepping in, closing the door behind me, I breathed in her lilac air. Surrounded by dozens of vivid memories, I felt claustrophobic and had to get out of there fast.

I went out and shut her door behind me, sure that I'd find better air up in my attic office, where I could think more clearly. But as I started to climb the stairs, it dawned on me that one devastating odor was already gone.

Damon, my seventeen-year-old, my firstborn, had been away at prep school in Massachusetts the past two months. The idea that I might never smell Damon again shattered whatever resolve I still possessed.

As I flashed on those photographs that haunted my dreams, wondering if they were enactments of things to come, my headache turned excruciating. Maddened, I charged up the stairs into my office and stuck my face right in front of a camera hidden between two books on homicide investigations.

"Why, Mulch?" I yelled. "What did I ever do to deserve this? What the hell do you want from me? Tell me! What the hell do you want from me?"

But there was no response, just that little lens staring back at me. I grabbed the lens, tore it free of the transmitter, and crushed it under my heel.

Fuck Mulch, or Elliot, or whatever he called himself. I didn't care that I'd just showed him we knew about the bugs. Fuck him.

Panting, wiping the sweat off my forehead, I decided to destroy all the bugs in the house before their presence destroyed me.

Then a dog started barking across the street, and someone began to pound on my front door.

CHAPTER

5

I OPENED MY DOOR to find a short, fit, and attractive brunette in her midthirties looking like she wanted to be anywhere but on my front porch as she held out her detective's badge.

"Dr. Cross," she said. "I'm Tess Aaliyah. I'm with Metro Homicide."

"You are?" I asked, because I'd never met her before.

"Came on board last week from Baltimore PD Homicide, sir," Detective Aaliyah replied. "While you were solving the massage-parlor murders and the baby kidnappings."

For a moment I was puzzled, didn't know what she was referring to, but then, like a window opening a crack, it came back to me. Even though those cases felt like they'd enveloped me a lifetime ago, not a week, I nodded, said, "No partner, Detective…uh…"

"Aaliyah," she said, cocking her head to study me. "Chris Daniels is my partner, but he evidently shattered his ankle this morning lifting weights."

I winced, nodded, said, "Daniels is a good guy."

"Seems that way so far," she agreed. She swallowed and looked at the porch boards.

"How can I help you, Detective?"

Aaliyah let out a short, sharp breath before looking me in the eye. "Sir, there was a body found down the street a few blocks, at a construction site. Female African American. She's been badly mutilated, and I'm sorry, Dr. Cross, but your wife's badge and ID are there as well. Is your wife here?"

I almost collapsed right there, but I grabbed the doorjamb and choked out, "She's missing."

"Missing?" the detective said. "Since…"

"Just take me there," I said. "I need to see this for myself."

It was a two-minute ride, which I spent in a near catatonic state. Aaliyah kept asking me questions, and I kept saying, "I need to see her."

There were patrol cars ahead, and yellow tape, familiar things in my life, but I got no solace from them. I have entered murder scenes too many times to count, but I have never been as frightened of what I was about to see as I was that morning, walking next to Aaliyah, past a patrolman and through a gate in a chain-link fence that blocked off the construction site.

"She's in the bottom, sir," Aaliyah said.

I walked to the edge and looked down into the hole dug for the foundation.

Crushed stone and rebar filled the bottom of the excavation, ready for cement. A woman of Bree's height, build, and hairstyle lay on her right side, her back to me. Streams of dried blood caked her skin from scores of oval wounds to her entire dorsal side. She was wearing the same bra and panties Bree had been wearing on Good Friday. And that was Bree's watch.

I staggered a step closer to the edge, felt bolts of lightning go off in my head, and thought for certain I was going to fall in there with her. But Detective Aaliyah grabbed hold of my elbow.

"Is it her, Dr. Cross?" she asked. "Bree Stone?"

I stared at her dumbly, then said, "I have to go down."

We went to a ladder, and how I climbed down it, I'll never know. Every step broke my heart. Every handhold was my last.

I stepped through the crisscrossed rebar and around the front, seeing that the earrings were definitely the same ones I'd given Bree on our anniversary.

An alien moan came up out of my gut.

Taking another step, I saw that her face had been beaten beyond recognition, and that the wounding pattern had continued down the front of her body, as if someone had used garden clippers to snip off ovals of her skin every five or ten inches of her entire body, right out to the engagement ring I'd given her and her wedding band, right out to bloody stumps where the tips of her fingers should have been. Her mouth was open, and her teeth were missing.

"Oh, dear Jesus," I whispered in shock, sinking to my knees in front of her. "What has that sick bastard Mulch done to you?"

CHAPTER 6

"IS IT YOUR WIFE, DR. CROSS?" Detective Aaliyah asked.

I stared at the desecrated body lying there before me, saw the hair, the skin color, the height, the weight, the jewelry, and said, "I don't know. I think so, but I don't know for certain. She's…she's unrecognizable like this."

"Where were you last night?" she asked.

Scanning the body for something, anything, that said definitively whether it was Bree or not, I replied, "I was home, Detective, watching reruns of *The Walking Dead*."

"Sir?"

"The television show about the zombie apocalypse," I said. "My boy Ali loves it."

"And he was there with you?"

I shook my head again, felt tears trickle from my eyes, and said, "He's gone too. They're all gone. My entire family. Haven't they told you? John Sampson? Captain Quintus? The FBI?"

"FBI?" she said. "No, I caught this on my way to work, but why don't we get out of here, let forensics do their job, and you tell me what I need to know."

I knelt there for several more moments, staring at the body and seeing images of my life with Bree playing in the air, making it all surreal and soul killing.

"Dr. Cross?"

I nodded, got wobblingly to my feet, and managed to climb back up the ladder without incident. We went to her unmarked car and got in.

"Let's hear it," she said in a calm, professional manner.

Over the next thirty-five minutes, I laid out the insanity of the past few weeks for her, trying not to leave out any important details.

"I first learned of Thierry Mulch when he started sending me strange, taunting letters about the massage-parlor murders, calling me an idiot and proposing theories about those killings that, I admit, proved invaluable in ultimately catching the man responsible. Then a man named Thierry Mulch who claimed to be a website entrepreneur went to my son Ali's school and gave a talk there.

"I did a Google search on the name. It turned out there were only seven Thierry Mulches that I could find on the web. And one of them *was* an Internet entrepreneur. Because I was chest-deep in the investigation of the mass killings at the massage parlor, I didn't give the coincidence much thought beyond that.

"But it turned out Mulch had been giving me and my family a lot of thought," I told the detective. "He bugged our house with audio and video. I think he used them to learn our habits and routines, because in a matter of hours last Friday,

Good Friday, he managed to kidnap them all, including my son Damon, who goes to school up in the Berkshires in Massachusetts."

"How come I haven't heard a word of this?" she asked. "And how do you know Mulch took them?"

"Give me a chance to explain."

Aaliyah nodded, and I told her how Mulch used my daughter's cell phone the night of Good Friday to send me pictures of my family, tied up, duct tape across their mouths. He also sent texts threatening to kill them all if I got the police or FBI involved. Late the next afternoon, John Sampson, my best friend and partner at Metro, came to my door, concerned that I hadn't reported to work or at least called in to explain why I was out.

"I got John to leave and did not tell him a thing, but Mulch didn't care," I said, digging in my pocket for my phone. "I began getting these pictures every hour on the hour."

I handed her the phone, told her to call up Photos. She did, and I saw the horror on her face as she looked at the pictures on the tiny screen showing each and every member of my family dead of a gunshot wound to the head.

"Are they real?" she asked.

"No," I said. "But I didn't know that then."

I told Aaliyah how I disintegrated after seeing the pictures. I walked the streets of Washington like a zombie, praying someone would blow my head off. In the end, I went into a meth house with a wad of cash and told the addicts I wanted to die, that I'd pay them to kill me. Someone obligingly tried, hitting me with a piece of metal pipe.

A girl who once lived with us, a recovering addict named Ava, found me and brought me home. I told Ava about the pictures just before I passed out from the concussion I'd sustained.

"Ava is very bright, and excellent with computers," I said. "While I slept, she transferred the pictures to a laptop and blew them up enough to see they were doctored."

Ava took that information to Sampson and to Ned Mahoney, my former partner in the Behavioral Sciences division of the FBI. Ava convinced them that my family was not dead.

Sampson and Mahoney found a way to sneak into my house without being detected by Mulch's bugs. It turned out that there'd been a rape in Alexandria, Virginia, committed by a man who called himself Thierry Mulch. DNA evidence gathered at that crime scene had been matched to the DNA of a brilliant but erratic computer engineering student at George Mason University who'd disappeared about two weeks before.

"His name was Preston Elliot, and given the sophistication of the electronics Mulch put in my house, we believed and still believe that Elliot and Mulch are one and the same. We left the bugs in my house and decided that I would continue acting as if I thought everyone in my family was dead in order to convince Mulch/Elliot that I was completely devastated—a victim, and no threat.

"We also decided to keep everything about the hunt for my family quiet," I said. "Days went by, and now a week. And we hadn't heard a thing from him. Until this."

Expressionless, Detective Aaliyah mulled over everything I had told her for several minutes. Finally she said, "You think Mulch, uh, Elliot is responsible for your…for the Jane Doe's death?"

"He *is* responsible," I said. "There's no question."

Aaliyah thought for several beats, and then asked, "What does he gain from doing all this to you and your family?"

"I've stopped asking," I replied. "But whatever sicko obsessive reason he's got for targeting me, on my end, it feels like torture, like he's trying to drive me to the brink again and again, hoping that sooner or later I'll jump off."

She cocked her head and asked, "Will you?"

"If that is Bree in that hole, honestly, I don't know."

CHAPTER

7

ON THE WHOLE, MARCUS SUNDAY was pleased with the way things were proceeding. There'd been a few deviations from the original plan, but he still felt right on target.

Sunday was riding in the front passenger seat of the Durango, raptly focused on the screen of a laptop computer and the video feed transmitting from a tiny camera, hidden weeks before, high up in a tree that overlooked the construction site.

He'd seen it all, how Cross fell to his knees in front of the body and stayed there for a very long time, looking crushed.

"The end is near," he said to Acadia, who was in the backseat. "Did you see the way he was begging right into the camera in his office before the cop banged on his door? Begging's a classic indicator. Isn't it, Mitch?"

The driver, a hulk of a man in jeans, hiking boots, and a Boston Red Sox jersey, nodded, said, "It is, Marcus."

Acadia wasn't buying it. "How would you know?"

Mitch Cochran had no neck to speak of. His massive head

seemed to her like an extension of his shoulders as he glanced back and said, "Before I said fuck it all, I was in Iraq. U.S. fucking Army. Guarded Abu Ghraib prison. I saw interrogations. It's like Marcus said, they beg before they crack. All of them."

Acadia remained unhappy. "But how long can we wait for that to happen?"

"It won't be long now," Sunday assured her. "Mulch has killed Cross's wife, and the rest of his family remains under mortal threat."

"How long?" she demanded.

Sunday grew irritated, growled, "You can't put a firm timetable on a project of this magnitude, Acadia. Haven't I told you again and again that the construction of a monster begins with the destruction of a man?"

"You've said a lot of things," Acadia shot back. "Like that Cross would crumble the night we sent those pictures."

"Cross was in pieces," he snapped. "He still is and it's growing worse. Didn't you just see that with your own eyes? He's disintegrating."

Acadia was silent for several long moments before saying, "More I think about it, sending those photographs was a mistake."

"A mistake?" Sunday replied, clearly annoyed.

Acadia said, "You went for the short-term shock value of having Cross see his entire family murdered with gunshot wounds to the head. But you were also giving away leverage. You did the same thing by dumping her there. A dead person can't be helped, Marcus. A dead person can't be saved. There's less motivation now for him to become the perfect killer you want him to be."

"Your understanding of the animal condition is shallow at times, Acadia," Sunday sniffed. "This is all timing."

"What's that supposed to mean?" she said, crossing her arms.

"Ever watch a dog trainer at work?" he asked. "I mean a real trainer, someone who teaches hunting or attack dogs?"

"My shithead of a daddy ran coonhounds."

"Then you know what the predator-prey response is?"

"I can guess," she said. "Critter runs in the woods, a dog chases it. Tries to kill it. It's in its nature."

"There you go," Sunday said, snapping his fingers at her. "And the way trainers build that predator-prey response is by taking something away from the dog, something that the dog values highly, like a bone or a toy. They let Bowser go for days thinking his favorite bone or toy is gone for good. Then they show it to him attached to a rope. When that dog goes to chase his toy, the trainer jerks it just out of reach—all the time, just out of reach. Isn't that right, Mitch?"

Cochran downshifted and slowed, saying, "The dog goes fucking crazy, doing anything in his power to have that toy again. That's when the trainer steps in and takes total control of the situation, uses the toy as a reward for a job well done."

He glanced at Acadia. "And how do I know *that?* We had fucking dogs at Abu Ghraib. Lots of 'em."

Cochran took a right turn onto a muddy road a few miles south of Frostburg, in rural northwestern Maryland. They passed a ramshackle farm, and Sunday heard the echoes of pigs squealing in his mind. The road wound up into an oak forest clad in new lime-green leaves.

A mile into the woods, Sunday started looking at the trees closely, and then he said, "That's it. Those birches on the right. Park over there."

CHAPTER

8

COCHRAN PULLED THE DURANGO almost to the drainage ditch next to three birches that grew close together, almost as if they were shoots of the same tree.

"We've got ten minutes still," Sunday said, and he turned his attention to the laptop again. But Cross was nowhere to be seen around the construction site.

"You can't go in early?" Acadia asked, sounding irked. "I told you seventy-two hours is the limit of how far we can push things. That window's closing fast."

Sunday checked his watch. "We're at sixty-seven hours. We'll make it."

"I gotta go number two," Cochran said.

"What are you, in kindergarten?" Acadia snapped.

"Maybe *that's* my problem, I'm too fucking childlike." Cochran laughed, got out of the car, and walked off.

Sunday looked off through the windshield in silence, and then said, "That farm we passed brought back memories. Mulch grew up in a hellhole like that."

"The fabled origins?" Acadia asked.

"Whence Mulch sprang. And where Mulch died."

"Ever been back?"

"Not even close," Sunday said, checking his watch. "I think I'm good to go now."

"Sure you don't want one of us along?" Acadia asked.

Sunday shook his head and said, "It took me a long time to find this guy and gain his trust. I don't want to spook him in any way, especially not now, when he's proven so resourceful."

"Don't forget the honey," Acadia said, and she handed Sunday a small gym bag with a Nike swoosh on it.

"I'm not back in fifteen, you and Cochran come looking, but slow, right?"

"Armed?"

"Definitely."

Sunday got out, smelling the rot of spring everywhere around him. It had started to sprinkle. He decided he liked the light rain. Hitting the new leaves on the trees, it would soften all other sound and give him a chance to check out the scene before he fully committed.

Sunday slid down the bank, then found and followed an overgrown logging trail, mindful to keep the bag raised so the brambles and thorns would not tear it. Soon he smelled wood smoke and slowed to a creep. He approached a ledge that overlooked a clearing and, beyond it, a swollen creek.

To his right and below, hard by the creek bank, there was a plywood-and-tarpaper shack. Smoke curled from a stovepipe that jutted from the roof. An old blue Chevy pickup with a capper sat between the shack and a barn of sorts.

Sunday noticed the sheet across the window that faced in his direction was fluttering, and he knew he'd been spotted. So he held up the bag and climbed over the ledge and down into the yard. A door creaked open. A big male Rottweiler came bounding out toward him.

Sunday stopped and stayed perfectly still, his eyes watching the dark space beyond the door as the dog growled low and circled him, taking his wind. When the dog barked, the door opened wider, and Sunday crossed to the shack. He climbed the stoop, passing a chain saw and a gas can, and went inside.

"That necessary every time?" Sunday asked the muscular bald guy crossing the dim space to a crude kitchen. His name was Claude Harrow.

"Every time," Harrow replied. "Puts a man's mind at ease, 'specially now that you and I done crossed a dark line together."

The dog came in behind him. Sunday shut the door and stood there until his eyes adjusted and he could make out the Formica table, lawn chairs, busted couch, and woodstove in the corner. The walls were bare except for a large Confederate flag and a framed eight-by-ten photograph of Adolf Hitler in full salute. The dog went to the stove and lay down by the stove, head up, watching Sunday.

"Looked like it all went according to plan," Sunday said, smelling bleach and seeing a washtub close to him on the floor. Two butcher knives and a pair of tin snips were soaking in three inches of chlorine and water.

"Well, what'd you expect? Amateur hour?" Harrow replied, and he turned to him, revealing a thin, nasty scar on his right cheek and a tattoo of a flaming sword on the side of his neck.

Sunday noticed a mirror on the table and saw the traces of white lines on it. He frowned. "Thought we agreed no tweaking during the game."

"We said during, not after," Harrow replied. "Don't worry. It's just a pick-me-up. I been up all night and had the jitters by the time I got back here."

Sunday debated whether to press the point, decided not to, and held out the gym bag, saying, "Balance on the first is there, plus a down payment on number two."

Harrow motioned for him to put it on the table, asked, "How soon?"

"Tonight. The older boy."

Sunday could tell Harrow didn't like that.

"That kind of short notice and tight turnaround is gonna cost you," Harrow said.

"How much?"

"To pull it off clean like that? Hundred K more on the back end."

Sunday didn't like renegotiations. "Quite a jump in pay."

"Hell of a risk I'm taking. Cops involved, right?"

"I think you'd do it even if I weren't paying you a small fortune," Sunday said, setting the bag down.

"I might," Harrow agreed, smiling for the first time. "Cops aside, I do enjoy and appreciate the cleaning work."

"You'll let me know when it's done?"

"Man's gotta get paid, don't he? You want coffee?"

"Sorry, I have to catch a plane, be in St. Louis by five, no ifs, ands, or buts," Sunday said, heading toward the door.

"And if you aren't?"

"Bad stuff happens."

CHAPTER

9

JOHN SAMPSON ARRIVED AS I watched the body bag being brought up out of the hole.

Built like a power forward in the NBA, he looked as weak as a kitten when he came to me with tears welling in his eyes. John and I have been brothers in all but genetics since we were ten years old. When the big man threw his arms around me, it was everything I could do not to dissolve right then and there.

"Jesus Christ, Alex," Sampson said hoarsely. "I came as soon as I heard. Is it true? Is it—"

"I think so, but I don't know for certain, and I won't until tomorrow at least—and that may be the worst part," I said in a dull voice as they put the body bag on a stretcher and wheeled it over to the medical examiner's van.

I kept trying to think of the body in the bag as being someone other than Bree. But Mulch, he—

"You want me to take you home?" Sampson asked.

"No," I said. "Home's not a good place for me. Mulch

watches me there, enjoys my suffering, and I won't contribute to his enjoyment anymore. I just need to go for a walk and get my head straight."

"Want company?" he asked.

"I'll see you later at work."

"Sugar, you can't work when something like—"

"John, I *have to* work when something like this is going on," I said firmly. "It's the only way I'll stay sane."

Sampson looked like he wanted to tell me something, but Detective Aaliyah came over, said, "Dr. Cross, I have—"

"John, this is Tess Aaliyah," I said. "She's new, from Baltimore, and she caught this case and needs to be brought up to speed on what the secret task force has found out about Mulch."

"Secret task force?" Aaliyah said.

"Exactly," I said, and walked off, trying to convince myself that that wasn't my wife's body in the back of that coroner's wagon.

But grief and loss have a way of crippling the best intentions even in the strongest of minds.

Within a block of leaving the crime scene I was lost in memories of my first days with Bree, how she'd rescued me from a long loneliness with an unshakable love, the kind I'd thought I'd lost forever. Then the likelihood that she was gone hit me like a freight train and I began to choke and sob right there on the sidewalk.

Every woman I'd ever loved had ended up dead or so traumatized by the violence woven through my life that she couldn't bear the sight of me. My first wife, Maria, died in a drive-by shooting when Damon was a toddler and Jannie was just a baby. A madman took Ali's mother hostage, and even though we managed to rescue her, it permanently fractured our relationship. And now Bree, the absolute love of my life, might have been swallowed up by the darkness that had shadowed me without pause almost since the moment I became a police officer.

What about my kids? What about my grandmother? Were they completely doomed to follow my loves into the shadows and the darkness? And what about me?

Was I already there? I asked myself as I walked on, wiping tears from my eyes. Had I ever left? Could I ever leave?

On autopilot, I took a route I'd taken a thousand times with my children. Every morning, or as often as was possible, I'd walked them to their school, Sojourner Truth. I did it for years, and as I retraced those steps, I was soon drowning in memories of Damon, Jannie, and Ali as each headed to the first day of first grade.

Damon had gone willingly, eagerly. It was all he and his friends had talked about. But Jannie and Alex Jr. had been nervous.

"What if I get a bad teacher?" Jannie asked.

Ali had asked the same thing, and in my mind, suddenly Jannie and Ali were right there, together, both six, and both looking at me for a response. I squatted down to them and pulled them in close to me, rejoicing in their smell and their innocence.

"There isn't anything I wouldn't do for you," I said. "And I love you. That's all you need to know."

"Love you more," Jannie said.

"Love you more," Ali said.

"Love you more and more," I whispered. "Love you—"

A woman said, "Dr. Cross?"

CHAPTER 10

STARTLED OUT OF THAT perfect vision of my life before Thierry Mulch, I was shocked to find myself at the fence around the Sojourner Truth playground. It was deserted. I thought I heard the school bell sound for recess. But where was the laughter of my children?

"Dr. Cross?"

Blinking, I turned my head to see a tall, pretty African American woman in a blue pantsuit standing beside me on the sidewalk, her face painted in concern.

"Yes," I said, almost recognizing her, feeling irritated and not quite knowing why.

She looked at me closely, said, "You don't look well."

"I'm just…where are the kids? The bell rang. It's recess time."

"It's Easter vacation," she said.

I looked at her like she was a stranger in a dream.

"Dr. Cross," she said. "Do you know who I am?"

I did suddenly and felt myself grow irrationally angry. "You're Dawson. The principal. You're the one who let Mulch in. Where have you been? We've been trying to find you."

My expression and tone must have frightened her, because she took a step back. "I'm sorry. I was on vacation, I don't—"

"Thierry Mulch," I shouted. "You let that sick fuck into Ali's school. You let him near all those children!"

"What?" she said, her hand going to her lips. "What's he done?"

"He kidnapped my family," I said. "He may have killed my wife. He may be getting ready to kill Ali."

The principal was horrified. "My God, no!"

I saw how strongly she reacted, and it shook me out of the fugue state where I'd been wandering.

"We left messages for you all week here at the school," I said. "The FBI. The police."

"I'm so sorry," Dawson said, her voice quivering. "I was in Jamaica, visiting my cousins, and I only just got back. I was going to my office to get ready for next week when I saw you standing here. How can I help? Anything."

"Tell me about Thierry Mulch. Everything you know."

Dawson said that Mulch had contacted her out of the blue, first by e-mail, and then by phone. He said he was a web entrepreneur who had had several successful ventures but was looking for a different demographic and a bigger audience. His idea was to create a social-media platform for the six- to twelve-year-old crowd that could be accessed only by verified members of that crowd.

"To keep out the perverts?"

"That's right."

"Not a bad business concept."

"That's what I thought. So when he asked to come speak to the kids, I saw it as an opportunity. And he checked out completely. I mean, his company has a legitimate website. Here, come into my office, I'll show you."

We went to the front doors of the school. She opened them and we went inside, turning on lights. The odors in the hallway were so familiar and so intertwined with memories of my children that I stopped breathing through my nose.

In her office, Dawson got on her desktop computer, typed, and then frowned before typing again. With a sinking expression, she said, "Either I've got it wrong or the website's gone offline."

The principal started rummaging in her desk, said, "But I've got his business card here some—here it is!"

"Don't touch it!" I yelled, coming around the desk quickly as she shrank back. "I'm sorry. It's just that we'll want to fingerprint it."

In a thin voice, she said, "He wore thin white gloves."

"Of course he did," I said, wanting to punch a wall. "But just the same. Do you have a plastic sandwich bag?"

"Will an envelope do?"

"Yes."

She got me an envelope and I used a pair of tweezers to pluck the business card from the drawer and place it on her desk.

"I've got a photocopy of his driver's license too," she said.

"We've already got one of those, but thanks," I replied, studying the card and then taking a picture of it with my smartphone.

Thierry Mulch, President, TMI Entertainment, Beverly Hills. It gave a phone number in the 213 area code and an address on Wilshire Boulevard. It also had a web address—www.TMIE1.info—and an e-mail address, TMulch@TMIE1.info.

I was about to drop the card into the envelope and take it with me downtown for processing when something about the URL and the e-mail pinged deep in my recent memory.

"Try www.TMIE.com on your computer."

Principal Dawson frowned, typed the URL in, and struck Return. The screen blinked, and up came the home page of TMI Enterprises, a multimedia and social-networking company.

"This is it," she said. "This is his website."

"Click on 'Corporate Officers.'"

She did and the screen jumped to another page that featured pictures and short bios of the people running the company. At the top of the heap was someone I'd seen when I'd visited the website two weeks before: a blond surfer-type guy in his late twenties wearing thick black glasses and a black hoodie.

"That's not the picture of Mulch I saw on the other version of the website," Dawson said. "I saw the guy who came here, red hair, red beard, everything."

"Will the real Thierry Mulch please stand up?" I said, and I felt the throbbing in my head start up all over again.

CHAPTER

11

MY HEAD WAS STILL pounding when I reached the sealed-off construction area on the third floor of Metro headquarters. Men in hard hats and respirator masks were using sledgehammers to bust down drywall. The air was full of gypsum dust as I went to the plastic sheeting that sealed off the destructing from the already destructed.

I started to cough and that only made the pain in my head worse. A part of me wanted to shut down then, to curl up in a fetal position right there in the dust and let it settle on me as I mourned my wife. But a greater part of me needed to keep pushing on. If I was to have any hope of saving the rest of my family, I had to keep moving, keep asking questions, keep fighting as long and as hard as possible.

I tore open the flap and stepped inside a large space already stripped down to the cement floors. In the middle, under a bank of fluorescent shop lights, stood eight desks. At them or around them, good men and women were working.

Ned Mahoney, my old partner at the FBI, was talking with Sampson. Mahoney spotted me and jumped up. "Jesus, Alex, I just heard. And I'm so goddamn…I don't know what to say except I promise you, we're moving heaven and earth to find this bastard."

I swallowed hard, patted him on the shoulder. Mahoney and I had worked together in Behavioral Sciences at Quantico. We'd toiled on too many cases involving the criminally insane to bullshit each other with psychological nuances and false premises.

"Ned," I managed. "If we don't catch him, he'll carve them all up in the same twisted way."

"That's not happening," said Captain Roelof Antonius Quintus, my boss, who was coming toward me with other members of the task force. "If that Jane Doe turns out to be Bree, he's killed a DC cop. At the very least, he's kidnapped a DC cop's family. For that, he *will* pay."

The rest of the detectives and FBI agents behind him nodded grimly.

"Thank you, Captain," I said, nodding to the others. "Thank you all for everything you're doing."

I got out the envelope I'd taken from Dawson's office.

"I went to Sojourner Truth and found the principal back from vacation," I told them. "I have a business card Mulch gave her when he went there to speak to the kids."

I handed it over to the captain, explaining about the fake website that was almost like the one a real Thierry Mulch ran.

"Everything was the same except the picture of Mulch. It took sophisticated computer work. The kind Preston Elliot could do in his sleep."

Quintus, Sampson, and Mahoney exchanged glances.

"Why don't you sit down, Alex," the captain said.

"What's going on?"

Quintus took a deep breath and pointed to a chair. Reluctantly, I sat in it, and I felt my eyes begin to burn even before Ned Mahoney spoke.

"Three days ago, the Fairfax County sheriff was called to a commercial pig farm in Berryville, Virginia," Mahoney began. "The owner found a human skull and a piece of femur in some machinery. Quantico ran the DNA and got three immediate matches."

I squinted at the light in the room, which suddenly felt too strong. "Three?"

Sampson said, "Semen taken from that rape scene in Alexandria, semen taken from the pants leg of Mandy Bell Lee's murdered attorney, and the hair sample Preston Elliot's mother filed as part of his missing-persons report."

It took several moments before I grasped the implications of all that. Ten days before, the attorney of country-western star Mandy Bell Lee had been found poisoned in his room at the Mandarin Oriental. That same night, a man who called himself Thierry Mulch had raped a woman in Alexandria.

Since we had clear DNA evidence linking the rape and the murder to Preston Elliot, we had been working under the assumption that the missing computer engineering student and Mulch were one and the same.

But Mulch was not Elliot. He could not be Elliot because the DNA match on the bones found at the pigsty was dead certain, which meant…

"Mulch killed Elliot and dumped his body in that pig barn," I said.

"We think so," Sampson said, nodding. "Pigs'll eat anything you throw at them."

I remembered something Ali had told me about Mulch.

"It fits. When Mulch spoke at Ali's school, he said that he'd grown up on a pig farm."

"So how do we think this worked?" Captain Quintus asked. "Mulch got Elliot's sperm before he killed him?"

"Why not?" Sampson replied. "It's a brilliant way for Mulch to throw us, isn't it? Plant a dead man's DNA at a rape scene and at a murder?"

"This sonofabitch is diabolical," Mahoney said.

"You're right," I said. "Mulch is diabolical. He's very smart, thinks long term, and is cruel and audacious, which strikes me as narcissistically evil."

Captain Quintus nodded. "Believes in himself above all others, thinks he's too smart to get caught."

"Which means he's gotten away with serious shit before," Sampson said. "It's mutually reinforcing with these guys."

Mahoney said, "What I'd like to know is, is Mulch acting solo, or are there others involved in what he's doing?"

CHAPTER

12

COULD MULCH HAVE KIDNAPPED my entire family in less than ten hours, starting with Damon at his prep school in the Berkshires, on his own?

On Good Friday morning, Damon was supposed to have taken a 7:45 jitney from campus to the Albany train station, but according to the driver, at the last minute, Damon told a friend that he was canceling because he'd gotten a ride to Washington.

But with whom? Mulch? Or someone else?

We hadn't been able to answer those questions because the Kraft School, like Sojourner Truth, had been closed for vacation.

In any case, I knew from personal experience that the drive from the Kraft School to DC takes at least seven hours, and Good Friday traffic had to have been thick. So let's say eight hours. That put Mulch in Washington around four.

Bree, Ali, Jannie, and Nana Mama were all taken in the following two hours. Theoretically, then, it *was* possible that

Mulch had done this alone. But if so, he'd acted with what felt like pinpoint and ruthless precision.

"My instincts say he had help," I said. "The sperm found at the rape and the murder scene supports that too."

"How's that?" Mahoney asked.

"Unless Elliot was a homosexual, it makes sense to me that Mulch had a female accomplice. She lured the kid in for sex, saved his sperm, probably from a condom, and Mulch killed him afterward."

"It fits," Quintus said.

It did fit. As if a fog bank were lifting, we were beginning to get a clearer view of the world behind us, a world I would have given my soul to return to.

I said, "Can someone go back to George Mason, back to Elliot's friends, ask them about any women he might have been seeing?"

"I'll do it myself," Mahoney promised.

I looked at Sampson. "Feel like driving?"

"Where we going?"

"That farm where they found Elliot's bones."

"Uh," Captain Quintus began, sharing a glance with Mahoney. "You sure you want to be working now, Alex?"

My breath turned shallow. "I can't just sit here and wait for more members of my family to show up dead, Cap. I refuse to. That's what Mulch wants and I just won't do it."

"Alex," Mahoney said. "Maybe—"

I glared at my old friend, said, "If I don't work, Ned, I'll be lost to Bree, and I won't be lost to her. Not now."

Mahoney nodded slowly and then gestured at Sampson and said, "But you're driving, John. With that head injury, he's still in no condition to be behind the wheel."

CHAPTER 13

IT TOOK SAMPSON AND me about an hour to get free of DC traffic and take blue highways out through Reston and McLean and on into the rural land you find the more west and south you go in Virginia. We rode most of the way in silence, but Sampson's pity and grief were as clear as if he'd spoken words of condolence or shock.

Sampson's mere presence, the living, breathing embodiment of my longest relationship in life other than Nana Mama, was the only reason I didn't completely crack up during the drive to the pig farm. But no matter how I tried to stop it, I kept flashing on images of Bree during our courtship. That first shared bashful smile. The first time I touched her fingers. The first time her lips met mine. How much she liked to dance and laugh. How committed she was to being a cop and a stepmother to my kids.

"You thinking about her, shug?" Sampson asked.

There were times when I could swear my partner was

clairvoyant. Or at least, he picked up on subtle changes in my body so perfectly that he could decipher my thoughts. Or it was an easy guess; I don't know.

"Yeah," I said, and fell quiet again for several long moments, swallowing hard at unbridled emotion. "John?"

"Talk to me," he said.

"I don't know how to..." I began and then faltered. "I can't..."

"Can't what?"

"Think of Bree as gone," I said through clenched teeth. "It's like my heart can't believe it. I didn't even get to say good-bye. I wasn't there to tell her how much I loved her, how she made everything in my life so..."

"Whole?" Sampson said softly.

"Anchored," I replied.

It was the perfect word for what Bree had done in my life; she was the person who anchored me, grounded me, kept me from washing away.

"We don't have DNA results yet," Sampson said.

"I've been telling myself that."

"And you keep telling yourself that, you hear?"

It started to rain. Sampson turned on the wipers, and the slapping sounded like nails being pounded by one of those air guns. I closed my eyes, reached up, and started rubbing at that spot on the back of my head where the junkie had hit me with a piece of pipe.

"Headaches still as bad?" Sampson asked.

"Getting better," I said, though that was an overstatement.

"You need to get that checked out again, Alex," Sampson said. "It's been, like, six days and you're still hurting. You should see a neurologist."

"Doctors said to expect the headaches," I said. "Part of the healing process. They could go on for months. And right now? I don't need another doctor to tell me the same thing."

My partner looked ready to argue, but then he spotted a sign ahead in the light rain that read *Pritchard's Farm: Specialty Pork.*

"There it be," he said slowing and turning.

We drove up a long dirt driveway bordered on both sides by trees that looked brilliantly green, all wet and new. It was spring, a time of rebirth. But it felt like November to me when we rolled into an orderly farmyard that reeked of a stench I can't even begin to describe.

As we climbed from the car, we heard a squealing din coming from a huge low-roofed building that sat on a bench of earth about a quarter mile from a picture-perfect farmhouse that looked recently built.

"Pork bellies been good to someone," Sampson observed.

A weathered woman in her forties wearing a green rain jacket, rubber gloves, and calf-high rubber boots over her jeans came around the side of the house. She carried a pitchfork and revealed smears of soil on her right cheek when she pushed off her hood and brushed back graying hair to look at us.

Sampson already had his badge out. "Mrs. Pritchard?"

"You here about the skull and the bone?" she asked.

"We are," I said.

"Expect you better talk to Royal about that, my husband," she said, gesturing up the hill with the pitchfork. "He's on up to the barn. It's feeding time. That's the reason he found them bones, feeding time, but I expect he'll be wanting to tell you that himself."

CHAPTER 14

WE FOUND ROYAL PRITCHARD out on one of several catwalks that crossed above the industrial pigsty. There were thousands of young pigs, or shoats, jammed into a pit that was easily a football field long and a quarter again as wide. A short, stocky guy in muddy rubber boots and Carhartt work clothes, Pritchard had a lit cigar in his mouth as he worked a set of hydraulic controls bolted to the railing of the catwalk.

Responding to the pig farmer's manipulations, a long line of feeders crossed above the sty from left to right, dropping corn in a steady, drenching stream. The pigs were going berserk in response, all trying to follow the rain of food, squealing and grunting so loud that it changed the pounding in my head, made it like the inside of a bell that was tolling.

Sampson got Pritchard's attention, and the farmer shut down the feeding system, which sent the pigs into a howling, squealing rage that seemed to join with the gonging in my head, speeding it, amplifying it, until I just couldn't take being in there any longer, and I ran blindly for the door.

Five seconds later, I burst out of the pigsty and ran on out toward the tree line in the rain, trying to control the excruciating pain that crackled from the base of my skull up. But the pain wouldn't stop, and I felt my stomach roll and thought I might be violently sick.

By the time Sampson came out with the pig farmer ten minutes later, however, the rain had cooled me down. My stomach was feeling better, and the ringing in my head had softened to a distant pealing.

"That smell takes some getting used to, even with a cigar to mask it," Pritchard allowed, looking sympathetic. "No doubt 'bout that. But I don't mind, you know? That's the smell a' money in there, sure as I'm standing right here."

"Pork futures are up, huh?" Sampson asked.

"It's the new white meat, ain't you heard?" Pritchard replied. "Price a' fatted shoats has doubled past three years."

"You found the skull and a bone?" I asked.

The farmer nodded. "I showed your partner where. Wasn't too far from where you was standing when you got to feeling kind of, well, piggish, what I call it."

"Tell him how you found the skull," Sampson said.

Pritchard shrugged. "One of them things. The hopper jammed out in the middle, and the corn was just pouring there, and every pig in the place wanted to be at the center. Anyway, I opened up the sides enough I could see the skull and bone there, plain as day, in the dung. Fished the skull out with a hook duct-taped to a pole. Sheriff's deputies used a claw thing to get the bone."

"Nothing else? No other bones?"

Pritchard's cheek twitched. "Not that I seen, but hell, there's three, maybe four inches of shit in there front to back. You're welcome to come rake through it after the gold on the hoof's up to weight and off."

"How long will that be?" I asked.

"Twenty days."

I have never been the sort of man who flies off the handle, but for some reason, I thought about the possibility there were other bones in that pigsty, and I just lost it.

"We're not waiting fucking twenty days," I shouted at him. "The fucker who dumped the body in there killed my god-damned wife! I'm getting a warrant and I'm getting those god-damned pigs out of there today."

"Christ, Detective," Pritchard said, looking offended. "I'm sorry about your wife, Jesus knows I am. But you're acting like I tossed a body in there."

"Did you?" I demanded.

Pritchard said, "Hell no. What the—"

I had seven inches and fifty pounds on the farmer. When I popped him in the chest with my right hand, he staggered backward and sat down hard in the gravel, shocked.

"You know a guy named Mulch?" I demanded. "He related to you?"

"Alex!" Sampson said.

I ignored him. "Is he?"

The farmer acted scared as he complained, "I don't know no one named Mulch, no, sir, and that's a fact."

"Mulch was raised on a pig farm," I replied angrily. "He came here specifically to get rid of that body. Mulch has to know you."

"No, sir," Pritchard repeated flatly. "Never even heard of

that name. Go down and ask my wife. Ellie and I been together since high school, and she'll tell you the same."

He looked at Sampson. "I called the sheriff second I fished out that skull. I could've just left it and it'd be fragments in the pig shit by now. Think on that."

It all went out of me then, and I realized what I'd done.

My shoulders sank and I squatted down next to him, shaking my head before I said softly, "Mr. Pritchard, I was way out of line there. I apologize. My wife…"

There was a moment of silence before he said quietly, "I understand, Detective. When my mom died, I wandered around in a haze for days."

I reached out my hand and helped him up. "Again, I'm sorry. I honestly don't know what came over me."

Sampson put his hand on my shoulder, said, "Think we better leave Mr. Pritchard to his chores."

I nodded, apologized a third time, and then walked away from the pig farmer, unwilling to look at the barn anymore, unable to block out the sounds of the ongoing riot inside.

Part Two

CHAPTER 15

AT 4:12 THAT AFTERNOON—actually, 3:12 local time—Mitch Cochran downshifted the Kenworth T680 tractor-trailer pulling an empty container chassis into the CSX rail yard in east St. Louis.

Sitting between Marcus Sunday and Cochran in the truck cab, Acadia Le Duc said, "Jesus, we're cutting this close. I told you and Dr. Fersing told you we didn't want to get anywhere near the outside limit, and we're pushing right on it."

"Have faith, darling," Sunday said calmly.

They were supposed to have landed in St. Louis an hour ago, but thunderstorms had delayed them, and it had taken a while to get through the paperwork at the truck-rental service.

"All I'm saying is if we have a catastrophe on our hands, I won't take responsibility," Acadia said.

"If it is a catastrophe, we'll call it an act of God and be on our way," Sunday said indifferently.

After expertly driving the tractor-trailer rig onto the scales,

Cochran jumped out and went inside a steel office building with the necessary lading documents.

Ten minutes passed. Then fifteen.

"We're not going to pull this off," Acadia said, frustrated. "We are—"

Cochran came running out of the building, climbed up into the cab, said, "They were backlogged."

"Jesus," Acadia said, wiping at sweat on her brow.

"Calm down," Sunday said as the truck began to roll forward. "We've got a half hour."

"You don't get it," she snapped. "It may be over already."

"If it is, it is," Sunday said. "And we'll have a cleanup job to do."

Cochran drove into a long wide gravel parking lot that abutted the rail lines. He maneuvered the rig to a gantry crane next to the tracks, stopped, and set the brakes. Cables whirled, swinging giant electromagnets above the rust-red container fitted with the solar panels.

The four magnets lowered. A worker positioned them. There was a loud clanking noise as they locked to the sides of the car, and then the cables began to retract. The forty-five-foot container lifted off the railcar as if it were no heavier than a box of Kleenex. The crane operator expertly swung the container and set it on the chassis behind them.

"We have twenty-two minutes," Acadia said.

The magnets released, and Cochran started the engine, put it in gear, and said, "Where to?"

"Get back on the interstate, go east to that truck stop we saw coming in."

"That'll take too long!" Acadia said.

Sunday said nothing. Cochran maneuvered through the

city streets by GPS and had them back on the I-70 heading east in nine minutes. When they had twelve minutes left, he got off at State Highway 203 and turned north into the Gateway Truck Plaza. Cochran pulled over out back by a field of weeds.

"Move!" Acadia said, holding a large duffel bag she'd retrieved from the sleeping compartment behind them.

Sunday jumped down, stepped around the diesel tank, and got up on the fifth-wheel frame between the cab and the container. He put a key in the lock of the custom hatch on the front end of the freight car. It wouldn't turn.

Had that kid in the rail yard back in Philly bent the hasp? He tried again, then jiggled the lock and twisted a third time. He thought the key was going to break off in the lock. Then something gave, and the hasp released.

He pulled it out, raised the bar holding the hatch shut. It swung open.

"Ten minutes," Acadia said, handing him the duffel.

"I'm putting my money on you," Sunday said and ducked into the pitch-black space.

Acadia glanced up at the leaden sky before following him and shutting the door behind her.

CHAPTER 16

WHEN THE HATCH OPENED twenty minutes later, they were both drenched with sweat. Acadia came out first, carrying the duffel, which was considerably lighter. Sunday had a large black plastic trash bag in his hands.

"Told you we were good," he said.

Acadia got down off the frame, wiped at the sweat on her face, said, "It was touch and go there, I'm telling you."

"What you're trained for," he said, setting the bag down and turning to close and lock the hatch.

"I left the field because I hated stuff like that. Still do."

"Sometimes we have to just push through the nasty tasks in life."

"That qualified," she said, and went back to the truck cab.

Sunday dug out a small plastic box filled with silicone earplugs. He mashed a chunk of one into the key slot so he'd know if it had been tampered with and then got down. Cochran had the engine going by the time he shut the door.

Sunday looked at the driver.

"Any visitors?"

"Couple of pickups went by," Cochran said, putting the truck in gear and pulling out. "Nothing to worry about."

Acadia said, "It's five twenty-two. Well, four twenty-two here. We've got until Monday morning, same time."

"Gotta be at the dock by six." Cochran grunted.

Sunday looked at Google Maps, said, "Piece of cake."

After they'd gotten onto I-70, heading west this time, toward the Mississippi River, Acadia said, "Why are we doing all this, Marcus? I mean really. Deep down, is this just payback for Cross savaging your book?"

Sunday looked at her sidelong for several seconds before flipping his hand dismissively. "If it was just that, I wouldn't have bothered. I *am* proving to Dr. Alex that I was correct and he was wrong. But mostly, Acadia? I'm doing it because I can, and because this little project and the logistics involved intrigues and amuses me a great deal. Does it continue to amuse you?"

He'd delivered the question in a hard voice.

Acadia hesitated.

But Cochran chortled in the driver's seat, said, "I can tell you it's kicking my ass, Marcus. Most fun I've had since Iraq by a long shot."

"Acadia?" Sunday asked, watching her closely.

Acadia seemed to struggle before she shrugged in resignation. "Ma always called me a shooting star, born to burn bright and brief."

Sunday smiled, reached over, and stroked her cheek. "The hell with a shooting star, am I right? Why not ride a comet?"

CHAPTER 17

ACADIA WAS GROWING INCREASINGLY uneasy about everything Sunday had gotten her into, but she said, "A comet sounds good too."

Rush-hour traffic slowed them, but within sixty minutes, they were pulling onto the scales at the new AEP River terminal north of the city on the Missouri side.

The woman working the scales said, "She's just fifteen hundred pounds?"

"She's riding empty while we test our experimental solar refrigeration and heating system," Cochran said. "How fast will it go downriver?"

"You'd be surprised. With the current up like it is, it's two and a half days to Memphis, maybe less. Five days to New Orleans, maybe less. Double that coming upriver."

"We'd like to be able to inspect the container at Memphis and then again at New Orleans."

"Long as you're there with the right papers, it shouldn't be a problem."

"Can you make us copies?" Cochran said. "I'm always losing stuff."

"I can give you two."

"Thanks. What do we owe you, then?" Cochran asked.

"Loading fee's one fifty. You'll pay the full freight at New Orleans."

Cochran handed her cash. She gave him the receipt and lading documents, said, "Pull on ahead. You'll see the dock on your right."

"Gantry?" he asked.

"New gantries aren't up yet. They'll be using the boom crane."

They drove to one of the freight docks on the bank of the river and pulled close to the *Pandora,* a container barge with a three-story white-and-blue wheelhouse at the rear. Cochran showed the crane operator and the barge captain the necessary documents. Cochran, Sunday, and Acadia watched as wide straps were run beneath the container and then hooked to the cable. The crane whirred. The container car rose, swung several times, and then was settled on the deck forward of the other fifty containers already stacked aboard.

"There was a lot of movement," Acadia said worriedly.

"Everything inside is strapped down or bracketed in place," Sunday reminded her before calling over to the captain, "We'll see you in Memphis to make an inspection."

Scotty Creel, a hearty man in his early fifties, nodded, said, "Just have that paperwork with you, and you'll have no problems getting through the gates. We'll be tied up there three, four hours Monday morning."

Back in the Kenworth, Cochran drove them south toward

St. Louis, said, "We got plenty of time before the flight. Let's get something to eat. Ribs? Gotta be good here."

Sunday turned up his nose.

Acadia said, "Marcus doesn't do pork."

"Oh, that's right, sorry," Cochran said. "Steak?"

"That'll do," Sunday said.

"And Cross?" Acadia asked.

Sunday glanced again at his watch.

He said, "Mr. Harrow needs time to finish his business. I'll wait until just before our flight leaves to have my first chat with Dr. Alex."

CHAPTER

18

I WOKE UP AROUND eight thirty that Friday evening, lying on the couch in my darkened office, my rain jacket over my shoulders, and my muddy shoes on the floor beside me. The headache that had tortured me the past six days had calmed somewhat.

Good nap. *Maybe that's all I needed,* I thought, before I fully awoke into the living nightmare again.

If that was Bree's body, what was I going to do with it?

She'd wanted to be cremated and have her remains spread in the Shenandoah, somewhere near the river, where she'd spent the summers of her childhood. I owed her that, I—

Captain Quintus flipped on the light, and I blinked and shielded my eyes.

"Alex, why don't you come on upstairs."

"What's going on?"

"Just wanted to talk some things through with you."

"I got time for a shower? I haven't had one in—"

"Go ahead," my boss said, then he slapped the doorjamb and walked away.

I felt better after the shower and a change of shirt from my locker, more alert than I had been in days. When I reached the third floor, the demolition team was long gone, and the floor had been swept clean. I went through the plastic sheeting and saw five people standing near that island of desks under the fluorescent lights.

Sampson looked like he had something left over from the pig farm on his shoe. I was about to tell him I had the same problem when I noticed Mahoney stirring a dark cup of coffee. Captain Quintus was drinking water, and Aaron Wallace, the DC police chief, appeared saddened.

Detective Tess Aaliyah was the only one who gave me a steady gaze.

She swallowed, said, "I wanted to tell you myself."

Questions exploded through my brain. Had they found Mulch? Had another member of my family turned up? Was I going to have to be tortured again, go to a dump scene to identify someone I loved? In the end, it was something even more unimaginable and cruel.

"The autopsy," Aaliyah said. "I was there, and…"

Her eyes were watering and she shook her head.

"What?" I demanded.

"We still don't have DNA, but the blood types match," she said. "And there's…"

Sampson cleared his throat, said, "She was pregnant, Alex. Six weeks."

Hearing about the blood type had made the grief real. Hearing about the baby was too much.

My head spun and I felt sicker than at the pig farm. I sat down hard in one of the chairs, put my face in my hands, the headache pounding with every bit of its earlier fury.

"I'm sorry," Aaliyah said. "Had you been trying?"

I shook my head bitterly, said, "This is a miracle and a tragedy at the same time. Can you believe that?"

"Shug?" Sampson said.

A great part of me wanted to rail at the sky and the moon, curse God and demand to know why I'd been singled out for this kind of punishment.

Instead, I gazed around at all of them and said, "Bree had uterine fibroids about five years ago. They removed them, but the procedure left scars. The doctors told us she'd likely never have children. A one-in-a-thousand chance, they..."

I don't think I've ever felt more bewildered in my life than I was at that moment. I didn't even hear Chief Wallace come over beside me, but I felt his heavy hand on my shoulder before he said, "Hell of a thing you're going through, Alex. Hell of a thing. Too much for one man to handle."

I nodded, cleared my throat, and in a voice tight with emotion said, "Chief, it's beyond anything I've ever had to deal with before."

He patted my shoulder again. "I can't imagine the stress."

"I'm still standing."

The chief took a chair, set it opposite me, and sat down on it, his forearms resting on his thighs, and his face twisted in anguish. "I know you're still standing. I know you're a fighter, and I know this is personal. That's what makes what I'm going to say now so hard."

I'd been nodding, but now I knitted my brow. "Chief?"

"Alex, for your own good, and because I respect you so much, I'm placing you on medical leave."

That made no sense. "What?"

"For the time being, I want you to take a break from this investigation, let us work on your behalf for once. I'm sorry, Alex, but I need your gun and badge."

For a moment, even those words didn't penetrate, but then they did and it felt like I was being tossed overboard.

"Chief, you can't do that," I pleaded. "I'm good. I'm handling this."

"No one in your situation could be good," Wallace said. "You showed up at your kid's school crying and then you ranted at the principal. You mistreated a cooperative witness this afternoon—hit him, as I understand it."

I looked at Sampson, not believing what was being said, and whispered, "You can't do this. I have to find—"

Captain Quintus shook his head, said, "Alex, we're all afraid that the injury to your head and the pressure of all that's happened to you is too enormous to be dealt with while trying to work. We want you to go to a hospital to meet with a neurologist who's waiting to do a baseline—"

"That's not happening," I said. "Not now."

"Alex," Ned Mahoney began.

"You think I asked for this?" I demanded, feeling the heat rise in my face. "Who asks for his family to be taken? Who asks for his wife to be cut to pieces? Who asks to be pounded and pounded and—"

Only then did I realize I'd been shouting at them.

"They say that's part of it, shug," Sampson said. "The anger. Coming from the concussion as much as from Mulch. You need help. You see that, don't you?"

"Of course he does, John," Mahoney said. "He knows the statistics."

"Gun and badge, Detective," the chief said sadly, holding out his hand.

CHAPTER

19

THE FIGHT WENT OUT of me then, like a liquid draining from my core in a matter of seconds. I handed my badge and gun to Chief Wallace, said, "Appreciate your concern."

"We'll get these back to you as soon as the doctors say it's okay," Wallace reassured me. "You're an incredible asset to this department and we know it."

I nodded, stood, went to my desk, and picked up a framed picture of my family and some mail. But I also managed to palm something valuable from the back of my department-issue laptop.

With the photograph in my right hand and the mail and flash drive in my jacket pocket, I headed for the plastic sheeting. Sampson and Mahoney fell in on either side of me.

"I'm not going to tip over, you know," I said as we went back through that demolition site.

"Just making sure you go to the GWU hospital," Sampson said.

"See the neurologist," Mahoney added.

I shrugged, said, "You're right."

We rode the elevator in silence. Sampson and I got out on one. Mahoney went to the basement to retrieve his car.

"Can I take a leak without you peeking over my shoulder?" I asked.

My partner thought about it, said, "I wouldn't put that duty on my worst enemy."

I managed a laugh and then walked around the corner and into a hallway that ran back toward the crime lab. I pushed the door to the men's room open loudly, kicked off my shoes, picked them up, and jogged down the hall in my socks, taking several turns before the staircase that led to the parking garage.

I opened the basement door in time to see Mahoney's taillights as he went up the exit ramp. Pete Koslowski, a sergeant and head of the motor pool, was an old friend. When I told him I needed a ride, he flipped me the keys to an unmarked car.

They were right, I thought as I climbed into the car. I probably did need to see a neurologist. But that would mean at least an overnight stay for observation, maybe two or three. I didn't have that much time to waste. Whatever was going on inside my head was going to have to wait.

My phone started ringing two minutes later.

Sampson called, and then Mahoney. I kept clicking the ringer off and headed for the house. I was going to need a few things. As I drove, out of the corner of my eye, I saw the phone screen lighting up every few seconds.

It lit up again while I was idling at a red light on New York Avenue, and I reached over to shut the phone off altogether.

Then I saw the caller ID.

It said *Mulch.*

When I answered, I heard shallow, raspy breathing, as if someone were trembling with excitement, and then an electronically altered voice said, “So good of you to take my call, Dr. Cross.”

CHAPTER 20

"DO YOU UNDERSTAND?" MULCH asked two minutes later.

Each and every word of my first direct conversation with the man who'd taken my family and butchered my wife was seared on my injured brain, and I couldn't reply.

"Do you understand what you need to do to see the surviving members of your family alive again?" Mulch asked insistently.

I couldn't answer him. My mind kept flashing on vague images from some movie I'd seen where each of a man's four limbs was tied to a different horse, all of them facing in different directions.

"Cross?"

"I can't, I…"

"Too late," Mulch said, sounding cold and hard through the static that camouflaged his voice. "Another one bites the dust. Look in your backyard and then call me back."

The static and connection died.

I stared at the phone, and then dug out a blue light from

the glove box, opened the window, and stuck it on the roof. Shaking from head to toe, I flipped on the siren and floored the accelerator.

Six minutes later I flipped off the siren, pulled the blue light, and turned onto my block. With every inch I drove, my fear and sorrow grew.

"Please, God, no," I whispered again and again.

But the closer I got to my home, the more I understood that the time for God had passed. There was someone, one of my children or my grandmother, dead in my backyard.

Mulch had done it once. He'd do it twice.

I no longer had any doubt of it.

I skidded to a stop in front of my home, took a flashlight, and circled to the narrow walkway that led around the side of the house to the backyard. Playing the beam about, I saw the foundation, the plywood walls of the addition, and the portable toolshed and toilet the contractors had brought in.

Where the rear fence of my yard met the gate that led out to the alley, my light found the body, and I was hit with the second shock wave of the day, a blow that felt supernatural in its strength, and pure evil in its intent.

But I didn't go down to my knees as I had earlier. I stood there, seeing Damon's class ring on his right hand, the chain and the St. Christopher's medal around his neck, and the stud and tiny loop earrings in his right ear.

He lay on the ground, his lower body twisted toward the wall, his torso and head turned to the night sky. His face had been battered beyond all recognition. And across his entire body, front and back, oval disks of skin were missing every four or five inches or so, as if Mulch had been trying to simulate a leopard's spotted pelt.

I tried to tell myself that it might not be my son.

But a thousand memories of Damon spun tragically around me. The air rang with a chorus of his voices: as a giggling toddler who'd loved to suck his thumb and curl up in my lap while his mom made breakfast on Saturday mornings; as a troubled five-year-old trying to understand why his mother had died; as a joyous, victorious ten-year-old after he'd almost single-handedly won a basketball game; as a young man who loved to laugh.

Damon had a beautiful laugh that came up out of his belly and seized his whole body. It was genuine and contagious, and one of the things I most loved about him.

Right then and there, I knew that I was doomed to pine for that laugh every day for the rest of my life. I wanted to cross the yard and take my firstborn in my arms, feel the weight of the man he'd become.

But I didn't. I couldn't.

With every passing moment looking at the corpse, I became aware that I'd been changed that day, irrevocably transformed into someone I no longer recognized.

Up until Mulch, I'd always considered myself a moral man, guided by principles; there were certain lines I'd never cross, or even contemplate crossing. But as I gazed at the desecration of my son, I knew that all my principles had been sacrificed, and all rules of conduct destroyed.

"This is not happening again," I vowed to my son before turning away. "I promise you that."

Flipping off the flashlight, I felt myself swell with righteous anger and went fast around the side of the house, only to pull up short, startled by the silhouette of someone standing there ahead of me.

CHAPTER

21

"ALEX?" AVA SAID IN a fearful voice. "Is that you?"

In the long frenzy of the day, I'd completely forgotten about the runaway girl who'd saved my life and my sanity in so many ways. When had she left the house? Last night? I honestly didn't know.

"Alex?" she said, her voice higher.

"It's me, Ava."

She ran to me, hugged me, sobbing: "Is it true? Bree?"

I held her to me, unable to tell her that Damon was in the backyard. "It looks that way," I said.

"Why?" she asked.

"I don't know," I said, pushing her back gently. "I have to leave now, Ava."

"Why? Where are you going?"

"To find Mulch." I kissed her on the cheek and started toward the house.

Ava hurried behind me, saying, "I'm going with you."

"No, you are not," I said.

"Please, Alex," she begged. "I can help you find them. I showed you how the pictures were faked. I can help. I'm good at that kind of stuff."

It was a bad idea to bring Ava with me for too many reasons to count.

But she *was* gifted with computers, and damn street-smart. She'd shown me that again and again. I thought about what Mulch wanted me to do to save the rest of my family, and I saw in an instant how it might work.

"You have a driver's license?"

"No, but I can drive. My mom's last shitty boyfriend taught me."

"Can you listen? Follow orders?"

Ava's chin retreated several inches, but she nodded. "I owe you and Nana Mama."

I dug in my pocket, came up with my house key, and opened the door.

"Go find Jannie's laptop. It's in her room."

"Where are we going?"

"I'm not sure yet," I admitted. "Just get the computer."

While she went upstairs to look for the computer, I got a bag of clothes and my backup weapon, an old .45-caliber Colt 1911. The pistol was bigger and heavier than the nine-millimeter Glock I had turned over to Quintus, but it had excellent balance, and I shot it well. At short range with the 230-grain bullets and the hot loads, it could drop a charging rhino in its tracks.

"I've got it," Ava said, looking at the gun as I tugged on a jacket.

"Good," I said. "Let's go."

"Do I need one of those?" Ava asked.

"One of what?"

"A gun?"

At first I dismissed it out of hand. Bringing her along was bad enough. Arming her was crazy, but I asked, "You ever shot a gun?"

She shook her head. "Seen it on TV."

"Little bit different in reality," I said, but I went into Bree's closet and reached under her nightgowns for the small Ruger nine-millimeter she sometimes kept in her purse when we went out somewhere fancy.

Ava reached for it, but I put it in my pocket, along with a box of bullets. "I'll see how you do along the way before I let you anywhere near it."

"But Alex—" she began.

"Follow orders," I said. I picked up the bag and left the house with her trailing. Locking the door, I realized that if I was to have any hope of catching up with Mulch before he killed the rest of my family, I was going to have to divorce myself from what had already happened. I was going to have to compartmentalize, focus on the task, and deal with my grief later. I was going to have to act as if I were on a case where I had zero emotional involvement.

We left with Ava driving and me riding shotgun with Jannie's computer in my lap. I never looked back. I couldn't bear the thought of it.

Ava was no polished driver, but she had grit and settled into the task with every bit of her little being. "Where are we going?" she asked again after I'd seen she could follow basic directions and not hit oncoming cars.

"Get across the bridge," I replied. "Head south until I tell you different."

Soon we were on I-95 in the far right lane heading toward Richmond, Virginia. My mind no longer felt fried. It had a purpose and began to click off the things I needed: money, lots of it, and a new phone, and a new car, and I had to tell someone about Damon.

Though I did not want to, I turned my phone back on. Rather than give in to my first impulse and dial Sampson, I called Detective Tess Aaliyah.

"It's Cross," I said when she answered.

"Where the hell are you?" Aaliyah demanded. "You need to be in a hospital. Everyone's looking for—"

"There's a male body in my backyard," I said. "I believe it's my son Damon."

Ava almost went off the road.

"My God," the detective gasped. "Are you there now?"

"I don't think I'll ever go back there, Detective," I said.

"Where are you?"

"Mulch has us heading in the general direction of hell," I replied, before lowering the window and hurling my iPhone onto the highway while going sixty miles an hour.

CHAPTER 22

IT WAS NEARLY DAWN that Saturday morning after Easter.

Tess Aaliyah had been in Alex Cross's backyard since eleven the night before, overseeing her second crime scene in less than twenty-four hours.

She'd welcomed the help from John Sampson and Ned Mahoney, allowing Cross's current partner to search the house and his former FBI partner to take charge of the gathering of evidence. From blood spatters, tire tracks, and marks in the dirt, they'd determined that the killer had brought the body into the alley behind the house and then dragged it through the gate into the backyard.

Mahoney's men believed the tracks were made by a pickup truck with bald tires. They'd also discovered that, like Bree's, many of the boy's teeth had been pulled.

Watching the corpse loaded into a body bag and wheeled out of the backyard, Aaliyah was thinking that in one sense the teeth pulling went along with the generalized mutilations of the bodies, but in another nagging sense, it didn't. The teeth removal and the clipped fingertips could be efforts to hide the victim's true identity.

But the DNA would give it away eventually. So why desecrate the body?

The detective understood, of course, that sometimes with the criminally insane, there was no specific reason for why they did what they did. But the almost uniform size of the oval cuts combined with the regular pattern made her believe that there was some sort of logic to it, twisted or otherwise.

She made a note to herself to ask Mahoney to run the pattern and the oval cuts through the ViCAP files to see if they had ever surfaced before, and then she followed the gurney bearing the corpse around the side of the house. As first light appeared in the sky, she saw that the media had descended on the scene.

Captain Quintus was on the front porch, and she went to him.

"Anything?" he asked.

"Lots," Aaliyah said. "I just can't tell you if any of it's usable yet. You?"

The homicide captain shook his head, looking drawn and exhausted.

Mahoney joined them, said, "Quantico computer lab called me ten minutes ago. The bugs Mulch put in the house? They were designed to transmit through Cross's wireless network, but where the feeds went is anyone's guess at this point."

Sampson came out of the house holding his phone. "Alex still isn't answering. He doesn't even have his phone on. We can't track him."

"Probably why he doesn't have it on," Mahoney said.

"He'll call in eventually, though, right?" Aaliyah asked.

"I don't know," Sampson replied. "Sounds to me like he's on a mission."

"Can I put out a bulletin on him?" Aaliyah asked. "Request that he be detained for questioning?"

"Questioning?" Sampson said. "For what?"

Aaliyah held up her hands. "Just doing my job here, Detective. I'd be asking the same thing of anybody who saw two murdered family members in the same day and then fled."

"We know Alex Cross a whole lot better than you do, Detective Aaliyah," Mahoney fired back. "He isn't fleeing. He's hunting."

"While suffering from a closed-head injury?" she said calmly.

"We don't know that," Captain Quintus replied.

"Really?" she said. "You all certainly sounded sure of it last night."

Silence descended on the group for several seconds before Quintus said, "I won't put out a bulletin."

"But Captain—" Aaliyah began.

"End of discussion, Detective. I won't do it."

CHAPTER 23

THEY HEARD SHOUTS FROM down the street. Several of the reporters and cameramen behind the barricade were having some kind of dispute.

"Another subject, sir?" Aaliyah said, turning away.

"Go on," he replied.

"I think we need the media on our side," she replied. "We need to tell them about the kidnappings and about Mulch, put his picture from the fake driver's license on television."

"That could open up a whole other can of night crawlers," Sampson protested. "My nickel opinion: the less they know, the better."

"I agree," Mahoney said.

"I don't," the homicide captain said. "Detective Aaliyah's right. We have to get them involved now. Someone somewhere could have seen Cross's kids, or his grandmother, or Mulch."

"Do you want me to talk to them?" Aaliyah asked. "The reporters."

"My job, Detective," Quintus said. "Go get some sleep. All of you. You're no good to Cross or his family if you can't think straight."

The homicide captain went down off the porch and out onto the street.

"Sorry if I stepped on any toes or poked any sacred cows," Aaliyah said to Sampson and Mahoney.

"Apology accepted," the FBI agent said wearily. "We're a bit sensitive when it comes to Alex. He's one of a kind."

"I know," she said. "Alex Cross is one of the reasons I wanted to become a cop in the first place."

Aaliyah climbed off the porch then, thinking that what she'd said was true. She'd read about Cross's exploits as a teenager and admired him almost as much as she admired her father.

The detective cringed. Her dad. Bernie. She'd promised herself she'd go knock on his door this morning. But she was simply too exhausted to make the hour-long drive.

Down on the sidewalk, Captain Quintus had an army of reporters surrounding him. Aaliyah went in the opposite direction, heading to her car.

As she got in and pulled out into traffic, her thoughts kept returning to Cross's last words to her. *Mulch has us heading in the general direction of hell.*

Us? Who was with Cross?

Mulch has us heading in the general direction of hell.

What did that mean?

On the one hand, it could be a figure of speech.

On the other, it could mean that Cross had communicated with the madman. Couldn't it? Or was that just a figment of her tired and frazzled imagination?

CHAPTER 24

"DON'T FRET, MARCUS," ACADIA chided. "You know Cross'll call you 'fore too long."

"I told him to call right back, and it's been hours," Sunday said coldly, looking straight ahead from the backseat of the Durango, watching out the windshield as Cochran drove them along that muddy road in the forest toward Harrow's place.

The rain had stopped. Dawn was coming on.

"He's got no choice," Acadia said. "Cross will— "

"I know he'll call," Sunday snapped at her. "The question is, why is he waiting so long? What's his angle? What's he doing?"

"Three birches coming up," Cochran said, and slowed to a stop.

Acadia handed Sunday another gym bag, said, "You're sure it's smart to end this all so soon?"

"We've made our point in Cross's mind," Sunday said. "Time to take care of loose ends and move on. That's how this game works, right? We keep moving. We keep everything in motion. That way, Cross stays off balance, can't focus, can't even find a target."

Acadia shrugged. "Your game. Your rules."

Cochran said, "Fifteen minutes?"

"Make it twenty," Sunday said, and got out of the car.

As the day brightened, he climbed down the bank, found that overgrown logging trail, and followed it again to the ledge above the clearing and Harrow's shack. Sunday saw wisps of smoke rolling lazily from the stovepipe and did not pause, continuing down the steep slope until he was at the edge of the yard.

Right on cue, the door opened slightly and the Rottweiler came bounding out. He circled Sunday, who stood stone still and let the dog wind him for a scent that might indicate a weapon. When the dog barked that he was clean, Sunday set off for the door, which opened wider.

He climbed the stoop past the chain saw and the gas can and closed the door quickly behind him, calling to Harrow, "Your dog's taking a dump."

"Long as it ain't in here," Harrow said, sitting down at the table. "You got the extra hundred K?"

"You get in and out clean?" asked Sunday, sitting down too and noticing the mirror was there again.

"Wasn't in that alley more than a minute, tops," the skinhead said. "You better have that extra we talked about."

"I've got it," Sunday said, unzipping the gym bag, opening it so Harrow could see the stacks of banded hundred-dollar bills, and setting it on the table. Then he dug in his pocket and came up with a packet that he tossed on the mirror. "Brought you a present too, for a job well done."

Harrow seemed instantly more interested in the packet than the money. “That blue crystal from AZ?”

Sunday nodded. “The real *Breakin' Bad* stuff, like before.”

“Oh Lordy,” Harrow whispered, eagerly opening the packet to reveal blue crystals that he spilled onto the mirror in a small mound. “Oh Lordy, Lordy, Lordy.”

The skinhead took up a razor, began tapping the crystals, and cut himself two big arcing lines of it. Then he reached in the gym bag, tugged out a hundred-dollar bill, and was rolling it up when somewhere outside the shack the Rottweiler yelped and started to whine.

“Fuck,” Harrow said. “Fuckin' stupid bastard.”

“What's the matter?” Sunday asked.

“Oh, I told you before, only thing causes Casper to make any noise 'cept that low growl is when he's gotten into a porcupine or a skunk,” Harrow said. “Fuck.”

The dog yelped again, and for a second, Sunday thought the skinhead was going to get up. But instead, Harrow looked back to the mirror, brought the rolled bill to his nose, leaned over, and snorted both lines, one in each nostril.

Harrow's head jerked back. His eyes stretched wide as a series of shivers worked through his body before this strange trembling smile came to his lips; it made that wormlike scar on his cheek look like it was alive and squirming.

“Ahhh,” Harrow said, highly pleased. “Little different than the last batch, but after the night I had, it just about makes things right.”

“Glad you like it,” Sunday said.

“Like it? I love it, man,” Harrow said, cutting another line and snorting it. Then he got up, blinking, and started toward the door, saying, “You can bring old Harrow the *Breakin’ Bad* blue anytime you—”

The skinhead stopped in midstride, and his hand shot out for the counter. He caught it and steadied himself.

“You all right?” Sunday asked with concern.

“Yeah, just…diz…”

Harrow weaved on his feet and then toppled backward onto the floor. His mouth went slack, his tongue lolled, and his eyes turned glassy and roaming.

CHAPTER

25

SUNDAY GOT UP, ZIPPED the gym bag shut. He went to the door and opened it, saw the Rottweiler lying on his side, slobber dribbling from his lips. There were two small darts hanging from the dog's left side. Cochran was walking toward the shack carrying a dart gun.

"Took two to drop that sonofabitch," Cochran said in awe. "That's a bear dose, dude."

"Get the darts, and then come in here and help me find the money I gave him yesterday," Sunday said as he reached down and picked up the chain saw and the gas can, which was nearly full.

He carried both inside. Harrow was still on the rough plank floor, rolling his head slowly and trying unsuccessfully to speak. Sunday stepped over him and set down the chain saw and gas can.

Cochran entered the shack, shut the door, and looked around at the squalor. "Not exactly a skinhead Suzy Homemaker, is he?"

"Start with the bedroom," Sunday said, grabbing Harrow under the armpits and dragging him six feet closer to the woodstove.

"I should have brought the gas mask," Cochran said before pushing aside a blanket that hung in a doorway and disappearing behind it.

Sunday got one of the butcher knives from the washtub on the floor and used it to cut two long narrow strips of fabric from the busted couch. Setting those aside, he picked up the can and poured gas on the floor and splashed it on the chest and legs of the skinhead.

Harrow's eyes widened. He managed to say, "No."

"Coming down off the first jolt, I see," Sunday told him in a conversational tone. "Mixed a bit of Rohypnol and a horse tranquilizer in with the blue."

Holding the gym bag from the day before, Cochran came out of the bedroom. He glanced at Harrow without pity. "Not exactly a rocket scientist either. Put it under his bed."

Sunday set the gas can down. "Skinheads don't like banks. Jews in control of their destiny and all that."

Sunday opened the woodstove door, was relieved to see that the fire was down to dully glowing coals. He took a strip of fabric and swung one end in onto the coals. He laid a small log in there to hold it. After positioning the rest of the strip down the front of the stove and onto the rough-hewn floor, Sunday took the other piece of couch fabric, soaked it in the gas, and then laid it end to end with the strip coming out of the woodstove.

"No," the skinhead whispered.

"Don't you fret none," Sunday said, adopting Acadia's accent. He tossed the knife back in the washtub. "With all that dope running in your veins, you won't feel a thing. Or not much, anyway."

Sunday grabbed the other gym bag off the table, went to the kitchen, and looked out the window. The dog was still lying there. The rest of the yard was empty. He nodded to Cochran. They went outside, shutting the door behind them without a glance back at Harrow.

"Torch the barn?" Cochran asked.

Sunday shook his head. "Leave it. There needs to be direct evidence of his involvement."

They hurried into the forest. At the rock ledge, Sunday paused a second to look back and was pleased to see through the window that flames were already dancing inside the shack of Claude Harrow.

It was tough Harrow had to end up like that, and so soon, he thought. Neo-Nazi serial killers are difficult beasts to find, much less seduce, and—

His burner phone rang.

Sunday saw a number he did not recognize. But he'd given the number to only one person in the world.

He punched Answer and said coldly, "What kept you, Dr. Cross?"

CHAPTER 26

I PAUSED BEFORE ANSWERING Mulch, still debating how best to play him. Finally, affecting a sullen monotone, I said, "I got hung up. Finding a son's body in the backyard tends to do that to a man."

"Hmm," Mulch said in that static-blurred voice. "And you told the police what I asked you to do?"

"No," I replied. "Per your orders, I've told no one."

"So you *do* understand?"

"I understand. I agree to your terms."

"Excellent," Mulch said. "Your surviving family members will very much appreciate your actions. So let's set a deadline, shall we? Say, twenty-four hours?"

"Thirty-six," I said.

"Twenty-four," he replied.

"I can't just do it. I have to develop a plan."

"Thirty hours," Mulch shot back finally. "And remember: I want proof. Video proof. And you damn well better be full in the frame, or there'll be one less Cross come tomorrow night. By the way, this is the last time this number will work."

"How exactly am I supposed to get proof to you, then?" I demanded.

"Go on Craigslist New Orleans an hour before the deadline," he said. "Click Casual Encounters and look for a personal ad from TM in the men-looking-for-women section. E-mail the video to the poster."

He hung up.

Setting down the phone I'd bought at a truck stop near Richmond, Virginia, the night before, I looked at Ava, who was curled up in a ball in the passenger seat. She looked played out.

I said, "You can leave anytime you want, you know. No hard feelings."

Acting a little insulted, Ava said, "I'm not going anywhere except with you."

I started the unmarked car. "All I'm saying is that, at some point, you might want to bail, and if you do, it's okay. I will never hold it against you. Ever."

Ava said nothing, just reached over and turned up the heat. We were in a campground in Glen Maury Park, three miles off Interstate 81, west of Lynchburg. She'd driven the entire five hours to get there while I'd used Jannie's computer to go through the flash drive I'd taken from the task force. The drive contained all the files and leads the six-investigator team had generated since my family was taken, as well as my own research into Thierry Mulch.

We'd gotten to the campground around three in the morning and found it empty. We'd slept, me in the front seat, Ava in the back beneath my jacket. I am a big man, and the front seat was probably the most uncomfortable place I have ever slept. But I passed out almost immediately and didn't stir until I heard Ava get out to go to the outhouse.

The five hours of sleep had evidently let my deep subconscious digest the bizarre and violent events of the prior day as well as everything I'd managed to read during the long ride to the park.

Now, in the gathering light, my short-term plan of attack seemed as plain as day.

CHAPTER 27

THE VERY FIRST TIME Thierry Mulch contacted me—by letter, during the investigation into the massage-parlor murders—I'd done a long Internet search and found only a handful of men spread out around the country who had that name. Every single one of the Thierry Mulches checked out, and none of them looked remotely like the red-bearded, red-haired man who'd shown up at Sojourner Truth.

There was also one other Thierry Mulch I'd come across, in an obituary. He'd died in a terrible car crash at age nineteen in West Virginia.

Had someone adopted the dead Mulch's identity? Maybe the man who had my family used the name only when he was dealing with me.

The dead Mulch was an extreme long shot, but we were going to check it out.

I put the car in gear, left the park, got back on I-81, and headed north toward the interchange with I-64 near the border with West Virginia. We stopped at a truck stop near Covington later that morning, and I bought gas, food, and coffee and withdrew another five hundred dollars from an ATM.

When we were well into West Virginia, almost to Lewisburg, Ava finally said, "Where are we going?"

"A small town called Buckhannon."

"Does it have to do with Mulch?"

"It might."

"Was that Mulch you were on the phone with this morning?"

"Yes," I said, as if I were talking about the paperboy and not a psychopath. But my only hope was to be dispassionate about doing what Mulch wanted, seeing it as a means to an end and nothing more.

After another long silence, Ava asked, "What does he want proof of?"

I glanced over to find her studying me intently. She was intuitive and smart, and I shouldn't have been surprised.

"Alex?"

I swallowed hard and said, "I don't want to talk about it right now."

She hardened. "I'm your friend in this, you know."

"I know you are, Ava," I said, feeling raw emotion get the better of dispassion. "I just can't talk about it until I figure out a few things. You're gonna have to trust me until then."

I could see she wanted to argue, but she bit her lip and did not reply.

We stopped in Charleston around eleven that morning and had an early lunch in a greasy-spoon café on the wrong side of town. Not surprisingly, we got a little scrutiny from the locals, both black and white.

I guess it wasn't often they saw a big African American male in his forties traveling with a seventeen-year-old white girl sporting tats and multiple piercings, but we had other deadly things on our minds and did our best to ignore the looks.

A waitress put a check in front of me and a piece of apple pie with vanilla ice cream in front of Ava. She'd already demolished a double cheeseburger, a hot dog, and two orders of fries, but she dug into her dessert like a starving woman as the waitress left.

I put down money for the tab along with a generous tip. When Ava finished and the waitress returned, she saw the tip and smiled. "Thanks."

"You're welcome," I said. "Is there a Verizon store close?"

"Sure," she said, gesturing over my shoulder. "Mile down the street."

"How about an electronics store?"

"They're all right there," she said. "It's a strip mall. Can't miss it."

"Appreciate it," I said. I tossed Ava the keys, and we headed for the door.

"Verizon?" Ava asked as we climbed into the car.

"I need a satellite connection and a data plan."

"Electronics store?"

"A video camera."

She thought about that, said, "For proof?"

I nodded but said nothing more about it. We left Charleston shortly after noon with a satellite broadband modem and a GoPro high-definition camera. I had the modem plugged into Jannie's computer and it was working like a dream. Neither my Internet connection at home nor the one at my office had ever worked that fast.

"Keep north," I said, typing on the keyboard until I found what I was looking for and then dialing the general phone number of the Morgantown Detachment of the West Virginia State Police.

When a female trooper answered, I said I was John Sampson, a DC homicide detective, and I was trying to track down the lead investigator in a twenty-five-year-old case out of Buckhannon.

"Twenty-five years?" she said skeptically. "I don't know if… who was the investigator?"

"Atticus Jones?" I said.

There was a long pause at the other end of the line before she replied, "Well, if you're going to talk to him, Detective Sampson, I'm afraid you're going to have to be quick about it."

"Why's that?"

"Last I heard, poor Atticus had terminal cancer."

CHAPTER

28

TWO HOURS LATER, WE walked into the lobby of Fitzwater's Gracious Living, a nursing facility in Fairmont, West Virginia. We'd passed the exit for Buckhannon on the way, but if the trooper was right, I had to make this visit first.

"Atticus Jones?" I said to the receptionist.

She gave Ava and me a critical gaze before saying, "You family?"

"No," I said, pushing one of my cards across the counter. "This is a business call. Mr. Jones used to be a—"

"Detective," she sniffed. "We hear about it all the time."

"Can we talk to him?" I asked.

She looked at Ava incredulously. "You a cop too?"

Ava, without missing a beat, said, "I get that all the time. Ever seen *Twenty-One Jump Street*?"

The receptionist giggled. "You *could* pass for high school, Detective…?"

"Bryce. Ava Bryce."

"You go on back then, Detectives," the receptionist said, buzzing us through a door. "He's down the hall there in the hospice lounge, but don't get the poor thing all riled up."

We heard Atticus Jones before we saw him, and he didn't sound weak to me at all.

"You complete frickin' idiot," he yelled. "Who is Genghis Khan? For Christ's sake, who is Genghis Khan?"

Then he fell into a hacking fit.

A frail black man with short silver hair and a boxer's nose, a former state homicide investigator, was sitting on a couch wearing a Pittsburgh Steelers sweatshirt and pants. He was watching *Jeopardy!* on the television and drinking a bottle of Yuengling bock beer. There was an empty beer bottle on the table beside him. An oxygen line ran from his nose to a tank on wheels.

"Detective Jones?" I said when he stopped coughing.

Jones took us in sidelong at first, swigging his beer before setting it down and putting the TV on mute. Turning slowly, he waved a bony finger at us.

"I am pushing eighty," he said. "And in my entire life I've never forgotten a face."

"Really?" Ava said, warming to him. "I'm like that too."

"Super-recognizer?" he said, studying her.

"Uh, guess that's what you'd call it."

"It is exactly what you'd call it, young lady," Jones said in a no-nonsense tone. "Saw a whole to-do on it couple months back on *Sixty Minutes*. You ever watch that show, Dr. Cross?"

I decided that if this guy was dying, I was going to live a hundred years.

I smiled. "You recognized *me?*"

"Told you," he said. "Saw you speak once."

"Where was that?" I asked.

"Seminar I took at Quantico 'bout ten years back. You guest-lectured one day. Criminal psychology."

"I make an impression?" I asked, taking a seat opposite him.

"Hell, I'd been thirty years on the job by that time, but yes, sir, you did teach me a thing or two. I will admit that."

"Nice to hear," I said, smiling. "I'm hoping you can pay me back the favor."

"That right?" Jones said, perking up. "How's that?"

"You can tell me about Thierry Mulch."

The old man's eyes narrowed, and his jaw set hard before he wagged that bony finger at me again and said in an emotional whisper, "I knew it. That evil, calculating, pig-farming daddy-killer. I knew it all along!"

CHAPTER 29

THE OLD DETECTIVE FELL back against the couch hacking so hard I thought he'd break a rib. But after thirty or forty seconds of this, he stopped, grabbed a plastic cup, and spit in it. He looked in the cup, then up at me.

"Good news," Jones said. "Blood, but no lung tissue."

I was still spinning from his remark about Mulch. Pig-farming daddy-killer?

"I'm sorry, sir," I said. "*What* did you know all along?"

"That Thierry Mulch is alive," the old detective croaked. "That's what you came to tell me, wasn't it?"

Alive?

I said, "But I read his obituary."

"Course you did. Don't mean a damn thing."

"Back up a minute. What makes you think he's alive?"

The old man reached up and thumped on his chest. "Always felt that way, in here. Never could shake the feeling. Why? What's he done?"

"If it's the same man, he killed my wife and son," I said.

"And he's holding my grandmother and my two other children hostage. He's threatening to kill them too if I don't do what he wants."

Jones looked appalled. "I knew that boy had gotten a taste for it."

"Taste for what?" Ava asked.

"Murder," the old detective said. "Thierry killed his father, and then another guy, probably a transient. I couldn't prove it, though."

"Time out," I said, waving my hands. "Could you start at the beginning?"

The detective hesitated before saying, "Be better if I could also show you, so you'd understand the lay of the land."

"You up for a ride down to Buckhannon?"

Jones laughed. "You'd have to sneak me out the back door. Otherwise that nosy gal at the front desk will be calling my daughter, Gloria, up in Pittsburgh 'bout it, and she'll have what my granddaughter Lizzie calls 'a cow.'"

I smiled again. "If you're up to it?"

"What else am I gonna do? *Wheel of Fortune*? I'm too far gone for that Vanna White."

"All right," I said. "We'll sneak you out the back."

The old man seemed to lose ten years then. He grabbed a walker and struggled to his feet. "Just have me back by seven. Gloria's coming down to pay a visit, have dinner. You got room for an oxygen tank?"

"We do."

"And you, young lady," he said, waving that finger at Ava. "Go in that fridge and get me the rest of that six-pack."

She glanced at me, and I said, "You think that's a smart idea for someone in your condition?"

"What's it gonna do, kill me?" Jones asked and then laughed. "Nah. A cigarette might kill me, but not a beer."

It took some doing, but soon we had Detective First Grade Atticus Jones, retired, up front and the oxygen tank in the backseat with Ava. Jones cracked a beer before I even got in the driver's seat and started calling out directions.

When we were finally heading south on the interstate, I said, "Can you give us the part of the story where we don't need to know the lay of the land?"

There was no answer for a moment, and then I heard a wheezing noise. Ava laughed softly. I glanced over. The old detective's eyes were shut, his mouth was hanging open, and he was gently snoring.

I guess two beers will do that to you when you're pushing eighty and close to death.

CHAPTER

30

ATTICUS JONES SLEPT UNTIL we were a mile shy of Buckhannon, where he seemed to hear some internal alarm clock because he came awake with a loud snort, looked around, and said, "Take Route Twenty south."

We rolled into the town, and as I turned onto the two-lane highway, I was surprised. I suppose I expected Buckhannon to be some idyllic backwater on a Saturday afternoon, and it *was* quaint, with older brick buildings and blooming trees everywhere, but the place was also bustling with dump trucks and pickups of every shape and size and crawling with ore rigs loaded with coal.

"There are mines here?" Ava asked.

"You are in Coal Central, young lady," the old detective replied. "Buckhannon's the county seat of Upshur County. You throw a stick in Upshur County, and there's a mine. You shake a dog, and a mining consultant will jump off before the fleas. That Sago Mine where they had the explosion back in 2006?

Killed those twelve men? That's just up the road there. Lot of money coming out of Buckhannon. Lot of black lung too. Killed my father. Killing me."

"You were a miner here?" I asked, surprised.

"Four years to get the money to go to West Virginia Wesleyan over there on the other side of town," Jones said. "Hated every minute of the mines but had to do it. Now, south of French Creek Road, you'll be looking for the signs to the Pig Lick Mine, up that Pig Lick Road. About nine miles out of town."

We drove past a mine-safety school and then traveled along the Buckhannon River, which looked beautiful in the spring sunshine. We reached Pig Lick Road fifteen minutes later.

There were warning signs about mining trucks and steep grades, and the dirt road had potholes and long stretches of washboard that had us bouncing all over the place even going slow. The enormous, bright yellow Crossfield Mining Company ore trucks laden with tons of coal, however, didn't seem affected in the least by the road conditions, and they scared the hell out of us as they barreled downhill going sixty-plus. But I managed to keep the sedan well out of their way through a series of switchbacks the Pig Lick Road made as it climbed the ridge.

Just below the top, however, an ore truck came up behind us, real close, and started honking for us to get out of the way.

"Don't worry," Jones told me. "You get to the crest there around the next bend and you'll find a place to pull off where you can see and he can get by."

The road was wider in the saddle and I did as he said,

swinging the car into a pull-off with a guardrail that separated it from a cliff that fell away several hundred feet to a narrow valley floor. The mining truck slowed as it passed. I saw a man in the passenger seat. He wore a blue uniform, sunglasses, and a yellow hard hat. He glowered at me as he went by.

CHAPTER

31

I SHRUGGED THE GUY'S anger off and gazed across the valley to where it looked like some giant had come along and lopped off the entire top of a mountain. The wound was almost a mile long and God only knew how wide. Dust rose off the top of the strip mine, stirred by the breeze and the dozens of trucks moving to and fro.

"Below us, that's Hog Hollow," Jones said. "That's where Thierry came from."

"The mine?" I asked, confused.

"No, no, that wasn't around back then," the old detective said. "But it's part of the story."

Jones cracked another bock beer and sipped from it as he explained that Thierry Mulch had been born into a family of pig farmers and moonshiners. Four generations of Mulches had lived in the bottom of Hog Hollow, the narrow valley between us and the present-day Pig Lick Mine.

Kevin "Little Boar" Mulch, Thierry's father, had gone to

school with Atticus Jones but dropped out at fourteen when his father, "Big Boar," died. The boy had to take over the family's affairs.

Little Boar married his second cousin Lydia when he was in his twenties and she was no more than sixteen. Lydia was a looker, which made Little Boar obsessively jealous. She was also bookish, which made him angry and resentful.

"Little Boar was ignorant and knew it but buried his own shame by always belittling Lydia," Jones told us. "Got worse after she had Thierry, who they called Baby Boar."

Addicted to his own rotgut hooch, Thierry's father became increasingly violent as his son grew up and revealed himself to be as bookish and smart as his mother. Little Boar put Lydia in the ER at St. John's Hospital on a number of occasions, once with a fractured arm, another time with a fractured jaw. Twice, Lydia brought Thierry into the same ER. His father had seen fault with how Baby Boar had done his chores and beat him with a barber's shaving strop.

"No one arrested the guy?" Ava said.

"Those were sadly different times, young lady," the detective said. "And from what I know, kids teased Thierry unmercifully as a child. They called him Pig Boy and would taunt him with 'Soooweeee' and 'Here, piggy, piggy!'"

When Thierry was thirteen, his mother met a mining engineer, someone from Montana or Oklahoma, and they had an affair. Without a word to her husband or son, Lydia left the family, took off with the engineer, and was never seen around Buckhannon again.

Everyone knew. People laughed behind Thierry's father's back, which made him get drunker, angrier, and even more reclusive. School became the boy's refuge, the only place he could go to escape his father's wrath.

"Smart boy, that Thierry," Jones said. "Real smart. And that was the shame of it all, what I think led to the killing."

Thierry wanted to go to college. Little Boar laughed at his son, told Baby Boar he would spend his life just like his father, tending to the hogs, but maybe Thierry could use his chemistry-class skills to make better moonshine. The farm had more than a hundred pigs on it, but Thierry's father said there was no money for something as useless as school.

The summer before what would have been Thierry's senior year, his father ordered him to quit high school, said it was a waste of time and he wouldn't stand for it. Right around then, a lawyer showed up in Hog Hollow with an offer to buy the Mulch property.

Little Boar owned twenty-six hundred acres, seventeen hundred of them barely tillable in the rocky bottom of the hollow and the rest considered worthless for generations, a steep, rocky ridge covered in hornpout hickory and other trash trees. Given that assessment of the property, the lawyer's offer was more than generous, in the high six figures. Little Boar refused to sell, said Hog Hollow and Pig Lick Mountain were sacred ground to the Mulch family and would always stay that way.

A month later, the offer was doubled, and Thierry's father refused again. The offer was tripled the month after that, and a drunken Little Boar pointed a double-barreled twelve-gauge at the attorney and told him to get off his property and never come back.

Jones took a sip, gestured toward the hollow, and said, "So

it's October first now, and school's on in Buckhannon, and Thierry's not there. About eight in the morning, I get a call from the sheriff. Thierry had just called in hysterical, said his father had fallen in with the hogs sometime during the night and they'd eaten most of him."

CHAPTER 32

FOR A SECOND I almost didn't believe my own ears, and then I said, "It's him, then. No doubt now."

I explained about Preston Elliot's skull and femur found at the commercial pig operation in Virginia.

"It *is* him," Jones crowed and slapped his thigh. "I knew it! When I got down to that farm about two hours later, I knew Thierry had killed his old man. I could just feel it; something about the way he moved when he showed me to the feedlot that the deputies had cleared. It was like he'd been relieved of some heavy burden."

When he got to the pigsty, Jones saw that most of Little Boar's flesh had been consumed already. Thierry showed little emotion, just gave this blank stare at what was left of his father. He told Jones that Little Boar had been drinking the evening before. The boy said that he did what he always did when his father was into his second jar of moonshine: he went to his room, locked the door, and read a book.

"Aristotle," Jones said. "He was reading Aristotle."

Thierry claimed he'd been deep into *Nicomachean Ethics,* reading about how man can best lead a good life, and had turned off his light around eleven. An hour later, he was roused by the pigs squealing, but that wasn't unusual. There were all sorts of turf battles in the sties. You just got used to it. Thierry said his drunken father must have gone out to see about the ruckus and fallen in.

"I told Thierry that he didn't seem too shook up about his daddy's death," the old detective recalled. "He said, 'I hated the sonofabitch, but even I wouldn't have wanted him to die that way.'"

That was Thierry's line and attitude during the entire investigation. Jones said he searched Thierry's room and found Aristotle on the table but also Dostoyevsky's *Crime and Punishment,* the story of a man who murders someone he thinks no one will miss.

Jones asked him about it, and Thierry shrugged, said he hadn't cracked it yet but that it was a requirement for honors English. Though his father had forced him to leave school, he'd been keeping up with the requirements.

The old detective said he tried every way he could to rattle the boy's story, but Baby Boar never wavered. Young Mulch had admitted readily that he'd thought about killing his father. Who wouldn't? The man was sadistic and in many ways deserved to die. And Thierry said that maybe someday, if it had come to it, he would have killed his father. But this was an accident, an act of God, and as fitting an ending as there could be for the man—eaten by his own hogs.

Jones said, "Autopsy showed a hairline fracture of Little Boar's skull, but the hogs gnawed and hooved on it so hard the ME couldn't say what had caused it."

Soon after, the old detective learned of the offers to buy the Mulch land. He pressed Thierry on that angle too. But young Mulch said the offers were news to him. Little Boar had never confided in him about anything.

Four months later, however, Thierry turned eighteen, and as the sole heir to the Mulch land, he signed a contract selling the property to the Crossfield Mining Company for $5.5 million. Turned out the worthless mountain was made almost entirely of coal.

When Jones pressed Thierry about the sale, Little Boar's son replied that he had no intention of being a pig farmer and that the sale was the practical thing to do, a way out, another act of God.

"He knew I didn't believe him," Jones said, shifting in his seat and adjusting the nose clip of his oxygen line. "He knew I was going to stay after him until I figured out a way to trip him up."

"So you think he staged his own death?" I asked.

CHAPTER 33

THE OLD DETECTIVE TIPPED his beer my way, said, "Thirteen months after he killed Little Boar. Took almost that long to get the estate through probate and establish that Thierry had a legal right to sell the land. But it went through and he turned the land over, got his money, bought a brand-new Ford pickup, and started partying hard."

The Crossfield Mining Company gave Thierry a month to sell the hogs and clear off the property. Two nights before they were set to bulldoze the pig farm, Baby Boar was seen drunk in town. Later that same night, around three a.m., someone traveling on Route 20 North spotted a fire burning up high on the ridge above Hog Hollow.

Jones gestured through the windshield toward the cliff. "Back then there was no guardrail here. Carrying a full tank of gas and going better than sixty by the trajectory, Thierry's new truck dropped two hundred and twenty-two feet and exploded in a fireball when it collided with a big boulder down there on the flat. It was a dry year and it lit the whole damn woods down there on fire, took them two days to put out the flames."

"Was there a body?" I asked.

"Squished pieces of one burned black as charcoal," Jones replied. "We recovered enough to say he was male, and that was about it. The fire that took the truck was incredibly hot, melted the steel, so hot the fire marshal thought there might have been a second accelerant on board, like naphtha or something. But we never found evidence of it. Then again, our chemical forensics weren't exactly first class back then."

I nodded. Naphtha was what was burned in camping stoves. It was extraordinarily combustible stuff. A truck soaked in naphtha that was also carrying a full tank of gasoline would have created an incredible explosion.

"How'd you identify Thierry?"

"Couldn't," the old detective said. "Little Boar believed in dentists less than in schools. Thierry had never been to a dentist in his life, and there was no such thing as DNA testing back then. Everyone just assumed it was him. Happened on the Mulch road in a Mulch truck with a male driver. Must have been a Mulch at the wheel."

"But you didn't think that added up?"

Jones shook his head. "No, I think he killed someone else, a transient or a hitchhiker, put him in the truck, and sent it flying off the cliff."

The old detective started to cough then, one of those long hacking sessions that shook his entire body. When he finally calmed, he said weakly, "I think we better start back, Dr. Cross. My daughter will be all shook up I'm not there when she comes for dinner."

"We'll get you back in time," I said and started the car.

One of those huge yellow ore trucks was climbing the last grade out of Hog Hollow, but I had plenty of room to pull out in front of it and start down the windy, pitted road to the state highway. The washboard was worse heading downhill because of all those massive trucks hitting the brakes before the tight turns, and I had to fight the wheel; the unmarked car shimmied as if a big dog had hold of the front bumper and was shaking it violently.

"What about the five million dollars?" Ava asked. "Where'd it go?"

The old detective had his bony hand on the dashboard, bracing himself, but he cracked a smile at me, said, "She's sharp. I was just getting to that."

"She is sharp," I said. I glanced in the rearview and saw her blush.

Jones said he couldn't find a record of Thierry depositing the $5.5 million in any bank in the state or in any of the states that border West Virginia.

"Was the check cashed?" Ava asked.

The old detective smiled again. "You got serious instincts, young lady. It took years to get Crossfield's attorney, a guy named Pete Garity, to talk to me candidly. He kept citing attorney-client privilege. But three years after Thierry's pickup was found burning with a body in it, I brought Mr. Garity a bottle of Maker's Mark and we got into it, and finally he admitted that young Mr. Mulch had been much shrewder than he appeared at first glance. The mining company had wanted to pay Thierry with a certified check, but he'd insisted on bearer bonds."

My head whipped toward him, and I was starting to say

the word *bearer* when I caught bright yellow motion in the rearview mirror. Fifty yards back, one of the ore trucks was coming at us like a juggernaut.

"Hold on!" I shouted and stomped on the gas.

CHAPTER 34

DETECTIVE TESS AALIYAH DRANK down her second double espresso since rising after six fitful hours of sleep and heading back to the office that Saturday afternoon. The murders were still in that critical forty-eight-hour window when most lethal crimes are solved, and she didn't want to waste a moment of it.

Aaliyah got to her desk around two and picked up a six-inch pile of files and reports, early forensic findings, and summaries of interviews patrol officers had conducted with Cross's neighbors.

She scanned through the early reports, finding the one that matched Bree Stone's blood type to that of Jane Doe, and another that matched Damon Cross's blood type to that of John Doe. There was a sticky note attached to the second report that said the FBI had pushed the DNA work on both bodies to the front of the line, but even in this day and age, it was roughly a fifty-hour process, which meant results on Jane Doe and Bree Stone were a day away, maybe more. And the tests on Damon would be back Monday at the earliest.

Setting those reports aside, the homicide detective started making a list of questions she wanted answered.

It was a long-standing habit, something her father had taught her. Now a retired Baltimore homicide cop, her dad believed that a mind was only as good as the questions it was asked and the orders it was given.

"Make a good list of questions and things to do and keep it running," he used to say. "Once you know the answer to a question or have fulfilled an order, mark it off and move on. That's how you create momentum."

First thing she wrote down was *1: How's Dad doing?*

After his wife, Tess's mother, died, a little over a year ago, Bernie Aaliyah had gone through a long mourning and depression. He was doing better, becoming increasingly independent, but he had been oddly guarded about his privacy recently.

It wasn't that he was cold to his daughter, not at all. He was just trying to rebuild his life, he said, and he was doing a good job at it, didn't need to talk to her every day or see her several times a week as he had in the first few months after her mom passed. She knew all that. But it had been a month since she'd seen him in person and four days since they'd spoken.

After that Aaliyah wrote in quick succession the questions and must-dos that popped into her head.

2. Did someone else have snipped skin like that? Ovals? ViCAP the MO.

3. Where was Damon Cross grabbed? His prep school? The Albany train station? Or on the ride home for Easter vacation?

4. Did Cross talk to Mulch between the time he took off and our conversation alerting me to Damon's body an hour later? Pull all phone records on every Cross phone.

5. Where is Cross? Put flags on all his credit cards and bank accounts.

Aaliyah did not think Alex Cross was in any way involved in the kidnappings or the murders. But her gut told her it was important to keep tabs on him, even if they were loose tabs, at least until he initiated further contact.

She decided to work backward through her list, first calling Ned Mahoney and asking if he and his colleagues in the FBI's white-collar crime units could research, open, and monitor all of Cross's accounts. Surprisingly, Mahoney thought it a very good idea, and he promised her he would.

Aaliyah had contacts of her own with the phone companies and soon had someone gathering the records she wanted. The detective then called the Kraft School and got a recording that said the offices were closed until classes resumed the following Monday morning. She knew the FBI had left messages with the school earlier, but Aaliyah left another anyway, asking the headmaster to give her a call as soon as possible. The matter was urgent and involved Damon Cross.

She hung up and was about to tackle the ViCAP request when she saw a long shadow cross her desk. She looked up and found John Sampson looming over her cubicle wall with a report in his hand.

"Read this," he said.

She took the report, saying, "You didn't sleep?"

"Not yet," he replied.

Aaliyah scanned the document. It was a ViCAP report on the mutilation patterns. She glanced up. "I was just about to do this."

Sampson grunted. "Great minds think alike."

Aaliyah smiled and returned to the report, which focused on a murder six years before in the northern Idaho town of Bonner's Ferry, hard by the border with Montana. A woman's body with oval pieces of skin missing was found floating in the Kootenay River. The second page of the report showed photographs. The dead woman was a light-skinned African American, and the oval cuts were very similar to the ones found on Jane and John Doe.

"The cuts," she said, feeling excited. "They're almost the same."

"Yes," Sampson agreed. "Just not everywhere on the body."

Indeed, the report indicated that only six pieces of skin were missing on the dead woman in Idaho. Dental records identified her as Katrina Moffett of Troy, Montana, which was about thirty miles upriver from where the body was found. Moffett, twenty-nine, a teacher in the local elementary school, had gone missing after friends dropped her at home late one night following a party at a bar called the Dirty Shame Saloon in the nearby town of Yaak.

Moffett's husband was serving in Iraq at the time, and her friends swore she was not carrying on any kind of affair. They did say, however, that since moving to the area, she'd gotten anonymous threats that featured racial slurs.

Not surprising, Aaliyah thought. *There are all sorts of Aryan nuts up there, aren't there?* Definitely. Ruby Ridge was somewhere in northern Idaho.

She went back to her reading and found that Montana state investigators had considered the same angle. They looked at everyone living in a five-mile radius of Moffett's home and were soon considering a young man named Claude Harrow as their prime suspect.

Harrow had recently been released from the Montana State Prison at Deer Lodge after doing six years for armed robbery. During that stint, he'd joined the Aryan Brotherhood, and he was an outspoken racist.

But Harrow's alibi of being one hundred and fifty miles from Troy the night of the murder was corroborated by four of his friends, all neo-Nazi sympathizers. Six months after the killing, Harrow inherited a small piece of land near Frostburg, in rural northwestern Maryland. He packed up and left.

At the request of Montana state investigators, the FBI kept track of Harrow in a database set aside for hate crimes. For the past three years, the neo-Nazi had been living on his inherited land, working as a part-time logger, attending skinhead functions, and doing little else.

Aaliyah looked up at Sampson, said, "Frostburg's what? An hour and a half from here?"

"Give or take," Sampson said. "Here's the best part: I ran Harrow's name through the Maryland DMV and he's got a 1988 Chevy pickup. How much do you want to bet his tires are bald?"

Aaliyah grabbed her coat. "Let's go look."

"Great minds," Sampson said, tapping his temple. "I've already requisitioned a car."

CHAPTER

35

THE MINING TRUCK CAUGHT up to us as I power-drifted the sedan through the oncoming switchback, gunning the accelerator instead of braking, trying to get the tires to skip off the ruts and washboard. The ore truck's massive fender barely brushed my car's rear bumper.

But I knew we were done for.

Control of the vehicle was wrenched out of my hands and given over to God and physics. The sedan went into a sickening twist that threw the rear end around hard. I got a snap look through the windshield and up into the cab of the mining truck as we spun down the road.

Trees and rocks whirled by as I threw my forearm across Atticus Jones's chest. The car tires caught on some deeper rut and pitched us up on two wheels. Ava screamed, sure we were flipping. But something about the next rut we hit caused the car to slam back down on all four wheels, and then it was heading straight down the mountain in the wrong lane of the empty road.

"The truck!" Ava screamed. "It's coming again!"

The ore truck was coming hard in its lane, and I suspected the driver meant to get up alongside of us and then bump us off the road into the woods. We were still going forty miles an hour when I mashed the brakes.

The mining truck shot by us. I hauled hard on the steering wheel, brought our car in behind the big rig, and released the emergency brake. He sped up, trying to outrun me, but by that point I was so infuriated that I would have driven off a cliff, fallen two hundred feet, and risked a fireball just to catch these bastards and find out why they were trying to kill us. I stayed with them the entire way down the mountain and caught up when they reached the T where Pig Lick Road met West Virginia State Highway 20.

There was surprisingly heavy traffic in both directions, other trucks from other mines and school buses and cars, and the ore truck was forced to stop at the sign. I pulled in close behind the rear of the truck where I couldn't be seen in their mirrors. I threw the car in park, bolted out, and drew the Colt.

I ran to the passenger side and sprinted along the flank of the ore truck. The brakes sighed. The truck rolled. I jumped up onto the running board and grabbed a metal handle meant to help passengers access the cab just as the mining truck began to accelerate out onto the highway in a tight curve that almost threw me off.

But when the truck straightened out and began to gain speed, I was still holding on. I tapped the window with the Colt. The passenger was that same guy who'd given me the glowering look at the top of the pass into Hog Hollow.

He'd been laughing then, and he still bore a smirk when he jerked at my tapping and looked over to find me aiming at him at point-blank range. Through the window I caught a subtle shift in his shoulders and suspected him of reaching for the door handle.

I aimed away from his head, just past his nose, closed my eyes to protect them from flying glass, and pulled the trigger. The Colt barked and jumped in my hand. The bullet shattered the window, showering the guy with hailstones of glass and turning the truck's windshield into a spider's web.

"The next one's going through your brain, asshole!" I shouted. "Stop this truck! Now!"

"What the fuck, man, are you insane?" the driver yelled.

"You're next!" I shouted.

CHAPTER 36

THE DRIVER DOWNSHIFTED AND slammed on the brakes, trying to throw me, but I held tight and kept the Colt aimed at the passenger's head until we came to a full stop right in the middle of the northbound lane of Route 20.

"You have a phone?" I demanded.

"What?" the driver whined.

"A cell," I said.

By now the passenger was shaking so hard he looked like he'd wandered into a cold-storage locker soaking wet. "I do."

"Call 911."

"C'mon, man," the driver said.

"Call!" I shouted. "Tell them I want the sheriff out here. Now!"

He reluctantly punched in the number, said some crazy guy had a gun aimed at him in the middle of Route 20 near Pig Lick Road.

That brought sirens ten minutes later, and flashing blue

lights and three cruisers. I was right where I had been, gun to the passenger's head, when they arrived. Deputies exited their cruisers with pistols and shotguns drawn.

"Put down your weapon!" one shouted.

I pulled it away from the man's head, holstered the gun, and climbed down. Putting my hands up, I yelled, "My name is Alex Cross. I am a homicide detective with the Washington, DC, police. These clowns tried to run us off the Pig Lick Road during the course of an investigation."

"Fuck," the passenger said. "A cop. Fuck, Billy, you said—"

"Shut up, Clete," the driver said. "Don't say a damn thing."

"Gun on the ground," a blond female deputy shouted, still aiming at me.

The driver got out while I put the Colt on the pavement. He shouted, "This crazy fucker can't drive, was going too fast, went into three-sixties up there in front of us, and next thing we know, he's up on the cab, gun drawn and shooting!"

"That's not what happened at all!" Ava yelled. She'd come up in back of me. "They hit us from behind, just like Alex said."

"No way!" the driver yelled. "No way."

"Everybody calm down!" called a frail voice.

I could hear the click of Jones's walker and the wheels of his oxygen tank crunching on the gravel.

The female deputy lowered her gun several degrees. "Atticus? That you?"

"Who the hell else looks like this?" Jones said as he came up beside me. "And these frickin' idiots hit us from behind, no doubt about it. They meant to crash us, for some goddamned reason."

The driver said, "This is bullshit. We're gonna get railroaded here. I want an attorney."

The passenger climbed out, spilling glass from the lap of his coverall. He looked at me like I was dirt, said, "They're lying, all three of 'em. But I can see where this is going. I want an attorney too."

After the deputies cuffed the two mine workers and put them in the backseat of a cruiser, the blond one, Anne Craig, came over and hugged Jones.

Deputy Craig looked at me, said, "I know who you are, Dr. Cross, and what's happened to your family. It's all over the news. I'm sorry, very sorry, for your losses. But why are you *here?*"

I hesitated. Jones said, "He's looking into the old Mulch case."

Craig rolled her eyes. She'd obviously heard about the case from Jones, probably several times.

"It could be connected to the man who has my family," I said.

"Really?" the deputy said.

"Looks likely, as a matter of fact," I replied.

She jerked a thumb over her shoulder. "These pukes involved?"

"I have no idea," I said. "You find out, you let me know."

"Need you to come into town to make statements," Craig said.

"Deputy, we're on a tight deadline," I told her. "I wasn't expecting all this."

"What kind of deadline?"

I glanced at Ava and Jones, said, "I can't say. But believe me, the safety of the rest of my family depends on me meeting it."

She studied me, then shook her head. "You discharged a firearm far outside your jurisdiction. I can't just let you walk without making a formal statement. I'm sorry, Detective Cross."

CHAPTER

37

IT WAS NEARLY FIVE THIRTY by the time we'd made our statements and were free to leave Buckhannon. I had less than a day to meet Mulch's deadline and no idea how to make it happen.

Atticus Jones was totally exhausted. He gave me his daughter's phone number and fell asleep before I got the car started. The front end of the unmarked car had a serious shimmy from the washboard and pulled hard to the right, but it remained drivable. I had Ava dial the old detective's daughter and put the burner phone on speaker.

"Gloria Jones," she answered.

I explained that I was a cop, that her father had been helping me, and that he would be a little late for dinner. In return, I got a ranting earful for sneaking him out of the hospice in the first place.

"My God, he's dying," she yelled at one point. "Can't you see that?"

Earlier in the day, I hadn't. Not really. But now Jones was

coughing and hacking in his sleep and looking terribly small and frail.

Amazingly, however, his energy picked up again when I pulled into the parking lot at Fitzwater's Gracious Living facility a little after seven.

Gloria Jones, a handsome, well-put-together woman in her late thirties, and the receptionist came stomping out, and they didn't have their happy faces on. They both laid into me this time, telling me how irresponsible I was even as they coaxed Jones into a wheelchair and rolled the old detective back to his room. I followed, took it all, and said nothing. Ava brought up the rear.

Jones finally yelled, "Goddamn it, Gloria, shut up for a second. Don't you see who this poor man is?"

She looked at me, puzzled, then shrugged and said, "Detective Cross?"

"Detective *Alex* Cross," Jones said.

Gloria blinked, said, "Alex…oh…I saw that story: your wife, your son, and…" She looked at me closely. "Why are you *here?* Why aren't you in DC?"

There was suddenly an expression of hunger on her face, a look that I thought I recognized. "What do you do for a living, Ms. Jones?"

She told me. I *had* recognized that hungry expression. And in one long, stretched-out moment, I realized she might be able to help me.

"Can we keep this between us?" I said.

She shook her head. "You owe me for almost killing my dad."

"The hell he does," Jones protested.

"Tell you what," I said to Gloria. "You help me, and once

I've got my family back, I'll gratefully tell you exactly what I've been doing here."

The old detective's daughter thought about that, then asked suspiciously, "What do I have to do in return?"

"Help me murder someone before two o'clock tomorrow afternoon."

CHAPTER 38

JOHN SAMPSON AND TESS AALIYAH drove up a muddy road out in the sticks southwest of Frostburg, Maryland. Suburbs gave way to truck farms and then to woods where drizzling rain fell.

"I heard you and Cross were boyhood friends," Aaliyah said at one point.

"Closer than brothers," Sampson replied. "The bond between us was instant. We were ten and he'd lost his parents, and Nana Mama, his grandmother, had brought him up to DC from South Carolina. She was a vice principal and everyone was scared of her. Me too, and she lived just down the street."

"You were scared?" Aaliyah asked, half smiling.

"Miz Hope's past ninety and she still scares me," Sampson said, allowing a sad grin. "We get her home and safe, and I'll be scared all over again."

Aaliyah laughed quietly and felt better because Sampson's attitude was that the Crosses *were* going to be saved. In her opinion, that kind of hope was still the best attitude for any detective to have. As her father had pointed out over and over again, cynical cops might be the stereotypical crime solvers, but they burned out fast. The detectives who stayed positive, who carried hope in their hearts, were the ones most likely to have stamina. She was glad that Cross's oldest friend was coming from that place.

"Miz Hope introduced the two of you?"

"Sort of," Sampson said, then gestured ahead. "It's coming up on this next turn."

They found a two-track drive that led down into the sopping forest toward a creek and Claude Harrow's property. A padlocked quarter-inch steel cable blocked the way. They parked and got out.

It had obviously rained hard sometime in the past several hours. There were puddles, and the tree limbs and leaves hung heavy and dripped. The air should have been full of ozone and fresh as spring. But it smelled like a doused campfire.

They went around the cable and walked down the soggy road, the smoke smell getting stronger. Sampson pulled his service pistol.

"You want to start from that position?" Aaliyah asked.

"When I'm dealing with possibly murderous skinheads, this is always my starting position," Sampson replied.

Aaliyah saw the practical wisdom in that and drew her weapon as well. They walked down the two-track lane, hearing the engorged creek, and then rounded a tight corner that revealed a clearing, a ramshackle barn, and a 1988 faded blue Chevy pickup. She guessed the pile of smoking ruins had been Harrow's home.

"This happened today," she said.

"Past eight or nine hours," Sampson agreed.

"No fire department?"

He shrugged. "We're in the middle of nowhere."

They stopped just shy of the clearing. Sampson yelled, "Claude Harrow!"

The two detectives stood there for several moments waiting for a response but got none. They eased out into the yard, a mud patch, really, with sparse and thorny weeds. Sampson called out again. The breeze shifted and for a moment Aaliyah smelled stale urine. Over the gurgling of the stream, she thought she caught a low moan but couldn't tell where it came from.

"You hear that?" she asked softly.

CHAPTER

39

"NO," SAMPSON SAID. "WHAT?"

Aaliyah stood there listening, and then shook her head. "Nothing."

She scanned the mud for footprints, seeing the vague impressions of several going back and forth between the burned building and the barn, and others crossing over toward the woods and a steep little hillside. She could already tell that the rain had marred the tracks, made them useless.

They went closer to what was left of the burned building: smoking posts and charred beams. A twisted black stovepipe jutted up out of the wreckage. Aaliyah walked around one way and Sampson the other. Moving closer to the black pipe, she spotted the woodstove. Its door was wide open.

Aaliyah took another two steps, smelled something like burned meat, and saw a chain saw—or what was left of it, anyway—a scorched toolbox, a charred gas can, and something else, partially buried in the blackened debris.

"I got a body," she called out.

"Sonofabitch," Sampson said.

When someone is burned alive, the corpse is often found curled up in a fetal position. This was the case here as well. The body was rolled onto its left side facing Aaliyah, knees drawn to the chest and hands wrapped around them. More often than not in these kinds of deaths, the victim is found with his chin tucked down to his chest and his arms wrapped around his head, as if his last instinct was to shield his face from the flames.

But this burned corpse wasn't positioned like that at all. The head was twisted upward, and the black, empty eye sockets seemed to be looking right at the detective. The victim's mouth was frozen open, as if his last utterance had been a scream.

"Stupid Nazi," Sampson said. "Fueling up the chain saw with the woodstove open. Rocket scientist of the year. How much you want to bet he was a meth head?"

Aaliyah saw how it could be interpreted like that but reserved judgment.

"Any tracks over your way?" she asked.

"Plenty of man tracks and a bunch of an animal of some sort," he replied. "We need to call this into the Allegheny County Sheriff."

She nodded, pulled out her cell. "No service."

Sampson looked at his, said, "So much for 'Can you hear me now?'"

Aaliyah backed away from the smoking debris and moved toward the pickup truck. The Chevy was parked under a tin-roofed shed that hung off the side of the cockeyed barn. There were landscaping tools in its bed, and shovels, pickaxes, ropes, and the like. Holstering her gun, she squatted to peer under the carriage at the tires.

Sampson joined her, said, "They seem bald to me."

The tires would have to be examined by an expert to say for sure, but they looked the part. What did that mean? If these tires and the tracks in Cross's alley matched, was Thierry Mulch also Claude Harrow, and vice versa? Was that the madman over there, burned to a crisp?

Or was it someone entirely different?

Aaliyah prayed that the potential evidence had not all gone up in fire and ash, and then she stood and walked to the doors of the barn. There was a steel bar and a padlock on them. The wind shifted and she could have sworn she smelled stale urine again, and then something new, another odor she recognized all too well.

Sampson stepped up beside her, and she pointed to her nose and sniffed. The big detective took a deep breath. His expression hardened, and he said, "That's blood rotting."

"I'm going in there," she said.

"Absolutely," Sampson said.

He went to Harrow's pickup truck, put on a pair of work gloves, and got the pickax. The blade hit the wood and chopped the hasp holding the lock with one blow.

Sampson dropped the tool, slid back the steel bar, and tugged open the doors. Pistol out again, Aaliyah stepped up, seeing in the gloom what looked like a horse barn that had been turned into a woodworking shop.

There were several stalls on the right wall filled with stacked lumber. In the center of the space stood band and table saws, an old lathe, and several other woodworking machines she couldn't name. There was a long wooden bench at the back of the barn, and hand tools hung on the wall above it. Flipping on the small Maglite she always carried, Aaliyah took another step, trying to get a better angle on all of it.

The dog exploded from the shadows without warning, a huge leaping Rottweiler.

CHAPTER 40

AALIYAH TRIED TO GET the gun around but instead felt crushing pain bolt through her right forearm as she was knocked off her feet by something with the force of a tackling linebacker.

She hit the wet ground hard. The wind was slammed out of her lungs, and her pistol and flashlight fell from her hands.

The dog instantly released his hold on her arm. His toenails ripped into her shins and thighs as his powerful legs scrambled for purchase. The Rottweiler lunged up her body, snapped at her face and neck with his bloody mouth.

Aaliyah tucked her chin down, trying to protect her throat.

The dog clamped down on her cheek and forehead and began to shake her. She screamed at the white-hot pain of the bite. That seemed only to inflame the dog to further violence.

As the detective felt her skin starting to tear, the attack dog suddenly hunched up stiff, from nose to tail, opened his muzzle, and released her head. Then he let out a mournful, bug-eyed howl, rolled off her, and howled again, over and over.

For a second, the detective remained dazed by the sudden ferocity of the attack, and then she realized blood was trickling down her cheeks and dripping from her forehead into her left eye. Her right forearm was throbbing and she thought she was going to be sick.

"Sampson?" she gasped.

He grunted. "Gimme a second and don't move."

She turned her head and saw him dragging the dog by a rope he must have gotten from the truck bed and looped around the animal's neck. The Rottweiler's head was down, no fight in him at all. When Sampson tied the rope tight to one of the shed's support posts, the beast immediately lay down, groaning and panting.

Aaliyah was sitting up by the time Sampson got back to her. He'd already taken off his jacket and shirt and was tearing strips off the latter.

"Stay put," he said. "He bit you something good."

"He...he came out of nowhere," the detective said, bewildered. "How did you get him off me?"

"Kicked him in the balls," Sampson said.

He was on his knees now, folding the rest of his shirt into a large pad that he pressed across the left side of her face. "Hold that."

Aaliyah held her hand up and pressed it to her skin, trying to ignore the sharp throbbing pain there. But she couldn't get away from the agony in her right arm. "I think he broke my arm."

"Hold tight a second," Sampson said as he wrapped and tied the longer strips around the makeshift pad.

Five minutes later, he helped her to her feet. Her arm was in a sling he'd fashioned from his jacket and her shoulder holster.

"Okay," Sampson said. "We're gonna walk right out of here and get you to a hospital where they can give you some painkillers, clean you up, and take a look at that arm. Maybe treat you for rabies too. Who knows if that dog ever got his shots."

"Not yet," she said, even though she felt dizzy and sick. "What about that smell?"

"It'll wait," he said.

"You've stopped the bleeding," she said. "Ten minutes more won't kill me."

Sampson hesitated, and then smiled. "You're a tough one. You remind me of my wife. Billie's like that too."

Aaliyah tried to smile, but it hurt too much. She asked him for her Maglite, which was still in the mud. Sampson got it for her, cleaned it off, and once again they started to probe the barn, looking for the source of that smell.

They found it under a bench in a galvanized bucket with a perforated lid: seven inches of coagulated blood. Was it human or animal? And where had it come from?

Sampson pointed to a ZipSnip cordless cutting tool hanging above the bench that looked like it had blood on the blade, but neither of them touched it. The throbbing in her cheek and forehead turned fiery, and she resigned herself to leaving the place to the Allegheny County detectives and a full forensics team. Or, better yet, the FBI. They had jurisdiction. This was an interstate kidnap/murder case after all.

As they walked back through the woodworking machines, Aaliyah tried to figure out where the dog had come from and why she hadn't seen him until he was in full attack mode. Remembering the angle at which the Rottweiler appeared, she went toward the horse stalls filled with lumber.

Aaliyah soon spotted a gap of about fifteen inches between the lumber pile and the far wall of the first stall. She shone her light into it.

A broken slat in the barn wall provided an opening big enough for a dog to get through. There was a filthy, ragged blanket on the floor, the dog's bed, she supposed, and what at first glance looked like the rawhide pieces people give dogs so they'll chew on those instead of the furniture. But then Sampson lit up a rear wall with a ledge on the top, and Aaliyah felt nauseated all over again.

Those weren't rawhide strips in the dog's bed or on that shelf right there in stacks, like Pringles chips without the can. They were curling ovals of black human flesh in various stages of drying.

CHAPTER 41

AT THREE IN THE morning, I set the GoPro camera and the harness on a picnic bench beside a deserted gravel parking lot lit by high-pressure sodium lights. Across the lot, there was a long, low yellow-and-silver prefabricated metal building that put me in mind of the commercial pig barn where Preston Elliot's bones had been found.

Aiming the high-definition camera at myself and turning it on, I felt a weight descend on my shoulders. I glanced angrily at the camera and tugged on latex gloves, saying, "I'm doing what you wanted, Mulch. When I'm done, you let someone go."

Then I drew the Colt, bowed my head, and prayed God would forgive me for what I was about to do. I'd had to kill men before, several of them, as a matter of fact. But in those terrible moments when I'd had to turn a gun or some other weapon on a fellow human, it had always been in self-defense, situations where there'd been only the instinct to survive and all moral conduct had been nullified by my right to live.

This was different. I was about to kill for no reason other than that I had decided one life *was* worth less than another. The weight of that was like no other I have ever felt or imagined—crushing, disintegrating, and wretched at its core. I wondered whether Mulch would see the agony of my predicament crippling my posture, worming through my mind, and gnawing at my skin like some flesh-eating bacteria.

Would he feed on it?

Is this what he wanted to see?

Was I his entertainment?

For much of the night leading up to that moment, I'd been thinking hard about Mulch, about what could possibly be driving him. Atticus Jones thought that Mulch had simply fallen in love with murder and with getting away with murder. Forcing me to kill for his amusement was just a twisted next step.

So be it, I thought numbly. *I'm dooming my soul to save the ones I love.* Feeling the torture of that, I set the pistol on the picnic table, picked up the GoPro, brought it close to my face, and whispered in a wavering voice, "This is how you want to see it, isn't it? From my point of view?"

Then I turned the camera away slowly, took the harness hanging from the bottom, and fit it and the camera on my head. After adjusting the camera so it could pick up the gun if my arm was extended to shoot, I set off toward the building.

The temperature was in the sixties, but to me it felt like the air had been heated to a hundred degrees or more. My breath turned labored. Sweat trickled off my brow and from under my arms. And yet my hands were clammy, as if I'd just touched the cold skin of a day-old corpse.

Hearing the gravel crunch under my shoes like so many tiny brittle bones, I turned my head and the camera, giving

Mulch multiple angles of the building. I drifted the camera across the sign for A. J. Machine Tool and Die before going around the near corner of the building and passing a closed loading dock. I climbed cement stairs to a door, twisted the knob, and opened it.

CHAPTER 42

INSIDE THE LOADING DOCK, the only light, a red bulb, revealed boxes, dollies, and hand trucks. With slow, soft steps I went to an interior door and hesitated there, my head bent, looking down at my gun hand and my gloved free hand, which hovered over the thumb latch. My shoulders trembled, and I wondered if I had the strength to press the latch, much less pull a trigger.

"Do it," I choked out softly. "Just do it."

Then I thumbed the latch and drew the door open. I raised my head, which raised the camera, and both shook ever so slightly, as if I were in the first stages of Parkinson's disease. I stepped through into the machine shop. Without pausing to look around, I pivoted and slowly shut the door so the click was no louder than the second hand ticking on my grandmother's clock.

The shop was lit like the loading dock, with red lights glowing in cages bolted high on the walls every thirty feet or so. At the rear of the space, however, several bright lights shone in an office with windows that were opaque for the first three feet and then clear, as if the manager liked his privacy but also wanted to be able to look out at his workers. I stood several long moments, peering intently over the tops of heavy metal lathes, drill presses, planers, cutting tools, and bending devices, until I saw dark movement behind the lower, opaque glass.

"He's in there, Mulch," I said in the barest of whispers.

Then I set off slowly through the machine shop, hyper-aware of everything around me, sidestepping rebar and pipe, pausing in the darkness next to two of the biggest machines to listen and peer out until I spotted a shadow moving behind the glass.

The side door to the office was open, throwing a thick shaft of light toward heavy-duty shelving that held stacks of sheet metal and steel bar. Ten feet from that light, I hesitated again, thinking I could not go through with it, that I could not sacrifice an innocent human being even if it meant saving another innocent human being who just happened to be more precious to me.

But could I imagine having to face another member of my family dead, beaten to a pulp and carved up for fetish reasons I couldn't begin to fathom?

I couldn't. I just couldn't. The war inside me echoed in the short, sharp breaths I was taking and in the jerky way I stepped into the dim light.

Wearing a green baseball cap and a green jacket that said SECURITY, an old black man sat with his back turned not ten feet from me, hunched over, facing one of those old rolltop desks. He was hunt-and-peck typing on a computer keyboard. The screen was big, but he craned his neck toward it as if he could barely see what he was working on.

"Sir," I said softly. "I'm here, sir. It's time."

The man froze for a long moment, then hunched over more and said, "Let me close this. One last letter to my daughter."

I just stood there, looking at his back, sniffling and feeling tears dripping down my cheeks. The computer screen went dark.

Atticus Jones swiveled in the chair to face me. Despite the shadows, I could make out his expression of resoluteness and courage. He licked his lips before he said, "I've lived a long life, young man, but the pain's too much. You're doing me a favor; nothing wrong with mercy. I want to see my wife again. I want to see my mother and my father. I want you to see your loved ones too. In this life, not the next."

"Yes, sir," I sobbed. "And may God have mercy on my soul."

Then Jones clasped his hands and bowed his head. A slat of light crossed his face, and then it was lost in shadow.

I raised the Colt shakily, the barrel wavering during several sharp breaths before the wispy white hair of his head steadied in the Colt's sights.

And I squeezed the trigger.

And I shot that wonderful old man dead.

Part Three

CHAPTER

43

SUNDAY HIT PAUSE, STARED at the dead man on the computer screen.

"Look it there, Marcus," Acadia purred. "Cross made it a mercy killing. Bet you weren't expecting that. I know I wasn't, but even so, it's made me hornier than ought to be allowed in civilized— "

He cut her off, snarling, "My love? With all due respect for your insatiable libido, please shut the fuck up."

They were in the living room of an apartment Sunday had rented in Washington's Kalorama neighborhood. He sat on the couch. She and Cochran stood behind him.

"Why should I shut the fuck up?" Acadia demanded hotly after a moment's pause. "Isn't this what you wanted? Cross a murderer, an existential man? Or are you just pissed that he's made it seem more like a blessing than a killing?"

Sunday wanted to spin around and slap her silly. But he restrained himself and said, "It has nothing to do with that. I'm thinking, Acadia. You've heard of that, haven't you? Thinking?"

"Screw you, Marcus," she said, and she stormed down the hall, went into the bedroom, and slammed the door.

"Don't matter," Cochran said. He came around to the front of the couch. " 'Bout it being a mercy killing, I mean. He did it, pulled the trigger. Straight up."

Sunday said nothing. Part of him agreed. But then he noticed a stirring in his gut.

Gut feelings had saved Sunday in more than one desperate situation. Gut feelings had led him to torch Thierry Mulch all those years ago, hadn't they? Gut feelings had made him a fortune, given him freedom, hadn't they?

They had, and as he continued to study that image of the dead man, Sunday realized that his stomach had gone nervous and acidic when it should have been calm and alkaline. Watching the video had made him feel vulnerable.

But why?

Why was he so agitated? However Cross tried to mitigate his crime, Cochran was right: he had done the deed. There was no doubt about that, was there? No. Cross *had* abandoned moral order. Cross *had* become a cold-blooded murderer. Cross *had* become a universe unto himself. *Just like me,* Sunday thought.

But something about the victim bothered him, something beyond the fact that the man appeared to have been terminally ill and eager for death. Something about that man seemed... well...off.

Sunday started up the video again. He watched every move and listened to every breath and sound Cross made before entering that machine tool-and-die shop. He studied the detective's face when he spoke to the camera and then the scene in which Cross walked into the office and revealed the old, withered black man asking to be delivered from his suffering.

For the most part, the victim's face had remained in shadow, but for several seconds before the shot, as the old man clasped his hands and bowed his head, a slat of light traveled over his features, revealing it in sections.

"And may God have mercy on my soul," Cross said and shot him.

"Told you," Cochran said, and he walked into the kitchen.

Sunday backed the video up and played that light traveling over the victim's face three times until the pieces gathered in his mind like a jigsaw and made his stomach lurch so hard he thought he was going to puke.

Atticus Jones.

Atticus fucking Jones.

Detective Atticus fucking Jones of the West Virginia State Police. Or what was left of that nosy sonofabitch, anyway.

How the hell had…? What the fuck did this…?

For the first time since Sunday had set his entire diabolical scheme in motion, a shiver of doubt passed through him. Somehow, Cross had found the man who'd investigated his father's death. Somehow, Cross had gotten to the detective who'd looked into the fiery passing of Thierry Mulch all those years ago. And then Cross had killed Jones to satisfy Sunday *and* put the old bastard out of his misery?

But why the security jacket? Was that what had become of Atticus Jones? Had the great detective been doomed to the pitiful life of a night watchman?

Was it a coincidence? How was that possible? What were the odds?

Ten thousand to one, Sunday decided. No, make that a

hundred thousand to one. No matter how random the universe could seem at times, this was no random event. No way.

It was a message. Cross was telling Sunday that he was on his trail.

Sunday tasted bile creeping up his throat. Then he swallowed hard at it, growing scornful and defiant.

That trail is cold, Cross, he thought. *Thierry Mulch disappeared in flames two and a half decades ago. By killing Atticus Jones, you honestly did me a favor; you eliminated one more potential witness against me.*

He stood and walked past the kitchen, where Cochran was eating cold Chinese food and drinking a beer, and went down the hall to the closed door of his bedroom. He opened it, found Acadia lying on her side in the bed, reading a book.

"Far as I'm concerned, this is your gig now," Acadia said, not looking his way. "You and Cochran can go to Memphis and handle it. I'm done."

CHAPTER 44

SUNDAY SET ASIDE THE video in his mind, stared at her, said, "That right? You're done?"

Acadia almost nodded, but then seemed to think better of it. She took a sidelong look at Sunday. Their eyes locked, and her defiance gradually waned until she dropped her chin and looked away, saying, "Just a figure of speech, Marcus. Back there you treated me like I was…"

"Stupid?" he asked, softer now.

She glanced at him angrily, nodded.

"I'm sorry," he said. "One thing you are not, Acadia, is stupid. And I'm sorry if I made it sound that way. There was just something off about that video."

Acadia nodded again, this time with more confidence, and looked directly at him. "What was off?"

Sunday hesitated, thought about telling her, but decided against it. "I haven't figured that out yet."

"You don't think the video's real?"

"Oh, it's real enough, as far as I can tell," he replied. "You'd have to have a real expert to doctor something like that."

She thought about that, said, "In any case, Marcus, just so we're on the same page here, you've made your point, right? Turned Cross into a killer? Proved your hypothesis?"

"I think so."

"So which one are you going to let go?"

Without hesitation, Sunday said, "None of them. They're all sticking around just a little while longer."

Acadia's expression hardened, and she sat up. "That wasn't the plan," she said. "That wasn't what you told—"

"Plans change, things evolve," Sunday said coldly. "Until I figure out what Cross was up to with that tape, he gets no mercy. Absolutely none."

"So what are you going to make him do?"

"Why, I'm going to make him kill again, of course."

CHAPTER 45

FOR WHAT FELT LIKE the hundredth time, I watched myself shoot Atticus Jones at point-blank range, felt my stomach drop when the terminally ill man lurched and fell into the shadows, blood pooling on the floor.

"Don't worry, Alex, Mulch will buy it," Jones croaked. "Gloria's friend is a genius. Mulch will absolutely buy it."

Sitting in a chair beside the old detective's bed at the nursing facility, the computer in my lap, I chewed on the inside of my cheek before saying, "Mulch doctored those photographs of my family. I'm just afraid he'll anticipate me using the same tactic against him and respond accordingly."

"He'd have to be a CGI expert to spot the flaws," Gloria Jones said flatly. She was sitting on the other side of the bed, drinking yet another cup of coffee and eating the last of the burgers Ava had brought in.

Jones's daughter was an award-winning news producer at

WPXI, the NBC affiliate in Pittsburgh. The night before, after I'd told her what I had in mind, she'd bought into the plan and went far beyond what I'd hoped, contacting Richard Martineau, an old friend of hers who worked in computer-generated imagery out in Hollywood.

In fewer than six hours, Martineau had done a masterly job, taking the GoPro footage and inserting the fake head wound and the blood that ran from it so convincingly. But I was still uneasy, thinking I might have gone too far in agreeing to let Jones be the victim.

If Mulch did recognize the old detective, I had no idea how he'd react. We'd all discussed it, of course, and ultimately I'd come over to Jones's point of view: that recognizing the detective would upset Mulch, maybe enough to throw him off his game, maybe enough that he would make a mistake.

But what if seeing the detective triggered a more brutal response? What if he decided I'd gotten too close, and he responded in the worst way? How would I deal with that? How could any man deal with that sort of loss?

For the most part, I'd been able to box off thoughts of Bree and Damon, except during those six hours when Martineau had worked on the video and I'd retreated to a nearby motel room to sleep. In bed, behind a locked door and before I'd collapsed into unconsciousness, I'd been unable to keep a lid on my roiling emotions. Though as far as I knew, there had been no definitive matching of Bree's and Damon's DNA with the bodies, I could not help fearing they were both dead and gone.

Bree could be gone.

Forever.

Damon could be gone.

Forever.

And there was the real and terrible possibility that Nana Mama, Jannie, and Ali would soon be gone.

Forever.

That word—*forever*—had released a wave of anguish that broke my resolve and my faith, and I'd curled up in a fetal position, feeling like I'd been gut shot and sobbing like there was no tomorrow.

But when I'd awoken to Gloria Jones pounding at my door and seen the video, I'd taken heart. It was totally convincing. For all intents and purposes, Atticus Jones had died there onscreen. For all intents and purposes—

"Do you think he'll let one of them go?" Ava asked, shaking me from my conflicted thoughts.

"We can hope so," I said. "But I'm not counting on it."

"So what are you going to do?" Gloria Jones asked. "Just sit here and wait to see if a member of your family shows up somewhere?"

"Ball's in Mulch's court," her father said. "Not much else he can do."

I thought about that a few moments and then shook my head. "I think I'll go to the Berkshires, try to figure out how Damon was taken."

"That's a ten-hour drive, at least," Gloria Jones said.

"I'll fly out of Pittsburgh, go to Albany," I said. "His classmates and teachers should be returning today from their Easter break. Classes start tomorrow."

I knew it was a weak angle, but I got to my feet anyway; it was the only one I could see at the moment. Looking over at Ava, I said, "You still in?"

She nodded, but then bit her lip. “Could I ask Mr. Jones one more thing before we leave?”

The old detective’s eyes were closed; his breathing was shallow, and he looked so frail, he put me in mind of a baby bird that had fallen from the nest.

“Dad?” his daughter said in mild alarm, getting up from her chair.

“I haven’t given up the ghost yet, Gloria,” her father said with his eyes still shut. “What can I do for you, young lady?”

Ava asked, “Did you ever track down Mulch’s mother?”

Jones’s eyes opened and he looked at her, puzzled. “Why?”

Ava shrugged. “I don’t know. Maybe he contacted her? I mean, Little Boar abused her too. She left because of that, right?”

The old detective cocked his head in a way that indicated he’d never seen that angle, and then he said, “You’ve got a real future in this game, you know that?”

Ava flushed, said, “It just made sense to me.”

“Makes sense to me too, now that you mention it,” Jones croaked. “And the answer to your question is no, I did not try to track down Lydia Mulch.”

Ava looked at me, said, “Maybe we should do that instead?”

“It’s a good thought,” I said. “No doubt. But the trail on Mulch’s mother is thirty years cold. Damon disappeared from school less than nine days ago.”

Ava appeared crestfallen until Gloria Jones said, “Ava, how about you stay here with me awhile and we try to find Lydia Mulch together?”

Ava’s forehead wrinkled, and I could see she was intrigued by the idea but didn’t want to leave me.

"Do it," I said to Ava. "You'll still be helping even if you're not with me."

She paused, said, "You'll come find me when it's all over?"

I walked over and hugged her, saying, "Of course I'll come find you, Ava. You're family. Maybe the last family I've got."

CHAPTER 46

AROUND THREE THAT SUNDAY afternoon, in the community of Arbutus, a suburb of Baltimore, Tess Aaliyah parked on Francis Street in front of the modest bungalow where she'd grown up. The blue and white paint was fresh. The lawn looked like it had been cut that morning. Her late mother's flower beds were tended. And the dogwoods and the first azaleas were in bloom.

At least Dad's keeping the place up, Aaliyah thought, though she remained upset that he had not answered any of her phone calls last night or this morning, which was what had prompted this visit.

Aaliyah got out of the car. But before she started toward the house, she checked the bandage that wrapped her throbbing right forearm, looking for blood or something worse, a yellow or green discharge.

Yellow or green discharge?

Aaliyah shuddered at the thought.

On a day-to-day basis, not much bothered the detective. But the idea that she might have gotten an infection from Claude Harrow's Rottweiler had nagged at her ever since the emergency room physician mentioned the possibility. The nurses had stuck her with more needles than she cared to remember, and she'd been given a powerful antibiotic. Still, you never knew what might be festering in a neo-Nazi dog's mouth.

To her relief, except for a slight dark red discoloration—normal seepage—the bandages looked fine. Fortunately, it turned out that her arm wasn't broken. Even the wounds on her face weren't all that bad—mostly just superficial abrasions.

She crossed the lawn diagonally, heading toward the side door to the kitchen. Her dad's Chevy Tahoe was parked in the driveway. His surf-casting rods were in the ski carrier he used to transport them to the beach.

That's where he'd been. Fishing again. He'd probably been out all night.

Sighing with relief, she climbed the stoop, and she was reaching out with her good arm to knock when she heard a woman chuckle.

"Bernie, you're awful," she said, and chuckled again.

"I swear, Christine," Aaliyah heard her father reply. Then he chuckled.

For a moment, the detective was so stunned she didn't know what to do. She stopped herself from knocking.

Christine?

Aaliyah felt a pit open up in her stomach. Her mother had been dead fourteen months. *Christine?*

She'd known the day would come, of course, when her father would move on, find someone else to spend his life with.

He was only in his late sixties. It made sense. But she'd had no inkling of... *Christine?*

"Oh, hello," said the woman, startling Aaliyah.

She hadn't heard Christine walking over, but there she was on the other side of the screen door, a very tall and very pretty redhead in jeans, a denim shirt, and pearls. Aaliyah guessed she was somewhere in her fifties, maybe early sixties, if she'd had work done.

"I'm looking for my dad?" Aaliyah said.

The woman let out a quiet shriek of pleasure. "You're Tess?"

"That's me."

She grinned widely, opened the door, and extended her hand, saying, "What a wonderful surprise. I'm Christine Prince. Your father's been telling me so much about you."

"Has he, now?" Aaliyah asked.

"You're all he talks about," she said, and chuckled that chuckle.

"Tess?" her father said, coming up behind Christine Prince, limping slightly from the wound that had ended his career.

Seeing the rods on the car, she'd expected to find her father in his fishing clothes: the canvas pants, the windbreaker, and that goofy hat he wore with all the lures on it. But he had on a starched white shirt, creased khakis, and his shoes were shined.

"Hi, Dad," she said. "I was just in the neighborhood and—"

"What the hell happened to your arm and your face?"

"Dog bites."

"What? How come you didn't call me?"

"I did," she said. "About seventeen times last night and this morning."

Bernie Aaliyah seemed chagrined. He looked over at

Christine Prince before saying, "That damn smartphone's the stupidest gadget I've ever owned."

"Right," Aaliyah said, and she glanced at Christine Prince, who caught her skepticism right away.

"Bernie," she said. "I just realized I forgot my purse at the house. Pick me up in, say, an hour?"

Aaliyah's father hesitated and then said, "Sure. That'll do."

"It was so nice meeting you," Christine Prince said.

"You too," Aaliyah said, hearing the lack of conviction in her voice.

The older woman smiled anyway, nodded, and then walked past her and down the stoop. The detective stepped inside, said, "She seems nice."

"She is nice," her dad growled, turning away and walking into the kitchen. "She lives down the street in the Evanses' old house. Lost her husband in a car crash two years ago. We met three weeks ago, out walking."

"So you an item?"

He turned, frowning. "An item? Nah. She's just...I dunno. Nice. Funny."

"And pretty."

"You got a problem with that, young lady?"

She shrugged. "I guess I would have expected you to mention her. But then again, you don't answer your phone these days."

He sighed, said, "I should have called you back. But the fish were on yesterday, and..."

"You had a dinner date," Aaliyah said. "I get it."

"It's not like that," he said flatly. Then he changed the subject. "Saw you're working that Cross case. Good man, Cross. Wicked thing he's going through."

Aaliyah hesitated, and then realized it might be better to talk shop than Christine Prince. At least for the time being.

"You don't know the half of it," she said.

"Guess you better tell me all about it, then," he replied. "Coffee?"

"I'd love some, Dad."

CHAPTER 47

WHILE HER FATHER BREWED a pot, Aaliyah told him about the mysterious Thierry Mulch, about the complex and highly orchestrated kidnapping of Cross's family, about the condition of the bodies dumped at Cross's house, even about the fact that Bree Stone had been miraculously pregnant at the time of her death.

"Jesus," her father said, shaking his head. "Jesus, that's tragic."

She agreed and went on, describing the scene at Claude Harrow's place, focusing on the burned shack, the dog, and those ovals of drying skin.

"They a solid match to Cross's wife and kid?"

"Still waiting for the initial results from the FBI lab, but we're working under that assumption."

Before taking the rifle slug that shattered his pelvis six years before, Bernie Aaliyah had been one of the best homicide detectives in Baltimore. He'd basically taught her everything she knew about investigative work. So she was interested to hear his take.

He thought about it a few moments, poured her a cup of coffee, and then said, "Obviously, if the skin matches, Harrow's your killer, but unless he's the dumbest dick on the face of the earth, he's not this Mulch character."

His daughter nodded. "I don't think anyone plays with gas in front of an open woodstove. Not even raving meth heads."

"Exactly," he said. "So this Mulch, he kills Harrow after Harrow kills Cross's wife and son for him?"

"Looks that way from where I'm standing."

"Me too," he replied. "What does Cross think?"

"I don't know."

"Where is he?"

"Last the FBI told me, he'd bought gas in Fairmont, West Virginia. Stayed in a motel there last night too."

"What's he doing in Fairmont?"

"He's not talking to us. They took him off the investigation."

"That's not a good thing."

"I'm aware of that, Dad."

"Just saying," he replied, and then got a puzzled look on his face.

"What?" she asked.

"Probably nothing," he replied. "But your mom had fibroids removed, long before the cancer."

"Like twenty-five years ago," she replied. "I remember."

He nodded. "It's why we couldn't have any more kids."

"And?"

"It's probably nothing," he said. "Medical advances and all that. But what are the odds of Cross's wife getting pregnant if she had the same kind of scarring as your mom?"

His daughter shrugged again. "Like I said, a tragic miracle."

They talked some more, and then Aaliyah glanced at the clock. "I should be going. And you've got your date to pick up."

Aaliyah almost laughed when her father flushed and said, "It's not a date."

"What is it, then?"

He struggled, and then said, "We're just two people who live alone going down to the harbor for a walk and some dinner."

The detective hesitated, then stood and planted a kiss on his cheek. "Whatever it is, she seems nice. I should have been nicer to her. Tell her I'm sorry for being a bitch."

"You weren't a bitch."

"Yes, Dad, I was."

They hugged and he promised to return her calls promptly in the future. She went to her car, and as she drove off she saw him hurrying to get the fishing poles off the Chevy.

"It's a date," she said, and she smiled wistfully.

Then she realized it had been months since *she'd* had a proper date.

But rather than dwell on the state of her own nonexistent love life, Aaliyah got back on 95 and drove, once again going through the facts of the case as she knew them. As she passed the exit for Greenbelt, her phone rang. John Sampson.

"Where are you?" he asked.

"On my way in," she said.

"Just talked to Mahoney. FBI lab made a preliminary match on the skin samples," he said. "They came from the same bodies."

"Shit."

"Yeah," he said. "But better to know."

"I'll be there in forty minutes, tops."

"See you then."

"Wait a second," she blurted. "Could you transfer me to the ME's office? Rodriguez? She did the autopsies."

He grunted and she heard him punching in numbers and then a ringing. Aaliyah had expected the pathologist's voice mail, but there was a click.

"Amy Rodriguez."

"This is Tess Aaliyah."

"Detective," Rodriguez said. "What can I do for you?"

"It's probably nothing," Aaliyah said. "But I was just wondering what the odds were of Bree Stone getting pregnant despite the uterine scarring?"

There was a long pause before the pathologist replied and flipped everything about the case right on its head.

CHAPTER

48

I REACHED THE KRAFT SCHOOL in the Berkshires around eight thirty that evening, pulled up to the gate and showed my ID to a security guard, who recognized my name.

"Everyone's in shock over your son's murder," she said sadly. "I didn't know him, but I knew who he was, always happy, always smiling. I'm so very sorry for your loss, sir, and I'm praying for Damon's soul. And your wife's."

Every word burned into my heart and brought new stinging to my eyes. "Thank you, I appreciate that. I really do. Can you tell me where I can find the new headmaster, Mr. Pelham?"

"I'd try his office in the administration building, Wiggs Hall," the guard said. "If he's not there, he's in the chapel."

I thanked her again, wiped my eyes with my sleeve, and drove into the campus, dreading the fact that I would have to go into Damon's room before the night was over. Steeling myself, I parked in the visitors' lot, got out of the car I'd rented at the Albany Airport, and headed up the walkway, past the admissions building, where Damon had worked as a tour guide. More than two hundred kids attended Kraft, and it was an unseasonably warm spring night, but I didn't see a single student around.

Wiggs Hall was beyond admissions, a big stone building covered in ivy. The front door was unlocked, and I went inside, smelled wood polish and then cigarette smoke. The door to the headmaster's suite was ajar. I knocked lightly and pushed it open, finding the outer office lit but empty.

Then I heard a man's refined New England–accented voice coming through an open doorway on the other side of the headmaster's secretary's desk.

"I've only just returned from St. Kitts, Mr. Baldwin, and I'm still getting up to speed on the circumstances, but I can state unequivocally that if that was Damon Cross, his murder had nothing to do with Kraft," he said. "He evidently lived in a very rough part of DC, where these senseless tragedies are commonplace."

I stood there forcing myself to take deeper and deeper breaths while he paused to listen.

Then he went on, said, "I understand it's a potential public-relations nightmare, Mr. Baldwin, but again, I can't control the home lives of students, especially those who come up here on athletic scholarships from crime-ridden ghettos. Kraft's reputation will be fine, I assure you, and I'll be sending a personal letter about the situation to all the parents in the next hour."

There was another pause, and I was wondering just how callous and self-serving the discussion was going to get before I heard him tell Mr. Baldwin that he would call with an update in the morning. Then he hung up.

I walked across the carpet and looked into the office to see a tanned, sandy-haired man wearing a blue polo shirt, collar up. He was seated, turned away from me, facing a computer screen. I'd met the previous headmaster when Damon transferred to the school two years before, but not Charles Pelham IV, who'd taken over last September.

I rapped twice on the doorjamb, and Mr. Pelham started, pivoted in his chair, and started again when he saw me standing there.

"Y-yes?" he stammered. "Who are you?"

Sensing the headmaster wasn't used to having a strange African American man of my size appear in his office unannounced, I said, "I'm Damon Cross's father."

Pelham stiffened, and then stood and came around the desk. "Mr. Cross. Dr. Cross. I'm so very sorry for your loss."

He was a small man with tennis-player arms. I shook his strong hand without enthusiasm and said, "Thank you."

"We can't believe it," he said. "I know I can't. I…I only just heard."

"Sure," I said.

"Well," the headmaster said, taking a step back. "How can I—"

"Help?" I said. "I'd like to start by talking to some of Damon's friends, whoever might have seen him last."

"Well," the headmaster said uncomfortably, "I'm sure that can be arranged. I'd have to contact the parents first, of course."

"Excuse me?"

He headed for his desk, saying, "To get their permission."

"For what?"

"To talk to you," Pelham said, seeming happier to have a desk between us. "This has evidently been very upsetting to many of the students and their parents, and I'd want to make sure I had their okay before I…"

He hesitated, obviously trying to choose his words carefully.

I chose for him, saying, "Before you let the police-detective father of a dead kid from the violent ghetto talk with them?"

The headmaster's lips wormed a bit; he cleared his throat and said, "I'm sorry you overheard that. I was speaking with the chairman of the trustees."

"About how Kraft had nothing to do with Damon's death," I said.

"Y-yes," he stammered again. "That's right. It's important that—"

I leaned across the desk, said, "It's important that *you* understand, *sir,* that the Kraft School *is* involved. At the very least, the Kraft School is *liable* for his disappearance, and if I don't get some goddamned cooperation here, I am going to scream to the press and then sue this fine educational institution into oblivion."

"As I understand it, Damon was killed in Washington, DC, while on vacation," Pelham said, his chin rising and his voice shaking. "We are in no way—"

"No, sir," I growled. "My boy was *taken* from this campus. He was supposed to have been in a jitney from school to the Albany train station. He never made it. Now, my boy was seventeen, a juvenile. It was this school's responsibility to make sure he got on that jitney, and he did not, sir."

Pelham blinked. "Well, I don't know—"

"I do!" I shouted. "The jitney driver told the FBI he had Damon on the list, but at the last second, Damon told one of his friends that he'd gotten a ride home. I want to talk to that friend and anyone else who saw him the Friday before Easter. Now!"

CHAPTER

49

PELHAM LED ME INTO the rear of the school chapel, a lofty space with a wraparound balcony. To his credit, the headmaster had arranged for counselors to be there to talk about Damon and to assure the students they were in a safe environment.

It was a packed house, standing room only.

The size of the turnout seemed to both surprise and alarm Pelham. But the number of kids who were openly mourning my boy touched me deeply, and I was almost overwhelmed with emotion when a few of them rose and talked about the son I did and didn't know.

"Damon was hilarious and smart and he'd give you the shirt off his back if you needed it," one boy said.

"He really listened to you," an older girl said. "And when he said he just wanted to be friends, he was serious. He was your friend."

A tall kid I figured played basketball said, "He wasn't the best player, but he was always the hardest worker. Always, and he made you want to work harder. I'll miss that."

There were a lot of heads nodding when Pelham and I walked up the center aisle. I honestly don't know how I made it. Pelham introduced me, and I saw the kids' faces change from interest to sadness and pain.

Fighting the ball of grief in my throat, I got some semblance of control and said, "Damon loved this school, and he loved all his friends and classmates. This place made him happy, which meant you made him happy. I'm hoping you'll honor his memory by helping me find whoever took him and killed him."

A pretty brunette in the second row started weeping softly. The boy beside her, a chunky redheaded kid in a blue Patriots hoodie, hugged her.

I said, "He was supposed to ride the jitney to the train station the Friday before vacation began. The driver said someone told him Damon had gotten a ride, but he couldn't remember who. Did any of you tell him that? Did any of you see my son that day?"

For several moments all I saw was confusion on the students' faces. Then the kid in the blue hoodie raised his hand and said, "We did, sir. Sylvia and me."

Sylvia went hysterical, and I went numb.

Ten minutes later, however, we were all in the headmaster's office. Sylvia Mathers had calmed down and was sitting on the couch with her feet tucked up under her and her arms holding her knees. Looking lost and defeated, Porter Tate sat beside her.

The boy spoke first, in a voice so low I had to sit forward to hear him.

"It was that woman, wasn't it?" he asked.

"What woman?" Pelham said.

"The one with the..."

"With what?" I asked.

"Dirty-blond hair and big tits," he mumbled.

Sylvia Mathers sent him a withering look, said, "You can be such an asshole sometimes, Porter."

"Hey, I didn't—"

"You did," she shot back. "It's all you and Tommy talked about on the ride, how Damon was teed up for big tits, and now he's dead."

"Back up," I said. "You saw Damon with a strange woman that morning?"

"Yes," Sylvia said.

"No," Porter said.

Now I was totally confused. "You saw her, Sylvia, and you didn't, Porter?"

The boy said, "No, I saw her, but she wasn't strange. I mean, I'd seen her before. I..." He looked at me bleakly, said, "Damon was my friend. I'm so sorry, sir. I wish I'd made him come with us. But it seemed chill. Damon was chill."

In fits and starts, their story came out. On the morning of Good Friday, Sylvia and Porter had left their dorms and passed Damon with his luggage. He was speaking with a woman in her mid- to late twenties. She had dirty-blond hair, wore dark sunglasses, was of medium height, and had the aforementioned large breasts, which, according to Porter, were encased in the same tight white top she'd been wearing the first time he saw her.

"And when was that?" the headmaster asked.

"I dunno," Porter said. "Like, ten days before that? She and Damon were across the street at Millie's, having coffee. I was there too, with Tommy Grant and Roger Woods. I mean, not *with* Damon and the lady. We were in the corner, kind of, I don't know, watching?"

"More like ogling, the way Tommy made it sound," Sylvia said, disgusted.

Porter said the woman and Damon talked for nearly twenty minutes and then left. Porter and his friends found Damon studying in his room later.

"At first he didn't want to talk about her," Porter said. "But then he told us she'd taken one of his tours that day and just wanted to ask more questions about the school and all, so they had coffee. She paid."

The headmaster tapped a pen on a pad of paper he was using to take notes. "Did he tell you her name? There'll be a record of her if she took a tour."

"Karla something," the boy said. "I can't remember. But Tommy would know."

"Why would Tommy know?" I asked.

"Because he likes to fish and her last name was like some kind of lure."

Pelham looked at me, said, "I'll find Mr. Grant when we're finished here."

After I'd come down hard on him, the headmaster had turned out to be a decent enough guy, and I nodded.

"Anything else?" he asked.

Porter looked at the floor, but Sylvia said, "Just that when I went by him, going to the jitney, I told Damon he was going to be late, and he said he'd be right there. But he caught up to Porter and said he had a ride all the way home." She choked, said, "Damon was a great guy, Dr. Cross. He was special and I..."

She broke down again. Porter rubbed her back, said, "They were like—"

"No, we weren't," Sylvia shot at him.

"Damon said he liked you, and you said you liked him!" Porter said. "What else is there?"

She rocked her head back, wiped away her tears, and said, "We liked each other, and that's what makes this so awful."

I reached over, patted her hand, and said, "Thank you for liking him."

Sylvia nodded, her lower lip quivering.

"Dr. Cross," Porter said. "There was, like, one other thing."

"Okay..."

"The lady, Karla, she said something to Damon, and he told us, and anyway we...we all thought she was messing with his head."

"Just tell them," Sylvia said.

"I am," he snapped. "She told Damon to leave his window unlocked and open because she just might climb in one night, and...you know."

The headmaster drew his head back. "Those were Damon's exact words?"

"I dunno. Yeah, I think so," Porter said. "I might be, like, paraphrasing, but go get Tommy Grant, he remembers everything that's got to do with sex."

CHAPTER

50

TOMMY GRANT LIVED UP to his reputation. A little while later, when Pelham brought in the hoops player who'd talked about Damon in the chapel, he not only knew the name of the woman who'd taken my son but remembered exactly what Damon had said about her.

"Her last name was Mepps, like the lure," said Grant. "And she had a tattoo of some kind of black cat on her left arm."

"She did not," Porter said.

"She did so," Grant shot back. "Most of it was covered, but you could see the tail for sure. And what she said to Damon was that he should keep his window unlocked and open because some day she might sneak out of the woods behind the dorm and climb in."

Sylvia sat up and frowned.

"And when was this?" I asked. "Do you know when this all happened?"

"Not, like, the exact date," he said. "But sure."

"Sure what?" said the headmaster.

"Sure I know when it happened, sir," Grant said. "It was the day before they found Carter."

My memory was jogged, and I remembered talking with Damon about Carter.

"The security guard who was killed?" I asked.

Pelham nodded but wasn't happy.

"And where was Carter's body found?"

As if already seeing the facts a news reporter could string together into a lurid story about the school, Pelham said nothing.

But Grant replied, "Sort of in the woods out behind North Dorm, but like far away, right, Mr. Pelham?"

The headmaster, with an expression that said he would never be able to fathom the adolescent brain, angrily barked, "And not one of you thought to tell someone about this before now?"

"About what?" Porter asked, puzzled.

Sylvia rolled her eyes, said, "What Karla Mepps said about coming out of those woods on the same night Mr. Carter was killed in those woods, you boob-obsessed morons."

"Oh," Grant said. "I didn't think about that."

Porter shook his head. "Me neither. I just remembered she was going to come in the window and you know. Nothing about the woods."

Sylvia looked like she wanted to slap them both, but she just sat there glaring at them when I said, "But you all got solid looks at Karla Mepps, correct?"

All three of Damon's classmates nodded.

"You'd be willing to work with a police sketch artist to help us get a sense of what she looked like?" I asked.

Sylvia and Grant said, "Yes."

Porter paused, then said, "Wouldn't a picture be better?"

I wanted to hug him. "You have a picture of her?"

"No," he said. "But they've got a security camera at Millie's coffee shop. It's how Clayton Monroe got bagged for stealing and got expelled last year. Unless they erase stuff that old, it's got to be there."

We tried to do it right then. Pelham got on the phone and tracked down Ward Brower, Millie Brower's son. Brower was more than willing to help, but he was at the emergency room with his mother, who was complaining of chest pain.

"He said he may have erased it all," Pelham said. "But maybe not. He opens at six a.m., but he said you could come by at five thirty tomorrow, when he gets there."

Although I was desperate to see the woman who may have lured my son to his death, I nodded and thanked Damon's classmates for their help.

"Are you going to do anything for him?" Sylvia asked. "Like a memorial?"

"Yes," I said. "Once I've got the people who killed him."

"Like, before the end of the year?" Porter asked.

"I'm sure hoping so," I said.

Pelham said, "Do you need a room, Dr. Cross? I could call the motel and see if there are vacancies, or we have beds at the infirmary you're free to use."

"I'd like to stay in Damon's room if possible."

The headmaster hesitated, and then said, "I can arrange that."

After sending the students back to their dorms, Pelham took me to North Dorm and Damon's room on the first floor. It faced those woods Karla Mepps had spoken of, the woods where Josh Carter, the security guard, had been bludgeoned to death in the pouring rain. Several kids were looking out their doors at me, and I nodded to them as the headmaster unlocked Damon's room.

He handed me a key and then his business card, saying quietly, "Anything you need, you call. And I'm genuinely sorry about the way I acted and spoke earlier. The board..."

"I understand, and thank you," I said, and patted him on the shoulder.

Then I took a deep breath and walked into the remains of Damon's life.

CHAPTER

51

I CLOSED THE BEDROOM door, stood there in the darkness, and breathed in through my nose. They say our sense of smell is our most primal, the one that can hit us the hardest, because it comes from the deepest part of the brain.

Smell kicked me like a mule that night, and right in the gut. Damon's window had been closed and locked for days. His scent permeated the place, and it was like he was suddenly right there in front of me.

I saw him gliding down the court at a game a year ago, when he'd come off the bench and scored three straight three-pointers, looking like he could never miss. I saw him the past Christmas. He was home, laughing his goofy lovable laugh at something Nana Mama had said. Then he was sitting on the couch the day before he'd gone back to school, Ali under one of his long arms, and Jannie under the other, all of them watching one of the college bowl games.

Was he dead? Were those memories all I was going to have of him?

I started to shake in the darkness. Fearing that more of these vivid memories would destroy me, I flipped on the light and stood there, blinking my wet eyes.

It was a small room for such a big boy, but it was neat and orderly, with posters of Chris Paul and Derrick Rose, the point guards who were his heroes, and others of Rihanna and the rapper Kendrick Lamar.

Over his desk there was a calendar with Good Friday circled in red and *Home!* scribbled next to it. I stared at that for the longest time before going on around the room, to his dresser and small closet, the door of which was plastered with photographs of him: playing playground ball, wearing snorkel gear in Jamaica, and standing in the suit he wore to the prom.

My hand went to my mouth and I turned toward his bed, which stretched sideways below that window Karla Mepps had threatened to climb through and…

Was that what happened? I wondered. Was she on her way to climb in Damon's window when the security guard saw her, maybe chased her before she beat him to death with a chunk of firewood?

Women, in my experience, are rarely involved in something so vicious. Clubbing a man and beating his brains in is more of a guy thing. So what kind of woman did that make Karla Mepps? And what did it mean in terms of Thierry Mulch?

I'd long believed that Mulch had at least one accomplice, and maybe more. There was too much distance and too little time for my family to have been kidnapped without, at a minimum, one other player involved. In my mind, I'd profiled the second fiddle as the kind of male toady that heinous criminals seem to attract, someone younger than Mulch but just as sick, an apprentice, even.

A woman in that role changed everything. It suggested twisted love, an attraction between monsters.

What would she look like? The boys who'd seen her said she was very attractive and well built. But would there be something in her body language that spoke of evil? Would I have seen something that Damon missed?

Part of me wanted to call Sampson and Mahoney and ask them to start running Karla Mepps through the criminal databases straightaway. But it was late on a Sunday night and there was a high probability that the name was an alias, and I was suddenly exhausted. Seeing my tortured reflection in the window glass against the inky blackness beyond, I told myself to sleep, that I would be no good to anyone if I couldn't think straight.

I sat on my son's bed, kicked off my shoes, and noticed the crucifix my grandmother had bought him last Easter. It hung above the headboard. Part of me wanted to yell at the figure on the cross, to demand to know the reason for my suffering. Instead, I got down on my knees to beg Jesus for help.

That's when I saw the snapshot taped to the wall by his pillow.

It was taken the day I married Bree, a portrait of me, my bride, and my family. Bree was radiant. Damon was as happy as I'd ever seen him. So were Ali, Jannie, and Nana Mama. And I looked like I'd won the Powerball.

Once upon a time, I thought, *you, Alex Cross, were the luckiest man alive.*

That broke me.

She's dead, I thought. *They're both dead.*

Grief welled up like a rogue wave. I got up before it could hit me fully, staggered to the switch, and turned off the light.

I groped over to Damon's bed, lay down on my side, curled up in a fetal position, and felt the wave hit like a tsunami. I sobbed my way into sleep.

CHAPTER

52

TWO MORE? HOW WAS I going to accomplish that?

The question tormented me as I trudged out of Damon's dorm at 5:20 Monday morning. It was still dark out. Blustering wind blew cold rain, pelting me with stinging drops as I followed the path to my car.

Two?

Then I realized that this intersection of paths above Damon's dorm was probably where Karla Mepps had intercepted him on Good Friday morning. Ignoring the fact that I was going to be wet and cold for hours, I stopped and stood there, wondering what she'd said to make him want to abandon his plans and do something as foolhardy as catch a ride with a stranger.

The easy explanation was her sexuality. Damon was seventeen, after all, and like most seventeen-year-olds, he had to be a slave to his raging hormones.

But I knew my son. Hormones or not, he wasn't someone

who did things impulsively. He was methodical, considerate. Mulch's accomplice had to have given Damon some reason beyond lust to go with her, I was sure of it.

Maybe I was guilty of wanting to think well of my son, of gifting him with noble attributes. But I vowed to press Karla Mepps or whoever she really was until she explained how she'd been able to swing Damon's decision and why.

The rental was right where I'd left it. Green leaves and dead pine needles were strewn across the windshield when I opened the door and climbed in. I was soaked through to my shoulders and calves, and I shivered as I started the car and turned up the heat.

I glanced at myself in the rearview mirror and saw a man I barely recognized, with sunken eyes and puffy skin and a blank stare that reminded me of other people I'd seen who'd suffered massive personal devastation. For a moment, I sat there, not sure if this man had it in him to go on and wondering whether he should turn fully to mourning. No, I decided. I didn't care what I looked like or how I felt. As long as there was a chance of saving any of them, I was going to fight.

Putting on the headlights, I prayed for the thousandth time that I would find them and rescue them. But I asked God for more than that. I drove through the rain toward the coffee shop, praying that before this was over, I would be able to confront Mulch, that I'd be given the chance to face him one-on-one and bring him to justice.

But for now, I remained under Mulch's control.

As soon as I'd woken, I'd looked on Craigslist New Orleans on my phone and seen the new ad. I'd opened it, wanting to believe that a member of my family had been released because of the video. Instead, it said, *Two more on camera in forty-eight hours, and you get all survivors. Fail, and you get none. Send reply here.*

Mulch was messing with my head and heart again, and I knew it. Had he figured out the video was fake? Or had he recognized Jones? Perhaps seeing the old detective had thrown Mulch, as we'd hoped. Was this change in the original deal because of that? Or was I just being played by the sickest of minds?

Swallowing against the acid that crept up the back of my throat, I drove out through the campus gate, turned right, and slowed to a stop at the blinking red traffic signal. The lights glowed in Millie's coffee shop across the main road.

Please let this bitch be on the tapes, I prayed as I climbed from the car. *Please give me a sign, a break, something to hold on to here.* Up on the porch, I rapped at the door. Ward Brower, a young, tired-looking man, came out from behind the counter, drying his hands on an apron.

He opened the door, sending forth the aroma of fresh coffee brewing. I walked in. "How's your mother?" I asked after introducing myself and shaking hands.

"Better," Brower said. "Can I get you some coffee? Pastry?"

"I'd appreciate that. Where's the surveillance disk?"

"Oh," he said, his face falling. "I checked as soon as I came in. That day and the day after it are already erased. It's automatic, I'm afraid."

CHAPTER

53

I THOUGHT I'D PREPARED myself for that possibility, but hearing the words stated so flatly at that hour of the morning on so little sleep, I felt crushed, as if God were purposely ignoring me, as if He'd completely damned me and my family and I wasn't worth His attention anymore.

"You okay, Dr. Cross?" Brower asked.

I lifted my head and looked at him with eyes blearier than his own. "No, I was hoping…I don't know."

"You want to sit down, sir?" Brower said, offering to help me to one of the tables.

"I'm okay," I said. "And I've got a long way to go. Can I get the coffee and pastries take-out?"

"Sure, straightaway," he said, glancing at me one more time as if he were afraid I might tip over.

My head felt scalded as I watched him pour the coffee and bag the pastries. If he said anything else, I can't recall it.

"How much?" I asked when he pushed the cup and the bag toward me.

"On the house," Brower said, bowing his head. "Sorry about your son."

Nodding slightly, I took the coffee and the bag as if I were breathing in confusion and exhaling defeat.

"How far you got to go?" Brower asked, looking concerned.

"What's that?"

"Where are you headed?"

"No idea," I said, then turned and walked toward the door, dreading opening it, feeling like I was exiting the coffee shop and entering a bleak, dark future, an eternity of hopeless pain, an end to all I ever was and all I ever could have been.

Headlights swung up the road as I pushed open the coffee shop's door and stepped out onto the porch. Falling torrentially from low, leaden skies, the rain billowed like curtains across the parking lot in the gray dawn. I crossed the porch, stepped down two stairs and out from under the eave, then stopped to let the cold rain whip my skin numb. I stood there, taking the brunt of it full in my face, feeling the icy water like needles and not—

"Alex!" a woman's voice called. "Detective Cross!"

I wiped my eyes with the soaked sleeve of my jacket, looked beyond my rental car, and spotted Tess Aaliyah climbing out of a DC Metro unmarked car.

She ran up to me, looking wired.

"We tried to find you," she said, her voice trembling. "But we couldn't until Mahoney tracked your credit cards and we figured you were going to Damon's school. So I jumped in a car and drove all night because I wanted you to hear this in person."

My stomach fell fifty stories. "Another body?"

"No," Aaliyah said, breaking into a beaming smile and starting to cry. "But there's a very good chance Bree is alive. And Damon too!"

CHAPTER

54

MY BRAIN REJECTED THE news out of hand.

A cruel joke. That's all that was.

Aaliyah looked at me with the same kind of concern Brower had shown.

"Alex, did you hear what I said?"

I said nothing, the disbelief and the fear of hope just locking me up.

"Bree and Damon are likely alive," she insisted.

"Don't tell me that unless you have DNA evidence!" I yelled. "Do you?"

"No, but—"

"Then I don't want to hear it," I said. "I can't."

"We have conclusive evidence that the female victim is not Bree," she said calmly. "The Jane Doe had no uterine scarring. The body you saw at the construction site belonged to Bernice Smith, a woman from northern Pennsylvania who'd gone missing two days earlier."

I said nothing, wanting to believe but petrified to do so.

"Dr. Cross," Aaliyah said, coming around me to show me a picture on her phone. "This is her. Mulch had a racist murderer named Claude Harrow put Bree's jewels and wedding ring on Bernice Smith. Harrow mutilated her enough to make you believe it could be your wife."

I looked at the rain-soaked screen, seeing a smiling woman who did look very much like Bree: same height, same athletic build, same basic facial structure.

Bree could still be alive?

"What about Damon?" I asked.

"Just awaiting the DNA, which should be in this morning, but if Mulch used one surrogate, I figure we'll find that John Doe is not your son."

I felt dizzy. "I need to sit down."

She grabbed me by the arm and led me up the stairs to the coffee shop, and we went in again, both of us dripping. Aaliyah got me to a chair and I sat down hard.

For two and a half days I'd endured the hell of their deaths. And now the woman in the foundation was definitely not Bree, which meant the body in my backyard probably wasn't Damon's. Though it was clearly possible that Mulch still planned to kill them, part of me wanted to erupt with joy.

Instead, I laughed caustically, said, "First the doctored photographs, and now this? Killing my family again and again? Mulch is trying to drive me insane, isn't he?"

"He's tormenting you," Aaliyah said, sitting beside me.

"Don't you let him, whoever he is," said the coffee-shop owner, setting two steaming mugs in front of us. "Don't let him do it to you. You just gotta be strong and stay true to yourself."

I looked at him appraisingly, said, "You've got experience with someone trying to drive you crazy?"

"I do," he said. "My ex-wife tried. She's still trying."

Something about the way he said it made me laugh, and the agony of the past few days lifted and was replaced by hope. They were alive! God had not abandoned me.

It was unspeakable that Mulch had killed and butchered two innocent people to make me suffer, but I was overwhelmed with gratitude that my family was alive. They were not safe, but they could all still be saved. Humbled, I put my face in my hands, shook with happiness, and thanked my Savior from the bottom of my soul.

Then I looked at Aaliyah through teary eyes and said, "You can't know how low I was when you told me."

"I could see it," she said, choking up and patting me on the thigh.

I cleared my throat and said, "Tell me about Harrow. And what happened to you?" I added, noticing some abrasions on her face.

"Harrow is dead," Aaliyah said, getting back to business. "We think Mulch killed him after the murders and burned his place down. I got my face scratched up there during the investigation; it's a long story. What about you? Where have you been?"

"Tracking Mulch," I said. "Also a long story."

"The headmaster said something about a woman taking Damon," she said. "And that there was possibly a picture of her here?"

"It got erased," Brower said sadly, back behind the counter again.

The door to the coffee shop opened with a tinkle of a bell and then shut.

"The FBI computer lab might be able to pull the erased

image off the hard drive," Aaliyah said. "It could take days, but it might be worth a try."

Days? I thought. *Did they have—*

"Excuse me?" a boy said. "Are you Damon's father?"

I looked over to see a string bean of a kid with wet red hair and bad acne, wearing a Kraft School hoodie, gray sweatpants, and flip-flops despite the weather.

"Yes?" I said.

"I'm Roger Wood, a friend of Damon's," he said awkwardly. "I was just having breakfast with Tommy Grant and Porter Tate, and they said I should come find you."

"Okay…" I said as the coffee-shop door opened and several more customers came in out of the rain.

"They said you'd want to see this," the boy said.

He held up an iPhone and handed it to me.

I took one look at the screen and wanted to scream.

Instead, I jumped up and bear-hugged the startled kid.

"What is it?" Aaliyah asked.

"He got her," I said, grinning wildly and handing her the phone. "He caught that bitch in living color."

CHAPTER

55

THE CURRENT WAS UP on the Mississippi River just north of Memphis. It tugged and punched at the moored barge *Pandora,* making Acadia Le Duc unsteady as she watched Marcus Sunday work at the lock sealing the cargo container. She was worried that things had gone far enough, that this game Sunday was playing was ultimately going to be a loser.

A guy like Cross didn't quit when it came to family, Acadia thought. If any member of the family was actually killed, Cross would hunt Thierry Mulch until his dying breath, which meant that he'd be hunting Acadia as well.

She didn't like that idea. She didn't like it at all.

Still, when Sunday pushed the hatch open and climbed through it, Acadia took a deep breath and followed him in, carrying a large canvas beach bag. Sunday shut and locked the hatch behind her and then flipped a toggle switch to illuminate the interior of the long, narrow space.

Sunday went immediately to a computer bolted to a stand, called up the screen, and studied it.

"Lot of sun the past two days," he said. "Really keeping the banks strong."

Acadia was barely listening. Her eyes were roaming over the elaborate life-support system keeping Alex Cross's family alive.

Strapped to bunks bolted into the walls, the five were intubated and on ventilators. They had nasogastric tubes inserted to prevent them from aspirating. Intravenous lines ran from their hands to the automated Harvard pumps that governed the flow of IV fluids.

Above each bunk there was a four-liter bag of liquid hanging on a hook. The average person can survive on one and a half liters of maintenance fluids a day. Each of the bags would sustain a patient for roughly sixty hours.

There were also three smaller bags hanging on each hook, all of which were linked to smaller pumps before they joined the main IV line. One bag held sixty hours' worth of midazolam, a relaxant similar to Valium. Another contained a two-and-a-half-day supply of morphine. The third was an equal amount of pancuronium. A molecular relative of the South American toxin curare, the third drug was a paralytic, used in surgeries or, as in this case, induced comas.

Acadia took it all in with a long sweeping glance, seeing no evidence of disruption or breakage. Sunday had bribed a brilliant, corrupt doctor with a cocaine habit to design the system and obtain the medications. The doctor had even helped program the automated infusion based on the weight, sex, and age of each patient.

Cross's ninety-something grandmother had been the trickiest. She weighed less than one hundred pounds, and she had a history of mild cardiac problems. Every time Acadia came into the container car, she expected to find the old woman long gone. Acadia went to her first. Nana Mama's heart rate was slightly up from the last time she'd checked. And her blood pressure looked a little low. But besides that, she was solid.

Satisfied, Acadia steeled herself for the side of nursing she'd hated in the four years she'd done it. She pulled down the old woman's sheet, changed her diaper, threw the old one into a garbage bag, and checked her Foley catheter for signs of infection. There were none. She emptied the urine bag, replaced it, then drew the sheet back up over her, unable to shake the idea that Cross would chase her for the rest of his life. He wasn't the kind of man who gave up, especially when his family was involved.

She glanced at Sunday, who was still studying the computers, and then at the array of medicines in the bags hanging off hooks above the old woman's bunk. She continued with her routine, checking the vitals and cleaning the other four. The Cross children were strong, Jannie especially. She had the heart and build of a serious athlete. Acadia caught Sunday looking at the girl's naked form with great interest and realized that he hadn't touched her since they'd taken the Cross family hostage. When she started working on Bree Stone, Sunday was almost leering.

"She's quite well put together, don't you think?" Sunday asked, moving around for a better view. "You can see why Dr. Alex would be so crushed by her death."

Acadia said nothing. She knew a thing or two about men. When they stopped wanting sex, you were in danger of being cheated on, dumped, or worse. Given the sheer audacity and scope of what Sunday had done already, she started to suspect that *worse* was the option he'd eventually settle on.

That suspicion built within her, and by the time she'd gotten the new four-liter IV bags and the drugs from the storage chest and swapped them out, it had become a conviction. Her time was growing short. Sooner rather than later, Sunday would kill her.

What was it he'd written in his book? That the perfect criminal was a universe unto himself? He works alone, or kills his accomplices? That was exactly what Sunday had written. But maybe—

"Acadia?" Sunday said. "Are we done here?"

She looked over at him, hesitated, but then came to a decision, thinking: *It's time to ride the comet.*

She said, "I'm just nervous about the intubations and the nasogastric tubes."

"Yeah?" he said with zero interest.

"They're showing signs of contamination," she said. "It could lead to sepsis, and we'd find the five of them dead the next time we came in here."

Sunday thought a few moments, said, "I don't like that. If they die, I want it to be at my hands."

"What I thought," she said. "But your quack doctor there told me that if this kind of contamination ever happened, we should remove the tubes and change the depth of the comas."

"Meaning?"

"Meaning they wouldn't be out cold like this, and they'd be able to breathe on their own without the tubes. But they'll still be so doped up, they won't move."

Sunday studied her, said, "What about food?"

"The IVs will carry them through the next check."

"Your call," he said finally. "You're the medical professional."

Acadia nodded, relieved. "It'll take me ten or fifteen minutes. You might want to go tell the captain so he doesn't come snooping around."

"Oh, he's..." Sunday said, then hesitated. "No, that's a good idea. Lock it up when you're done."

"Tight," she said.

At each bunk, Acadia reprogrammed the Harvard pump, cutting off the paralytic and lowering the dosages of the other two drugs by 55 percent. She also shortened the duration of the infusion so that about forty-two hours from that moment, they would all start to wake up.

Last, Acadia loosened the restraints so that in forty-five hours or so, one of them might be able to get free and help the others. If the change in the medications worked the way she expected, a few hours after that, by the time they reached New Orleans, they'd be able to pound on the walls, make enough noise to attract attention, and get themselves rescued before Sunday could return.

She'd done enough, she decided as she exited the container, locked the hatch, and tossed the triple-wrapped garbage bag to Sunday. She climbed down, looked up, and said, "So what happens when they get to New Orleans?"

He looked back at her, grinned, said, "I want it to be a surprise. But I guarantee you'll love it."

"What's the matter, Marcus? Don't trust me?"

CHAPTER 56

SUNDAY COCKED HIS HEAD at the question before saying, "No, it's just that at this point, there are a few ways this can go, all of them fantastic. For now I'll keep my options open but close to my chest."

He turned and went down the gangway to the docks where the barge captain, Scotty Creel, was waiting.

Creel said, "So how's the new system working for you?"

Sunday acted the entrepreneur, said, "So far, so good."

"You think this will work all over the world? Solar-based refrigeration?"

"Wouldn't that be something?" Sunday said, and he laughed. "I came up with this idea off the top of my head. We'll see you in two and a half days and let you know."

The captain said, "We'll be there faster than that. Probably less than forty-eight hours. I figure we'll be at the port before two or three Wednesday morning. River's really starting to move now, heading toward flood stage."

"Excellent," Sunday said.

But Acadia didn't think that was excellent at all. The Cross family might be coming around by then, but they certainly would not be capable of making much noise.

She followed Sunday off the docks, and they walked up the bank to a small lot where their rental car, a Chevy Malibu, was parked. On the road outside the fenced-in area, another Kenworth tractor-trailer idled with Cochran behind the wheel. They'd rented the rig in case something catastrophic had happened and they were forced to remove the container.

"I'll go tell him we're good," Sunday said, checking his watch. "We've got a few hours before the flight back, and he's going to want to eat. Any preference?"

"I'm not really hungry," Acadia said.

"Then you get no say," he said, and tossed her the keys and the lading documents they'd used to access the container car. "Follow us."

"Right on your tail," she promised, and got in the car.

Acadia threw the lading documents on the seat and started the car, seeing Sunday climb up into the passenger seat of the tractor cab. When he closed the door and was no longer visible through the tinted glass, she put the car in gear.

Following the rig east on Old Randolph Road, she stayed close. She fell back slightly on State Route 50 heading south and then caught up on the connector toward I-40.

Acadia waited until Cochran had fully committed to taking the eastbound I-40, a left-hand exit. She threw on her blinker as if to follow, but at the last possible second, she veered right onto Interstate 69, heading south.

Her heart beat so hard she could feel it in her throat.

Thirty seconds. A minute. Her cell phone began to ring.

She glanced over at it, feeling panic rise. Should she say an animal ran across the road, she'd swerved to avoid it, and she'd be right along?

No, Acadia decided, and she hurled the phone out the window. Once you made a move like this on someone like Marcus Sunday, there was no turning back. She'd ditch the car as soon as she could and rent or steal another. And she'd need all the cash she could get her hands on.

Acadia understood that she knew too much about everything. When Marcus decided to come after her—and she had no doubt he eventually would—she wanted to be able to go a long, long way at a moment's notice.

CHAPTER

57

SUNDAY LISTENED TO ACADIA'S phone ring once and then go to voice mail.

"Say what you have to say," her voice drawled.

It was the second time he'd heard the message since Acadia had gone south instead of east.

"Maybe she's going to the airport ahead of us," Cochran offered. "Expects us to take the shuttle over to meet her."

Sunday dismissed that possibility out of hand. His agile mind was running full tilt, spinning out motives and scenarios to explain Acadia's actions. His lover was an extremely smart woman. Sometimes she envisioned the future as well as he did. She was also a survivor and could be lethally ruthless if her survival required it. Acadia rarely acted on impulse. She put thought into her words and deeds. But then she acted and didn't look back.

She's running from me, he thought, *just as I knew she would eventually.* Sunday felt not a lick of anger at her abandoning him. He just hadn't expected it to happen so soon. Too bad; she was a certifiable genius in bed, and it was always nice to talk to someone who shared his active interest in death.

But when paths part, they part. Ordinarily, that's how Sunday would have handled it, chalked it up to randomness and walked on. But Acadia knew too much about him. He'd opened up to her more than to any other woman. He couldn't abide her using that information against him somehow, which meant she had to die. And sooner than—

Cochran coughed and broke Sunday's train of thought. "Any luck?"

Sunday gazed at the driver a long moment, recalculating, before he replied, "I'll try again."

He punched in Acadia's number. When it went to voice mail, he said, "Hey. We've been calling. Where are you?"

He paused, nodded, said, "That's what we kind of thought. We're going to gas the truck, get something to eat, and we'll take the shuttle to meet you."

He listened, said, "I dunno. An hour and a half, two hours?"

Cochran glanced his way, seeing Sunday looking at him quizzically.

"Sounds right," the driver said.

"Six, six thirty," Sunday said, and ended the call. "She had to take a pee. And the airport is right there."

Cochran bought it, said, "I had a girlfriend like that. When that woman had to go, she had to go."

"That's Acadia," Sunday said. "She has to go."

Cochran took an exit, went north underneath the interstate, and pulled into a Pilot truck stop. He parked at the pumps and started to get out.

"Want a coffee?" Sunday asked.

"Sounds good. Make it like you did last time."

Wearing sunglasses and a Kenworth cap that had come with the truck, Sunday got down out of the cab, went into the truck stop, and got two coffees that he took time to prepare according to a very precise formula. He paid with a ten-dollar bill and returned to the truck.

Cochran was already up in the cab, and he reached out for his coffee through the open window. Sunday handed it to him, then went around and got in the other side. Cochran had already taken a big swig of the coffee. There was foam on his upper lip.

"Damn it, Marcus," Cochran said. "What's in that? It's so damned good."

"I know, right?" Sunday said, pleased. "I added a little something, though. Do you taste it?"

Cochran took another drink, and said, "Cinnamon?"

"Close."

"Nutmeg?"

"You're good," Sunday said.

"No, this is good," Cochran said and drank more.

"Hey, do me a favor?" Sunday said. "Pull over there in the back of the lot. I have to look up something and I don't want to be bouncing all over."

"Sure, Marcus," Cochran said. "But watch the time. If we get it back past noon, they dun you for the full-day charge. Says so in that sheet with the copy of the lading docs."

"Thank you for thinking of my pocketbook," Sunday said. "And this shouldn't take long at all."

Sunday was right. It didn't take long at all after they'd parked at the back of the lot by several other rigs idling while their drivers slept. He made a show of opening the laptop and typing as Cochran lifted his cup for another sip.

But something stopped him before he drank, something that seemed to bewilder him. His fingers loosened and began to drop the coffee cup. Sunday snagged it before it fell.

Cochran slumped over to his left against the window, taking slow, shallow breaths. Sunday looked out the side-view mirrors, saw the closest movement seventy yards away, and dug in his pocket for a pair of latex gloves.

When he had them on, he twisted around in his seat, grabbed Cochran, and pulled him over onto his back. Cochran looked up at him blankly. But Sunday knew better. Though paralyzed, the man was fully in control of his mind.

"Some surplus pancuronium," Sunday told him matter-of-factly. "If I gave it enough time, you'd suffocate. But the truth is, you've been very useful, Mitch Cochran. I owe you a little mercy."

Despite Cochran's paralysis, Sunday saw hope flicker in his eyes.

Then Sunday reached up and over him, got a pillow from the sleeping berth, and smothered the man to death.

CHAPTER

58

I STARTLED AWAKE IN the front seat of the unmarked cruiser and looked around blearily, seeing farmland and tractors along the interstate, and then Tess Aaliyah hunched over the wheel, looking wired.

"Where are we?"

"North of New York City," she replied.

"I can drive."

"You had a head injury recently."

"Haven't had a headache or symptom in two days. Honestly."

She glanced at me, saw my sincerity, and then nodded. "I'll get off at the next stop. We need gas anyway."

"You're a machine."

"Why?" she said.

"You drove all night, and now you turn around and drive back?"

"Oh, believe me, I will crash in a big way when I get home to my bed. Right now, I'm just like a homing pigeon."

"I appreciate it. I appreciate everything that you've done for me. You're a fine detective. And you've done your dad proud."

She looked over at me, embarrassed.

"What?" I said. "You didn't think I knew who your father was?"

Aaliyah shrugged, said, "I try not to broadcast it."

"Must be hard to live in the shadow of a legend."

"Sometimes," she said, and then she seemed eager to change the subject. "I wonder if we'll get a match on Mepps."

I'd contacted John Sampson and Ned Mahoney before we left the Kraft School, and was buoyed at first by the DNA tests, which had come in at last, confirming that neither body in the morgue belonged to a member of my immediate family. Then I'd had to come to grips with the fact that two innocent people had died simply because they looked like my wife and son. In its own way, that knowledge was one more torture Sunday was inflicting on me.

Pushing that pain aside, I had gotten Sampson and Mahoney up to speed on all that had happened to me in the prior two days, and then I'd forwarded the JPEG of Damon and Karla Mepps at the coffee shop. Ned had promised to run the image through facial-recognition software that would search through a broad cross section of state and federal databases, including criminal records, driver's licenses, and passports.

The problem was that that could take even longer than the DNA testing. In the movies, someone feeds a picture to a computer, makes a few keystrokes, and out pops a name. In fact, facial recognition is a laborious process based on complex algorithms that tax even the fastest of computers.

"Mahoney said the search might take hours," I told

Aaliyah. "Or it could grind on a few days before the system finds a match or admits defeat."

"Like it did with that picture of Mulch from the fake ID?" she asked.

I nodded. "Either he's not in any of the databases or he altered his face for that picture."

She put on the blinker and took the Ramapo exit off Interstate 87. My cell phone rang. I checked it and saw it was Gloria Jones calling.

"This is Alex Cross," I said.

After a loud sigh of relief, the television news producer said in a lower, more conspiratorial tone, "Let me get Ava and find somewhere we can talk. Call you back in two minutes."

"Okay," I said, wondering what was up.

Aaliyah pulled into a gas station, headed in to use the restroom. I filled the tank. It wasn't until after the detective had returned with a Diet Coke and a bag of Kettle Chips and we'd gotten back on the highway, this time with me behind the wheel, that my cell rang again.

Aaliyah said, "Take 287 South. It's quicker to DC."

I nodded, answered the cell, put it on speaker, and set it up on the dash so Aaliyah could hear.

"Ava?" I said.

"I'm here, Alex," she replied. "You won't believe what we found!"

"I had very little to do with it," Gloria Jones said. "This was all Ava."

"Well, I'm in a car with Detective Aaliyah of DC Metro Homicide," I said. "We'd both like to hear whatever you've got, but Ava, I have something wonderful to tell you."

"Yes?"

"It's complicated, but we believe Damon and Bree are alive."

She gasped. "But—"

"Mulch had someone else kill and mutilate people who looked like Damon and Bree. The DNA doesn't match."

For several moments there was no reply, but then I heard her sobbing, and tears welled in my eyes all over again. They were alive. I had a chance to save them. Ava could feel that hope as strongly as I did. Wiping away my tears, I saw that the exit for Suffern and I-287 was coming up in five miles.

"What did you find, Ava?" Aaliyah asked.

"Okay," Ava said. She sniffled, and then told us.

It took a few moments for her discoveries to penetrate my tired brain, but when they did, I almost drove off the road.

"That's where I am," Ava said. "I'm trying to figure out what happened to her after that."

"I already know what happened to her after that," I said.

"What?" Ava, Aaliyah, and Jones cried all at once.

"Ava? Gloria? I hate to do this, but I promise I'll call you right back."

Over their protests, I grabbed the phone and ended the call.

"Take 287 before you tell me what the hell is going on," Aaliyah said.

I glanced at the exit before veering away from it, staying on I-87, heading east toward Nyack and New York City.

"Where are you going?" she demanded.

"Omaha," I said, handing her my phone. "Call and get us on the next flight out of JFK or LaGuardia."

CHAPTER

59

SIX HOURS LATER, WE were driving north through Omaha. We passed a playground full of young children and a soccer field where older kids, eleven or twelve, were practicing on a blustery spring afternoon.

"Every kid I see seems vulnerable now," I said to Aaliyah, who was driving. "Part of me wants to roll down the window and shout at their parents to never let their kids out of their sight. Absolutely never."

For several moments, the detective did not reply. She'd been annoyed and on edge from lack of sleep and from the blowback she'd gotten from Captain Quintus when she'd called him after booking our flights to Omaha.

But at last, she sighed and said, "I can understand the feeling."

Feeling was what had brought us to Omaha. I knew much of the story, but I wanted to run Ava's discovery by the people who knew the case best. And something in my gut said that would be better done in person and on-site. Captain Quintus had disagreed, but the tickets had already been bought, and so there we were around four thirty that afternoon, driving past the Omaha Country Club into the bedroom community of Raven Oaks.

We followed the GPS on Aaliyah's phone into a development of upscale homes, some with tennis courts and others with pools, until we reached the North Fifty-Fourth Avenue circle, which ran out to a cul-de-sac with six homes on it. As soon as we turned onto the road, I saw the unmarked car parked by the curb and told the detective to pull in behind it.

We got out and started toward the car. My attention went immediately to the big white house at the end of the cul-de-sac and stayed there until I climbed into the unmarked car's backseat.

"Alex, I wish we were seeing each other under better circumstances," said the petite woman sitting sideways in the front passenger seat. Omaha police detective Jan Sergeant had aged little since I'd last seen her, seven years before.

"I do too, Jan," I said.

Sergeant's partner, Brian Box, sat behind the wheel looking straight ahead with an expression I remembered. Box had gone gray since I'd last seen him, but he still looked as if he'd bitten into something that didn't taste quite right.

I'd met the two detectives eighteen months after a brutal mass murder had taken place in that white house on the cul-de-sac before us. The Daley family of Omaha—Calvin, Bea, Ross, Sharon, and Janet—were found dead in their home two nights before Christmas. Their throats had been cut with a scalpel or razor.

I'd gotten involved after a second mass murder in suburban

Fort Worth. The Monahan family—Alice, Bill, Kenzie, Monroe, Annie, and Brent—were found at home with their throats slit.

I'd worked the case for the FBI but ultimately had been unable to push the investigation beyond a psychological profile I wrote of the unnamed suspect.

"We couldn't have done this over the phone?" said Box.

"I thought you'd want to hear it in person, Box," I said. "And I needed to see the scene again, and I wanted Detective Aaliyah to see it as well."

"We're not going in there and upsetting those people without cause," Sergeant said.

"No need to go inside. We can do this from here."

"So, out with it," Detective Box said.

"Tell us about Bea Daley," I said.

Box shrugged, said, "Nice woman. Housewife. Devoted to her husband and her kids. Did charity work, PTA, that sort of thing. But quiet."

"What about before she married Calvin?" I asked.

Sergeant said, "I believe she was born in Helena, Montana, and attended the university in Missoula before marrying Calvin."

"Next of kin?" Aaliyah asked.

"Dead, as we understood it," Sergeant said. "This is about Bea?"

"She's the key," I confirmed. "She's the reason her entire family was murdered that night."

"You have proof of that?" Box said, turning in his seat for the first time and looking highly skeptical.

Aaliyah and I told them about Thierry Mulch and his runaway mother, Lydia. Then we explained that Ava and Gloria

Jones had searched for Mulch's mother on Ancestry.com under both her maiden and married names and gotten nothing. But then, remembering that Atticus Jones had thought the man she'd run off with was from Montana or Oklahoma, they did searches in both those states.

"They found a record of a Lydia Mulch changing her name in Butte, Montana, about six months after she was last seen in West Virginia," I said. "She changed her name to Bea Townsend."

Detective Sergeant sat up, intent on what I was saying, but Box looked unimpressed.

"Six months later," I said, "Bea Townsend marries Calvin Daley in Omaha and gets yet another name. Daley was a mining engineer. I don't have it confirmed yet, but I'm betting he worked in Buckhannon as a consultant around the time Lydia Mulch disappeared. It just all adds up."

"Adds up to what?" Box cried.

"Motive," I said.

"For whom?" Sergeant asked.

"Thierry Mulch," I replied.

"The son who's officially dead?" Box scoffed.

"And the man who's taken my family," I said, keeping my cool and talking to Detective Sergeant. "Can't you see it, Jan? Rather than a mysterious intruder who leaves no evidence and no link to the crime, now you've got a homicidal son scorned and bent on revenge. He plans, waits for the night of a snowstorm, slips in, kills everyone in the house, and then vanishes without a trace."

Sergeant was staring off into the distance as she said, "I do see it."

"Fuck, c'mon, Jan," Box began. "This is—"

"Right," she said. "It fits, Brian. Think about it: the ME said that Bea Daley was the last to die."

I nodded. "Mulch wanted her to feel it. He killed her family first, showed her the bodies, or maybe made her watch her husband and children die, and then he slit his own mother's throat."

CHAPTER

60

THERE WAS AN EXTENDED silence in the car. Down the street, a woman in her thirties came out of the house where I believed Thierry Mulch had slaughtered his mother and her second family. A little boy walked by the woman's side as she went to the mailbox, and she gave us a long glance before they went back in.

"I still don't buy it," Box said at last.

"Why not?" Aaliyah asked. "It looks obvious to me."

"Yeah?" Box said. "Except there was another mass murder exactly like this one. You tell me you've got Mulch connected to that one too, and I'll start believing that this dead guy is behind it all."

"Smart man," I said.

"Dr. Cross," Detective Sergeant began.

"No, he's right," I said. "I do need that and I don't have it. Can we use a desk and a computer at your office?"

Box said, "Are you—"

"It's the least we can do," Sergeant said.

Twenty-five minutes later, Aaliyah was working at a computer in the Homicide bureau of the Omaha Police Department, and I was making phone calls. I called Ned Mahoney first, hoping we'd gotten some kind of match through the facial-recognition software, but so far, he said, it was still searching. I told him about Mulch looking like a suspect in the Daley slayings.

"Anything that links Mulch to the killings in Fort Worth?" he asked.

"Not yet," I said. "I'll let you know."

I called John Sampson next and brought him up to date. He was with our computer experts looking through the files of Preston Elliot, the dead programmer whose bones were found in the pigsty in rural Virginia.

"Get anything yet?" I asked.

"Not so far," he admitted. "But they found some encrypted files about an hour ago. So maybe we'll get lucky once they break them."

Then I called the Fort Worth Police Department looking for Detective J. P. Vincente and found out he was now Lieutenant J. P. Vincente.

"Alex Cross," Vincente said. "Fuck, man, I am so fucking sorry about the world of shit that's whirling around you now, my brother."

Vincente was smart and profane, and I liked him a lot. He'd come up from poverty and was a tireless worker and an all-around good guy.

"Appreciate it, JP," I said. "I need some help that might help you."

"With what?"

"You ever hear the name Thierry Mulch come up during your investigations into the Monahan murders?"

After a pause, he said, "Name doesn't ring a fucking bell. Why? Who is he?"

"The son of Bea Daley, and the sonofabitch who took my family."

It took a while to explain. When I'd finished, Vincente said, "Name doesn't click for me. But let me pull up the file."

"Look for anything that connects the mother to Mulch or West Virginia or anything that sticks out."

"I'll get back to you," he promised and hung up.

Detective Sergeant took us to an excellent steak house for dinner. The meat was amazing—Omaha, after all—but I had little appetite and turned down all offers of alcohol. I was trying to juggle so much at the same time that I couldn't chance anything that might cloud my judgment.

Aaliyah looked exhausted around nine o'clock when she said good night and went to one of the rooms we'd rented at the Hyatt. I felt exhausted and unsure of where to go or what to do next beyond flopping into a bed.

There was the deadline for delivering video proof of a double killing. But Gloria Jones and her friend in LA were already putting something together. All I had to do, she said, was find a place to film my part in the fake murder sometime later the following day.

There was nothing for me to do in the meantime.

That frightened me. As long as I was moving, trying some new avenue of investigation, I was able to keep my family's situation from getting to me. Now, however, lying on my bed and staring at the ceiling, it came back down on me like a crushing force.

Yes, there was hope that they were all still alive, but linking Mulch to the Daley murders had made me realize that he would not hesitate to kill my entire family when the time came. But when was that time? How long was he likely to keep playing me? Did I have enough time to find them?

I considered a promise to God: I'd leave this life of constant investigation if my family were returned safely to me. But then I remembered something Nana Mama had told me back when I was fifteen or sixteen.

You can't bargain with God, Alex. You can state your good intentions, you can imagine the life you want, but you can't negotiate with Him. He holds all the cards.

Lying on the bed, I closed my eyes and imagined my family as vividly as I could. We were in the new addition. My arm was tight around Bree's waist, and I smelled her as if she were right there. Ali was pretending he was in a gunfight behind the new furniture. Jannie was with Damon on the couch, laughing at their younger brother. Back in the kitchen, I saw a shadow and—

My cell phone rang. A Texas area code.

"You ready for this?" Lieutenant Vincente said.

CHAPTER 61

I SAT UP, TURNED on the light, said, “Go ahead, JP. I’m ready.”

“Okay,” he said. “So Alice Monahan was born in Alaska, graduated from Deerfield Academy in Massachusetts, and did her undergrad and MBA at Rice University.”

“Smart lady,” I said.

“Very,” he said and laughed. “That’s why I almost missed it.”

“Tell me.”

“For some reason, we had her transcript from Deerfield under her maiden name,” he said. “If I hadn’t dropped the papers, I wouldn’t have seen the bottom of the transcript and the fact that she attended high school in *Buckhannon, West Fucking Virginia,* her freshman and sophomore years before transferring to Deerfield. Her father was a high-profile geologist who had a two-year contract with the mines.”

My heart raced. Buckhannon! What was the likelihood of a coincidence like that? Two women who lived in the same small town in West Virginia end up slain in the same gruesome manner? A million to one? More like ten million to one. This was no coincidence. Mulch knew Alice Monahan. I was sure of it, but I wanted the evidence straight in my mind.

"What was Mrs. Monahan's maiden name?"

"Littlefield."

"Years she attended Buckhannon High?"

It took Vincente a few seconds, but he found it and told me.

"She and Mulch would have been in the same graduating class had she stayed," I said, feeling pieces starting to snap together. "And she was a great student and so was Mulch. My guess is if we compare Mulch's transcripts with hers, they took classes together."

"So, you're thinking Alice did some mean-girl shit to him and he took revenge?"

"It feels right," I replied. "She's smart, well-to-do. He's smart and lives on a pig farm. Maybe, after the psychological release Mulch got killing his mother and her second family, his thoughts turned to Alice and her family."

"Like his thoughts have now turned to you and yours?"

The question unnerved me, but I said, "For whatever reason, JP."

"Hey, you know who you should talk to about Alice Monahan?"

"Who's that?"

"That fucking Harvard guy who wrote that book about the cases. What's his name?"

"Sunday," I said. "Marcus Sunday."

CHAPTER

62

SUNDAY SIPPED A DOUBLE espresso and kept his eyes on the highway. It was already half past ten; he was ten miles out of Little Rock, and he had a long ride ahead of him. But he welcomed the journey. *It's the drifter and the hunter in me,* he thought. *I am simply one of those men born to roam and kill.*

He was also like the philosopher Epicurus, seeing good and evil linked with pleasure and pain. A good meal was pleasurable, and therefore good. A hangover showed the evil potential of wine.

But his thoughts about the pleasure that could be derived from pain were more complex and contradictory. Indeed, as his mind drifted toward Acadia Le Duc, he drove on, feeling the pleasure of her coming pain and knowing that was going to be good.

Very, very good.

A smile crossed Sunday's face and he glanced over at Cochran's laptop computer. It was the only thing he'd taken from the truck.

Before leaving the rig, he'd wiped the interior down completely, shut the drapes, and then waited for an upsurge in activity at the truck stop. He left the truck idling, as sleeping drivers often do, doors locked, and strolled behind the convenience store, looking for cameras.

Seeing none there, Sunday slipped into the scrub pines that abutted the truck stop and headed south. He walked five miles and then trashed his trucking cap before calling a cab, which had brought him to an Enterprise.

While waiting for the pickup he'd rented to be serviced, he'd gotten on the Internet using Cochran's laptop and started monitoring four of his bank accounts as well as all activities on his credit cards. In the past few hours, nearly twelve thousand dollars in cash had been taken from the accounts via ATMs in Memphis and across the river in Arkansas.

Worse, close to one hundred and eighty thousand dollars had been wire-transferred to accounts in Mexico he'd never heard of. There was only one person who could have pulled this off, only one person who could have gotten copies of his ATM cards, the passwords, and the bank account numbers and routing information for those wire transfers.

Acadia.

She was a bright, larcenous creature, wasn't she?

He'd seen that she'd dropped the Malibu with Avis at the Memphis airport and then somehow gotten across the river to make the withdrawals. But how? He assumed she was using her own credit cards, but unfortunately he had no way of getting into her accounts. That pissed him off. *She thought to find out my numbers,* he fumed, *but I didn't think to learn hers.* Which meant it was a crapshoot as to which of the three places he thought she might run to she'd actually gone.

Before he could consider them each again, he heard a phone ring. It was his legitimate cell phone, the one he used in his professional and writing life. He dug it from his pocket, saw an unfamiliar number on the screen, wondered if it might be Acadia, and punched Answer.

"Marcus Sunday?" a man said.

"You're talking to him."

"I'm sorry to interrupt your evening, but I got your number from your publicist in Los Angeles, and—"

"Whom do you write for?" Sunday asked. He'd had a flurry of stories written about him when the book came out, but none in months.

"I don't write for anyone. This is Alex Cross. Do you remember me?"

CHAPTER

63

FOR THREE SLOW BEATS, time stood still for Sunday, and for once in his life, no thoughts flickered in his brain.

"Dr. Sunday?" Cross said. "Hello?"

Then time and Sunday's mind lurched back into sync. Talk to Cross? Now, this *was* interesting.

"Right here, Special Agent Cross," Sunday said. "And of course I remember you."

"I'm not with the Bureau anymore."

"No?" Sunday said, feeling excited, dueling. "I hadn't heard that."

"Look, I know you've got reason not to talk to me after the review I gave your book, but are you aware of my situation?"

"Situation?" Sunday said with slight imperiousness. "No. I've been overseas and have only just returned. What is your situation?"

"A guy named Thierry Mulch has killed several people in the DC area and has taken my family hostage."

"Jesus," Sunday said. "I'm sorry to hear that. I wouldn't wish that on my worst enemy."

"Thank you," Cross said. "Ever heard of him? Thierry Mulch?"

Be calm, Sunday thought. *Carry on smoothly.* But what was Cross's game? How much did he know? How much should Sunday say? He decided to go on instinct, his intimate ally in the past.

"I can't say I've ever heard the name, as unusual as it is," Sunday replied. "Who is he?"

"The son of Bea Daley," Cross replied.

Sunday's mind whirled with the implications of that statement. Cross now had a link that, to Sunday's knowledge, no one else had. But that link in no way indicated that Cross had connected Mulch to Sunday. He was positive of that.

"You must be mistaken, Dr. Cross. Bea Daley's son, Ross, died in the house with the rest of the family."

"Turns out she had another son in another life before she met Daley."

"What? Where? In Montana?"

"Buckhannon, West Virginia," Cross said. "Bea was Lydia Mulch back then. She met Calvin Daley when he worked as an engineer at a coal mine there, and ran away with him, leaving her son behind. She changed her name legally in Montana and then moved to Omaha and married Calvin. That story she told people about being raised in Montana was fiction."

"So what are you saying?" Sunday said coolly. "You think this Thierry Mulch character killed the Daley family?"

"I do," Cross said.

"But the killer left no evidence," Sunday said. "So you can't say for sure. Or can you?"

"Not good enough for a jury, if that's what you mean," Cross admitted. "But there's more. Alice Monahan? She was once Alice Littlefield."

"Correct. Born in Anchorage, I think."

"That's right," the detective said. "And she graduated from Deerfield Academy after spending two years in Buckhannon High School."

"I…I didn't know that."

"It was there in the evidence." Cross sighed. "But no one attached any significance to it until now."

"Well," Sunday said, making a point of sounding dejected, "I guess my perfect criminal wasn't so perfect after all."

"Oh, Mulch was close to perfect," Cross said. "Had all sorts of people believing he was dead for decades. No one suspects a ghost in a series of mass murders."

"So why exactly did you call me?"

"I don't know," Cross admitted, sounding as if he was bearing a heavy burden. "J. P. Vincente thought you might have come across something that we could use to help us find Mulch before he kills my family."

"You don't know where this Mulch is?"

"We have no idea."

Cross sounded frustrated and sincere, and Sunday's shoulders relaxed before he said in a soothing voice, "I'm afraid I can't help you, Dr. Cross. I'm terribly sorry, and sorry for your…horrible, horrible situation."

"Sorry I wasted your time."

"You didn't waste my time," Sunday said. "You actually did me a favor."

"Yeah? How's that?"

"You gave me the heads-up," he replied. "I'm going to have

to amend the book now, and I should probably start by researching Mr. Thierry Mulch and Buckhannon, West Virginia. That was the name of the place, wasn't it?"

"Correct. And while you're at it, would you amend the quotes you attributed to me? They're not right."

"You tell me how you want them to read," Sunday said. "And I deeply apologize if I misquoted you."

There was a silence before Cross said, "Apology accepted."

"Good. Where are you, Dr. Cross? DC?"

"Omaha. You?"

"Memphis, for a reading. Last week was Philly, and after this I'm headed to Austin," Sunday said. "Say, would you agree to do an interview when this is all over?"

Cross hesitated, then said, "Sure, with a tape recorder running, maybe," and hung up.

Ignoring the dig, Sunday grinned, buzzing on the adrenaline his conversation with the detective had triggered and the satisfaction he got knowing that even if Cross had learned of Thierry Mulch's past, he had no clue where to find Mr. Mulch now. Sunday clearly had the upper hand and was still two, maybe even three steps ahead.

Laughing and gleefully pounding his fist on the steering wheel, Sunday put the gas pedal to the floor and shot forward through the night.

CHAPTER

64

I HUNG UP THE phone with Marcus Sunday feeling like I'd hit yet another dead end. Why had I called him? If the FBI and police had never heard of Thierry Mulch in connection with the Monahan and Daley murders, why should I expect Sunday to have come across his name?

Because you are grasping at straws, Alex.

As soon as I had that thought, I got angry with myself. Damn right I was grasping at straws. My family had been gone for ten days. For ten days, Mulch had been playing me like I was a puppet, and he was a cruel puppeteer. I would grasp at any straw, string, or thought if it might help me find Bree, Nana Mama, Damon, Jannie, and Ali.

It was nearing midnight, however, and I realized there was nothing else I could do, no other straws I could reach for. I put my phone on Do Not Disturb and fell into a deep sleep.

I surfaced groggily shortly after three a.m. and then tried to force myself back to that deep, dark respite from reality.

Instead, I was cast into dreams where I saw Mulch as that red-bearded guy who'd gone to Ali's school slipping alongside the Daleys' house in a snowstorm carrying the knife that would kill the mother who had abandoned him. Mulch was inside then, a Grinch creeping past a glowing Christmas tree. He climbed the staircase, pushed open the first bedroom door. There were forms lying beneath the covers of a queen-size bed.

When Mulch eased back the blankets, I saw that woman who now lived in the Daleys' house. Beside her, my son Ali, not her son, was curled up in a fetal position. Mulch put the blade to Ali's neck and pulled backward sharply. Blood misted the air.

I screamed and spun in my dream, raced down the hallway to the next bedroom. But Mulch was somehow already there, and he was done with Damon and Jannie. The hallway got longer as I ran on, trying to protect Bree.

Mulch came out her door before I got there, and he smiled at the blood dripping off the knife before beckoning me to follow him to the last bedroom door.

When I got there, he was standing by my grandmother, who looked exactly as she had the day she came to get me when I was ten: that loving but no-nonsense expression, her teacher's crisp posture, the blue dress she'd worn with a matching hat and handbag, and the white church gloves.

As if unaware of Mulch raising the blade toward her throat, Nana Mama looked at me and said softly, "Alex, are you ready for a new life?"

"No," I said.

"No?" my grandmother chided gently. "Then your thinking is wrong, young man. That's the difference between folks when it comes down to it. Their thinking defines them. So I'll ask you again, are you ready for a new way of thinking?"

"No!" I screamed as the knife cut into her with a sound like thumping. "No!"

The thumping became pounding in my brain so loud I thought my skull would split before I jolted awake, sweaty, and looked around the hotel room wildly. It was almost five a.m.

The pounding startled me that time. Someone was knocking on my door.

"Hold on!" I shouted, struggling to my feet and realizing I'd slept in my clothes. God only knew what I smelled like.

At the door I peered through the peephole and saw Tess Aaliyah moving like Jannie had as a girl when she had to pee, rocking from one agitated foot to another, her face screwed up in concentration.

My stomach did a flip, and I bowed my head, prayed, "Dear God, please give me the strength to handle whatever it is she has to tell me."

Then I opened the door.

"I thought you were dead for a second there," Detective Aaliyah said with relief. "Don't you answer your phone?"

"I had it on Do Not Disturb. What's going on?"

"Mahoney and Sampson have been trying to call you the past hour," she replied. "They wanted to be the ones to tell you, but it is what it is."

Her face broke into a smile. "The facial-recognition software got a solid hit on that photo of Karla Mepps. Mahoney and Sampson think they know who she is."

CHAPTER

65

THE FACES OF NED MAHONEY and John Sampson filled the laptop screen. Aaliyah and I were in Aaliyah's room, linked to them through Skype.

"The biometric analysis keyed on a Louisiana driver's license," Mahoney explained. "I'll send it over in a second."

"Who is she?"

"Acadia Le Duc," Sampson said. "She's a former nurse turned freelance photographer. The New Orleans address on the license is old, and we have nothing current, but her name, Acadia, came up in those encrypted files on Preston Elliot's computer. Elliot evidently did some work for an Acadia."

"Where?"

"Looks like DC," my partner said. "The notes in the file said 'Acadia. Work complete. Services owed. Kalorama.'"

"When was the file created?"

"Three months ago," Sampson said. "It was last updated two weeks ago."

I digested that, said, "So she was in DC just before my family was taken."

"Looks that way," Mahoney agreed.

"We have access to her credit cards?"

"Not yet, but we're working on it."

"Ms. Le Duc have a record?" Aaliyah asked.

"Nothing as an adult," Sampson said. "But we got bounceback on her name in juvey files in…uh, Jefferson Davis Parish, Louisiana."

"With your permission, we're going to put out a blanket bulletin on her," Mahoney said. "Every agent and police officer in the country will have seen the face of Acadia Le Duc by tomorrow."

At first I thought that was a good idea, but then I balked.

"Can we wait on that a day? Find out more about Le Duc first?"

"Why?" Sampson asked.

"I guess I'm nervous over what Mulch might do if we announce to the world that we've identified his accomplice."

My partner glanced at Mahoney, who said, "We'll do it your way."

"Thanks. Listen, I'll follow up on that juvenile report. Where was it?"

The FBI agent looked at his notes, said, "Jefferson Davis Parish. Courthouse is in the county seat, Jennings."

With promises to keep my phone on and check in every hour, I ended the Skype call, looked at Aaliyah, and said, "I'm starving."

"I am too," she said.

We went downstairs to the hotel restaurant, and I ordered four eggs, toast, bacon, potatoes, and coffee. Aaliyah ordered oatmeal and fruit. While we waited for the food to come, I looked up the number for the Jennings, Louisiana, police department on the Internet and then called. A female dispatcher answered. I identified myself and asked if there were any detectives or officers still around from the year that Acadia Le Duc got a sealed file in juvenile court. After a long pause, I was told I'd need to talk with the Jefferson Davis Parish sheriff's office.

Our food came. Sensing that this might be a long hard day, I ate it all before looking up the sheriff's phone number. The deputy who answered the phone said that Sheriff Paul Gauvin fit my search criteria, but he was at a training seminar and wouldn't be back for an hour or so. The deputy said he would give Sheriff Gauvin my number when he called in.

Even though it was early, I called the court clerk in Jennings, Louisiana. Surprisingly, he answered the phone. Figuring I'd get shot down on the juvenile file, I asked if he could call up all civil and criminal files on anyone with the surname Le Duc.

A few moments later, he returned and said, "There's something from the late nineties on the girl, but it's sealed. There are two old lawsuits regarding land boundaries that are more than twenty years old. And there are several old criminal cases involving the father, but Jean, well, he has been dead for years, since the late nineties."

The way the clerk said that last bit—emphasizing *the late nineties*—sounded odd, so I said, "How'd he die?"

"His gators got him," the clerk replied. "Any more than that, you need to talk with the sheriff. He worked all that nasty business back then."

The clerk hung up before I could get another word in, and

I was left spinning my wheels, waiting for a call from Sheriff Gauvin but wondering if the way the clerk had said the words *the late nineties* was meant to tip me off that Acadia's sealed juvenile case had something to do with her father's death by gators.

It kind of made twisted sense if that was so. Thierry Mulch had fed his father and Preston Elliot to the pigs, after all. How had Mulch and Acadia met? Did one monster sense the other and, what, confide? I'd seen it before, usually among male serial killers who'd taken on younger apprentices.

But an alliance between monsters of different genders? I couldn't come up with an example of it, other than Bonnie Parker and Clyde Barrow, and that seemed a weak case, at best, because they were bank robbers who happened to kill, not murderers who happened to kidnap.

CHAPTER

66

IN A CRANKY, FOUL mood around eleven thirty that morning, Sunday sat in the rented pickup truck watching a small tan bungalow down a side street in Corpus Christi, Texas. Summer had come early. It was blistering hot out, ninety-two in the shade, and humid beyond belief. Worse, he'd barely slept in the past thirty hours, and he'd been pissing in a bottle since leaving Memphis.

He'd dozed off and on since arriving around six twenty, but he'd woken up whenever a car or pedestrian had passed, and he was sure that Acadia had not gone into the house. He was also positive that no one had left in the almost five hours he'd been sitting in the heat, turning the AC on every few minutes and wanting to punch out the window.

There was always the possibility that Acadia had gotten here first and had put her car in the garage before six twenty. Or he could have guessed wrong. But when he'd considered the three places she'd be most likely to head in times of turmoil, he'd followed his gut and come here first. How long should he give it?

His head was starting to spin and pound, and he knew he was in no condition to make decisions. He'd have to give in and sleep.

Sunday was just about to turn on the car, and the AC, and shut his eyes for an hour when, in the rearview mirror, he spotted a green Mini Cooper turning onto the street. He immediately slid across the bench seat, head down, and waited until the Mini passed, then he glided out the passenger door and galloped down the sidewalk wearing blue shorts, a sleeveless T, running shoes, sunglasses, and a visor pulled down low over his eyes.

The Mini slowed. The bungalow's garage door rose as the car turned into the short uphill drive. Sunday slowed too, eyes patrolling the suburban street and seeing it deserted in the blistering heat of day. When the Mini's nose passed into the garage, he took one last glance around and exploded diagonally toward it.

The Mini was inside. The door engaged and began to lower. Sunday dove over the security beam and then barrel-rolled into the garage. A second later, he was crouched behind the left rear bumper and the garage was closed off from the street.

Sunday froze as the driver's door opened and shut, and he heard footsteps walking across the floor to a set of wooden stairs. A key turned in a lock. The door opened and stood ajar. Sunday heard the first beep and made his move, dancing along and around the front of the Mini and up the steps as more beeps echoed in the garage.

A loud buzz sounded, signaling that the security code had

turned off the system. In a heartbeat, Sunday was through the door and on her from behind, clamping one hand over her mouth before she had the chance to scream and driving her across the hallway and up against the wall.

He ground his hips hard against her rear and pushed his face close to the left ear of a terrified redheaded woman dressed in purple hospital scrubs.

"Hello, Jillian," he growled. "Just getting off shift?"

CHAPTER 67

A FORMER CLASSMATE OF Acadia's in nursing school and the closest his ex-lover had to a best friend forever, Jillian Green squealed into Sunday's hand, sounding so much like a sow going to slaughter that he almost laughed.

"Where is Acadia?" he snarled. "And if you scream or lie, I will hurt you. I don't want to. But I will. Do you understand?"

Tears welled in Jillian Green's eyes and she nodded, trembling.

"Please, Marcus," she whined when he removed his hand and turned her to face him.

Jillian was thick and busty, not at all his type, but he was still happy to press against her with his forearm across her throat and say, "Where is my girl?"

"I don't know," Jillian said desperately. "I haven't heard from her in weeks."

"Wrong answer," Sunday said, pressing his arm harder against her throat and grabbing one of her pinkies. "Now, try again, or I will snap this finger and then another before I crush your larynx. Do you understand, Jillian?"

She was weeping again, but she nodded.

Sunday released the pressure on her throat but held her pinkie firmly.

Jillian sobbed, "Don't hurt her, please."

"Hurt her?" he said, acting taken aback. "I'm not interested in hurting Acadia any more than I'm interested in hurting you, Jillian. I just want the money she stole from me yesterday. I want it back in my account, and then I'm moving on. No hard feelings. Truth is, she and I have been on the outs for a while now, and while I can take the abandonment, I cannot abide a thief."

"You promise you won't hurt her?"

"On my dear mama's soul," Sunday assured her.

Jillian swallowed, said, "Last I knew, around midnight, just as I was going on shift, she had car trouble and said she wouldn't be coming here after all."

"Okay," he said reasonably. "Where did she say she was going?"

"Her apartment in New Orleans," she said, a little too quickly.

Sunday could spot a liar a mile away, much less six inches. He smiled, said, "So she's going to her mother's."

A wave of fear pulsed through Jillian's face. "Marcus, no, she—"

He pressed against her throat again, said, "Shhh, now. No more of that. I'm going to need a place to sleep for a few hours. I can crash here, right?"

"That's not a good—"

He increased the pressure on her throat again, and she gulped and nodded.

Sunday released her and let her lead the way. As they crossed through a small, tidy kitchen, he saw her hesitate as she passed a block of knives on the counter.

"Don't even think about that, darlin'," he said.

"What? I was wondering if you were hungry."

He was, but that could wait. He said, "I just want to sleep for now. I'll eat later, and then you'll be rid of me."

From the stiffness of her posture as they entered the hall, Sunday knew she was having a hard time believing him. But that was okay. He was having a hard time believing it himself.

Jillian stopped, gestured through an open door, said, "There's an extra bed in there you can use."

"No, no," he said, pushing her forward. "I was thinking we'd sleep together so I'd know if you got up or tried to make a phone call."

"I wouldn't," she said, her voice cracking as she went through the door at the end of the hall.

"Just the same," Sunday said, following her into the master bedroom, a tasteful and orderly space with a decidedly feminine touch.

"I need to take a shower," she said.

"That's a great idea," he said. "But later, after."

Jillian turned and, without meeting his eye, said, "After?"

"C'mon, now, darling, you take off those scrubs, show Marcus what he's been missing, and he'll show you what Acadia's been getting," he said.

"Please, Marcus," she whimpered.

"Take them off," he said. "Or I'll tear them off you."

Looking humiliated, she shed the top and bottom, and then took off her bra and panties.

"Well, Jillian, I must say, you've exceeded my expectations," Sunday said, shucking his running shorts. "You're an Aphrodite as Rubens might have painted her, pale and voluptuous. Now lie facedown on the bed and let old Marcus go to work on you. You watch; it'll relieve the unnecessary tension between us, Jillian. It'll help us both get a great afternoon snooze."

CHAPTER 68

TESS AALIYAH AND ALEX CROSS checked out of the hotel shortly after noon and headed to the airport. It was Cross's idea to set up there, and Aaliyah agreed with the strategy. If they had a break of any kind anywhere in the country, they wanted to be able to move as fast as possible.

They went to a café inside the airport and spent nearly five hours there, drinking coffee, eating, and reviewing every aspect of the case. They identified questions they wanted answered and let their imaginations and investigative instincts paint the space between what they knew and what they didn't know about Thierry Mulch and Acadia Le Duc.

The more time Detective Aaliyah spent with Cross, the more she respected him. An ordinary man—cop or otherwise—faced with this kind of pressure would have buckled long ago. But Cross just seemed to shrug the weight from one shoulder to the other, bearing the load with a grace she couldn't imagine. Based on his accomplishments, Cross could easily have been a know-it-all or a pompous ass, yet he was an excellent listener, gave of himself, and didn't seem to have an egotistical cell in his formidable body.

He also displayed a remarkable ability to compartmentalize. Though he and Aaliyah were talking about things that directly affected the lives of his family, Cross seemed able to divorce himself from what had to be disturbingly emotional aspects of the case and keep working the investigation rationally and logically.

When Aaliyah came back after a bathroom break around a quarter to five, Cross said, "We'll give it another couple of hours, then find a hotel again."

"What about the video of the killing you're supposed to make?"

"Gloria Jones is supposed to call me when she's ready for me," Cross said. "On another note, how's your dad's hip these days?"

As a general rule, Detective Aaliyah did not discuss her dad without his permission, but Bernie was an admirer of Cross's work and she didn't think he'd mind.

"I don't know if you know, but the entire right side of his pelvis was shattered," she said. "He gets around okay after four operations, but you can tell it still bothers him."

"The hip or not being on the job?"

She smiled. "Both."

"I remember what a machine he was," Cross said. "Must have made him crazy. To be done with his career, I mean."

"Oh, it did at first," Aaliyah said. "I thought he was going to drive my mother insane, and he abused alcohol for a bit, but then Mom got sick, and she became the focus of his life until she passed, last year."

"I'm sorry to hear that. What does your dad do with his time now?"

"He fishes a lot, and putters in the yard, and he's got a lady friend."

"You okay with that?"

Aaliyah cocked her head, reappraised him, and said, "So it is true you've got telepathy and X-ray vision."

Cross chuckled. "Just a knack for reading body language."

"Then you should go play poker in Vegas."

"Does that mean you're not okay with his lady friend?"

God, he was good, she thought. Gentle, but relentless.

"I've met her only once," Aaliyah replied. "She's nice. And, I don't know, I guess I don't want to see my dad hurting anymore."

"That's perfectly understandable," Cross said. "And it must be tough for you because he's struggling toward normalcy and you're not a part of it on a day-to-day basis."

Aaliyah hadn't thought of it that way before, but she nodded, realizing that Cross had a vast reserve of emotional intelligence as well as an analytical side.

His cell rang at five thirty. Cross answered, listened, and said, "Yes, Sheriff, this is Alex Cross. What can you tell me about Acadia Le Duc?"

He listened again, then said, "I understand that it was sealed. You should know, however, that DC Metro Police and the FBI consider her an accomplice in a kidnapping and murder spree."

Cross nodded at Aaliyah and then listened without comment for nearly fifteen minutes. Finally, he said, "No, I wish you'd hold off on that until I can get there, but in the meantime, you should put that cabin under surveillance. And I'll let you know our ETA once I get a better handle on how we're going to do this."

Then Cross hung up, looking energized again, and said, "We need to get to Jennings, Louisiana, the quickest way possible."

CHAPTER

69

IN JILLIAN GREEN'S CONDO in Corpus Christi, Marcus Sunday awoke refreshed and with a pleasant dull ache in his loins. He checked his watch, yawned, and got to his feet naked.

Sunday left the bed in a shambles, with the blankets in a heap and long, thin tears in the sheets as if fingernails had gouged them. He pushed open the bathroom door and smelled bleach. He cocked his head, appreciating the sight of Acadia's BFF lying in the bathtub, water up to her neck, her eyes still bugged out from having been choked with his belt as he fucked her from behind.

He'd heard that being strangled during sex causes stronger orgasms in some women, and he'd decided to experiment. Jillian certainly proved the point, he thought. She'd gone off into la-la land there at the end, quivered unbelievably just before she'd died.

Sunday turned on the shower, waited until it warmed, and then climbed into the chill water with the dead woman. He paid the corpse no mind as he washed himself head to toe with antibacterial soap.

When he was done, he pushed her head under the bleach water. After three minutes, he pulled the plug on the tub, stepped out onto the mat, and dripped dry while using a washcloth to hold the showerhead and rinse Jillian's body with cold water. When he was done, he poured three capfuls of Drano into the drain, wiped down the shower controls with the washcloth, and brought it and the bathmat to the master bedroom.

Sunday stripped the bed, took the sheets and blankets to the washing machine. He put them in and added half a cup of Clorox before turning it on hot. He wiped down the machine knobs and found the vacuum. He vacuumed from the edge of the tub back into the master bedroom and then put on his running gear again. Then he cleaned his way out of the house, back through the kitchen and into the garage.

After removing the vacuum-cleaner bag, he wiped down the vacuum with the damp washcloth and then set the machine in a corner, as if it were always kept there. With the washcloth, he pressed the garage-door opener, waited until it was completely up. A kid on a bicycle went past but didn't look his way.

Sunday stabbed the switch and took off, vaulting off the top of the stairs, sprinting along the Mini Cooper, then hurdling the security beam.

He was down the street and in the rented truck thirty seconds later. He'd dump the vacuum bag at a rest stop out on I-10, heading east.

CHAPTER

70

A WIDE SWATH OF violent weather swept across the southern plains that evening. Thunderstorms delayed our takeoff and landing, so it was eight before we stepped off a United Airlines jet in Houston. The ride had been a rodeo, and there was talk of tornado activity throughout the night from eastern Texas into western Louisiana, which, unfortunately, was where we were headed.

"I'm praying this isn't a wild-goose chase," Aaliyah said as I drove a rented Jeep Cherokee out of the airport into a pelting rain.

"It's the strongest straw we've got to grasp at," I said. "Put Jennings in the GPS."

She did, and the machine told us we had a hundred-and-seventy-eight-mile road trip ahead of us. Luckily, most of the way would be on Interstate 10. We theoretically could be there around ten thirty.

But wind and rain buffeted the car and slowed us. Was this

trip worth it? Was it worth risking the drive at night with all the weather warnings?

I still thought so after going over what Sheriff Gauvin had told me over the phone. Gauvin had been new to the force the night Acadia Le Duc called in the accidental death of her father. Like Thierry Mulch's father, Jean Le Duc had a reputation for violence and booze. He'd beaten his wife and daughter several times, but both had refused to testify against the man.

The mother had a fresh black eye when Gauvin and the sheriff arrived on the scene—a cabin on the banks of a bayou outside Jennings—early one morning after a torrential rain. Acadia and her mother said Jean Le Duc had gotten wildly drunk the evening before and took it out on his wife before she and her daughter managed to barricade themselves in the windowless back room, their usual method of surviving his tirades.

They claimed to have spent the entire night there. Acadia went searching for her father when they found the cabin and shed empty. She went down by the dock, expecting to find him passed out on his airboat, a common enough occurrence. Then she heard a commotion in the pen where her father kept his pet alligators.

"All that was left was his right forearm, which conveniently had an identifying tattoo on it," Gauvin had said. "That and other evidence I won't get into led us to believe that Acadia and her mother, or Acadia acting on her own, killed old Jean and then fed him to the alligators. But we could never prove it, and most folks around here said, 'Good riddance.'"

Acadia left Jennings after graduation and moved to New Orleans to enter a nursing program at Loyola. That was a while back, but the sheriff said he saw her several times a year, when she came to visit her mother.

"So the mom knows how to get in touch with her?" I'd asked.

"Expect so," he said.

"If she got in trouble, would she head there? To her mom's?"

"She might," Gauvin said.

"What's the Le Duc place like?"

"The house is a dump, but there are outbuildings and the property's big," the sheriff said. "And it's on the Bayou des Cannes. Isolated. There isn't another house around there for a mile, maybe more."

It was, in short, the kind of place a madman like Mulch might keep five hostages. The sheriff offered to go out to Le Duc's mother's to ask some questions and have a look around, but I asked him not to, saying that I wanted to be there in case that *was* where my family was being held. Instead, I asked that the road into the place be monitored.

Shortly after ten, the rain eased somewhat, and I was able to relax my death grip on the wheel. The rain had been falling in sheets, and the glare off the wet road was forcing me to squint when my cell phone rang again.

CHAPTER

71

IT WAS NED MAHONEY. I answered and put the phone on speaker.

"Alex?" Mahoney said. "Where are you now?"

I glanced at Aaliyah, who said, "About ten miles west of Beaumont."

"Your hunch about Le Duc's mom might be paying off," Mahoney said. "We got access to Le Duc's credit cards. About five hours ago, she bought gas in Natchitoches. Four hours before that, she bought gas and food in Texarkana. She's driving a blue 2014 Dodge Avenger rental and heading in your direction."

I sped up and ignored the rain, which had started falling hard again.

"Any pictures from gas stations?" Aaliyah said.

"We've made the request," Sampson said.

I said, "Can you get the rental agency to track the car's GPS?"

"We've made that request too," said Mahoney. "Hertz

wants to comply, but they need to see a search warrant, which is being worked on as we speak."

"Where was she before Texarkana?" I asked.

"She's spent quite a bit of time in DC the past few months," Sampson said. "In and around Kalorama."

"We have an address?" Aaliyah asked.

"There's nothing under her name."

"Any other travel outside the District?" I asked.

"Lots," Mahoney said. "She was in a mystery bookstore in Philadelphia last Tuesday, and at the airport in St. Louis on Friday. On Saturday, she was back east, buying food at a restaurant in Cumberland, Maryland."

"Wait," Aaliyah said. "What time did she buy the food in Cumberland?"

There was a pause before Sampson said, "Ten twelve. She charged eighteen dollars and change at, uh, Café Mark on Baltimore Street."

"That's not twenty miles from Frostburg," Aaliyah said. "And it fits with the time Claude Harrow was killed and his place torched."

"I thought that too, Tess," Sampson said.

"You talk to anyone at that café?" I asked.

"Closed until seven tomorrow morning," Mahoney said.

"Any other purchases?" Aaliyah asked.

"Uh, yeah," Sampson said. "Later Saturday afternoon, she charged sixty dollars at the Harris Teeter food market on Kalorama Avenue and thirty-seven dollars at Secondi, a used-clothes consignment shop in Dupont Circle."

"Walkable from Kalorama," I said.

"Easily," Mahoney agreed.

"Maybe that's where Mulch is holding them," Aaliyah said.

It was entirely possible. Again and again in the past few months, Acadia Le Duc had returned to that neighborhood in my city to do her spending. She'd clearly been living in the area. With Mulch? I guessed yes. But why had she gone to St. Louis? And why was she in Louisiana now?

"What about this past Sunday?" Aaliyah asked.

"She didn't charge anything on that date, but she was busy yesterday," Sampson said. "She bought an early breakfast at Reagan National and then rented the Dodge at the Memphis airport about four hours after she landed. Last night she bought gas and got a room at the Hampton Inn in Fort Smith, Arkansas, then nothing until the gas buy in Texarkana."

I barely heard the last part of the report. My mind had rocketed back nearly twenty-four hours, and my hands began to shake.

"John," I said in a trembling voice. "Just to confirm. You said she got the car at the *Memphis* airport? And you said she bought something in a Philadelphia mystery bookshop?"

"Both correct," my partner said.

My hand shot to my mouth and the car swerved so hard I had to take my foot off the gas and hit the brakes.

"Jesus," Aaliyah said. "What the—"

"I think I know who Thierry Mulch is," I said. "Or is now, anyway."

Their voices came back as one. "What? Who?"

"Marcus Sunday," I said, feeling rage building inside me. "That Harvard guy who wrote that book about the Daley and Monahan killings, *The Perfect Criminal.* Jesus Christ, the egomaniacal sonofabitch was writing about himself!"

Part Four

CHAPTER 72

ACADIA LE DUC HAD timed her approach so it was pitch-black and pouring when she took the Evangeline Highway exit off Interstate 10. She headed north around and away from Jennings, Louisiana, for nine miles, and then turned the Dodge rental onto a muddy two-track path that she bounced along for several hundred yards across the top of a dike before parking where a rice field met a swamp.

When Acadia was a girl, she'd roamed for miles in these swamps. Now she confidently climbed out of the car into the driving rain and went straight into the tangle and vine with no light to guide her. As she had the night she'd snuck into the woods behind Damon Cross's dormitory at the Kraft School, she thought of herself as that panther tattooed on her arm and navigated by dead reckoning and by the swollen creeks that fed the Bayou des Cannes.

The panther skirted clusters of moss-covered cypress trees. She padded through overgrown tupelo groves and ancient pine plantations choked with kudzu. She fought her way through stands of reeds and knew just where to walk to stay out of the sucking mud. The rain was incessant, but it muted all sound, a good thing.

As Acadia moved, her thoughts turned to Marcus Sunday. It had been nearly thirty hours since she'd run. How was he taking it? Bad, she was sure, especially if he'd figured out she'd looted a few of his accounts. If she'd been a liability and a threat before, she was an exponentially larger liability and threat now.

Acadia not only understood everything about the Cross kidnapping plot and the two murders Claude Harrow had done for Sunday but knew Sunday's entire sordid story, how he'd made the money he'd gotten from selling his father's pig farm to the coal company disappear, how he'd managed to create a new identity after faking his death, and even how he'd had academic transcripts forged so brilliantly that he had gotten into Harvard.

Acadia also knew how Sunday had planned the death of his mother's family. She'd heard blow-by-blow descriptions of how he'd killed each and every one of them. She knew the same kinds of details about the Monahan slayings in Texas. In short, she simply knew too much.

Marcus was the smartest, most self-actualized man she'd ever known, an outsider who'd created his own rules, the most basic of which was his personal survival. Sooner rather than later, he'd start hunting her.

So Acadia had several choices. Did she keep going after tonight? Head for Mexico and the money she'd moved there? Or did she contact the police, maybe even Alex Cross, and cut herself a deal in return for immunity and witness protection? Or did she contact the police, give them enough information to nail Sunday and save the family, but then disappear into another life? Marcus had proven that it could be done, hadn't he?

An hour after Acadia entered the swamp, she still had not yet decided what she was going to do. The rain slowed a bit. She caught the faint glow of lights ahead and dropped her pace to a crawl. After every step she paused and listened to each rustle and snap in the woods around her. She sniffed the air for strange smells but caught only the washed scent of ozone and the perfume of rain. But the closer she got to those lights, the more her breath tasted of old and bitter memories.

The place where Acadia was born, raised, and forced to commit patricide appeared in bits and pieces through the leaves. Weeds surrounded the cabin, which pitched slightly off its stone foundation. The roof sagged, and the screened-in porch defied gravity. Somewhere to her left out there in the darkness, the old dock creaked and groaned.

Acadia got closer still and saw lights behind the threadbare curtains. She also heard a radio in the cabin tuned to a gospel station, and a television blaring the theme song to *CSI,* her mother's favorite show.

She stood behind a tree, studying the cabin and the yard for almost ten minutes. The old Ford pickup was parked beneath the big cypress. A few moths flitted beneath the porch eaves and around the bare lightbulb by the door.

The breeze shifted. Acadia wrinkled her nose at the smell of rank water and rotted meat coming from the bayou. Years had gone by, and her mother still fed the alligators that had fed on her father's corpse.

"Why wouldn't I?" she'd always say. "The gators set us free, didn't they? I owe them, don't I?"

For her part, however, Acadia had not gone near the backwater where her father's pets lived since the night the old bastard died. She'd go anywhere else around the twenty-acre homestead, but never, ever down there. Though not a superstitious person by nature, she thought of that sliver of wetland as cursed.

Above the noise of a preacher delivering a sermon of salvation on the radio, and Gil Grissom shooting his mouth off about X-ray analysis on the television, Acadia heard the rattle of pots and pans. Her mom was probably cleaning up after a late supper in front of the tube.

For several moments longer, Acadia stood there, just inside the shadows, racking her brain, trying to remember if she'd ever mentioned this place to Sunday. Maybe once. Maybe that very first drunken night when they'd met in a bar in the French Quarter, but never again. She'd made sure of that, telling Sunday that she'd been raised over on the Mississippi border northwest of Slidell.

Something intense must have been happening on *CSI* because the music coming from the TV got all creepy. Then she heard her mother start coughing and hacking. It was enough to embolden Acadia, and she finally stepped from the trees and cut across the yard toward the cabin.

Acadia thumbed the latch and opened the screened-in porch's door, expecting Mercury, her mother's beloved pit bull, to come charging out to meet her. Instead, she heard snores and spotted the old dog on his straw bed in the corner.

"Some protection you are," she said.

Mercury grumbled, sighed, and farted. The door to the cabin was ajar.

"Ma?" Acadia called as she gently pushed it open, seeing dishes drying in a rack by the sink.

She stepped inside onto the rough-hewn floor and saw her mother's overstuffed chair, empty except for the latest copy of *People* magazine open to the celebrity crossword. Several cans of Diet Coke sat on the TV-dinner table next to her ashtray and an open pack of Pall Malls. *CSI* had given way to a commercial that touted a breakthrough in fabric softeners. The preacher on the radio had shifted from salvation to a theme of damnation and hellfire for all sinners before God.

"Mama, where are you?" Acadia called louder. "It's me."

Her mother's frail voice answered from her bedroom. "I'm back here, baby doll. Can you come give me a hand? With the rain, my arthritis is acting up."

"Be right there," Acadia said, and she walked past piles of newspapers and older editions of *People* magazine and a plastic bag full of empty Diet Coke cans.

In a short hallway that smelled of old age, she maneuvered through stacks of old magazines and boxes of moldy treasures her hoarder mother flatly refused to get rid of. Acadia pushed open the bedroom door, stepped in, and turned left, expecting to see her mother trying to button up her nightdress or tie her robe.

Instead, her terrorized mother lay on the bed with her arms, chest, and ankles wrapped in duct tape. The old woman whimpered, "I'm sorry, baby doll, he said he'd shoot me if I didn't."

Before Acadia could run, the cold muzzle of the pistol bumped the back of her head.

"Don't you move now, lover," Sunday whispered behind her. "I found this in the closet and I think the safety's kinda loose on a hair trigger."

He pushed her toward an overstuffed chair, saying, "Admit

it, you're shocked. But you've got to remember, I've got the superior mind, Acadia. Total recall. You said that first night that you grew up in the seat of Jefferson Davis Parish, and after that you always said it was Slidell. Ha. How's that for a memory?"

"Marcus," she said. "You left me no—"

The butt of the gun clipped Acadia hard behind the ear, and stars exploded and blew her straight into darkness.

CHAPTER 73

THOUGH THE STORMS HAD slackened and Tess Aaliyah was able to drive seventy miles per hour, we were still a solid fifty minutes west of Jennings, Louisiana, when I said into her phone, "Are we ready?"

"We are," Mahoney said. "Just do the smart shrink thing and keep him talking long enough for my men to triangulate."

"I'll do my best," I said, and handed Aaliyah's phone back to her.

Picking up the burner cell I'd bought with Ava back in West Virginia, I prayed that FBI techs using software I couldn't begin to comprehend would be able to quickly home in on the three cell towers closest to Sunday's position.

For the past fifteen minutes I'd been wrestling over what I should say to the man who had my family. By whatever name, Mulch or Sunday, he was a diabolical sonofabitch who would not hesitate to kill, and I was as nervous as I'd ever been punching in his phone number.

Sunday answered on the third ring and yawned before saying, "Dr. Cross? Is that you?"

"I'm sorry, Dr. Sunday," I said. "Did I wake you?"

"I was just about to turn off the hotel-room lights," he replied. "I've got a big day planned for tomorrow."

"In Austin?"

"That's right. You still in Omaha?"

"Back in DC, and again, sorry to call, but I could use your help."

"Well, of course," Sunday said, and he yawned again. "How can I be of service?"

"You know, I jumped to conclusions about your book," I said. "And I wanted to apologize again about that. I know we differ about the quotes you attributed to me, but I went back through the book earlier this evening and was really impressed how you got inside the perfect criminal's or, now, Thierry Mulch's mind."

There was a pause, and I heard what sounded like gospel music playing in the background before he said, "That's high praise coming from you, Dr. Cross. I truly appreciate that."

"You're welcome. So, anyway, I was wondering, now that you've had the chance to consider Mulch's background, if you had come to any kind of deeper insight into his character and what he might have done with my family?"

There was another pause, this one longer, before Sunday said, "As a matter of fact, Dr. Cross, Thierry Mulch is all I've thought about since you told me he was my perfect criminal."

"And?"

"Well, I don't mean to sound narcissistic, but I think I sketched him with remarkable accuracy."

"How so?"

"I stated quite forcefully in the book that the perfect criminal would have to be, in effect, an existentialist, someone who believed there was no inherent right or wrong, no ultimate moral code in the universe."

"I saw that," I said, glancing at Aaliyah, who took her cell away from her ear to make a keep-going motion with it. "You think Mulch is an existentialist?"

"I most certainly do," Sunday said. "Think of the drastic actions he's taken over the years. Killing his father to free and enrich himself before faking his own death. And then slaughtering his mother's family and the family of this woman you say Mulch knew when he was in high school?"

"Alice Littlefield," I said.

"Yes, so it would be much too easy to dismiss this man as insane," Sunday said, sounding as if he were spouting off at some academic symposium. "Quite the contrary, I think those drastic actions show that he is thoughtful and careful in the extreme but bold in his execution, which means that he knows that he functions outside the norm, that he thinks a moral universe is folly, and that his acts are simply a means to an end. No right. No wrong. Simply tools for his purposes."

I paused, glanced at Aaliyah, who shook her head.

"Interesting," I said. "And what end or purpose might that be?"

After a moment of silence, Sunday said, "I don't know. Perhaps we'll get to ask him that someday when you catch him."

"I look forward to it."

"As do I," Sunday said. "Now, really, Dr. Cross, I have a long day tomorrow and need my sleep."

"Just one more question?"

He sighed and said, "One more."

"In your research," I said. "Did you ever come across a woman named Acadia Le Duc?"

CHAPTER 74

MARCUS SUNDAY CLOSED HIS eyes to the sight of Acadia Le Duc sprawled unconscious at his feet, took a long, slow breath, and then said, "You couldn't forget a name like that if you tried. I can honestly say Acadia Le Duc's never crossed my path."

"Huh," Cross said. "That's funny."

"What's funny?" Sunday said, opening his eyes.

"Well, you said you had a book signing at Whodunit Books in Philadelphia last week, and according to her credit card records, Ms. Le Duc was there," Cross said. "She even bought one of your books."

Fighting the urge to kick Acadia in the head, Sunday said, "There were at least twenty-five people in attendance that night. Who is she?"

"Mulch's accomplice," Cross said. "We have strong evidence to link her to my son Damon's kidnapping, and we have several clear pictures of her. They'll be all over the news in the morning."

Sunday refused to give in to the sharp pains suddenly knifing through his skull, forced himself to sound shocked. "So, what, you think this Le Duc woman might have come to my reading in Philadelphia on Mulch's behalf?" Sunday asked.

There was a pause on the line before Cross said, "That would make sense, wouldn't it? You write about Mulch, he's going to want to find out about you, maybe even target you. So he sends in Acadia, or maybe he was even there with her."

Sunday almost smiled. He liked where this was going now. "You think Mulch could have been in the audience that night, right there in front of me?"

"Why not?" Cross said. "You were talking about him, weren't you? And you know how delusional criminals of this nature can be, always believing they're too smart to get caught."

I am *too smart to get caught, asshole,* Sunday thought. Then he said, "So, am I in any danger?"

"We suspect he and Le Duc might be stalking you. Perhaps getting ready to kidnap or kill you."

Sunday laughed nervously. "Seriously?"

"Seriously," Cross said. "Where was your reading in Memphis?"

For a moment, Sunday floundered, but then he snagged something from his memory of the prior day. "Booksellers at Laurelwood. God, I do so many of these things, I lose track sometimes. You think one of them was *there* last night?"

"We can put Acadia Le Duc in Memphis," Cross said. "She flew in from DC yesterday morning and rented a car at the Memphis airport."

"My God," Sunday said, feeling as if there were dogs close at his heels for the first time since Mulch had faked his death to get away from Atticus Jones. "Should I suspend the book tour?"

"No," Cross said. "Keep going. The FBI people will have agents at your event. Where is it in Austin, and when?"

Acadia moaned on the floor, and Sunday's head began to saw with pain. He'd believed that he'd covered every base, but Cross's questions were upsetting him, forcing him to ad lib at every turn. He had not had a reading the night before and he didn't have one coming up. Then he saw a plausible explanation.

"The reading was tonight," Sunday said. "I don't actually have another event scheduled until Friday night in LA, and that's at Diesel in Brentwood."

Acadia moaned again, and Sunday felt as if he were late for something.

"Diesel in Brentwood," Cross said, as if writing it down.

It dawned on Sunday that he'd been on the phone for almost ten minutes, and a nub of suspicion grew into a conviction that they were tracking him.

He started making noises like static and said, "Dr. Cross?"

Then he made more static noises before thumbing his cell off, prying it open, and ripping out the battery.

Despite the odd twist Cross had put on the facts, he thought there was an excellent chance that the detective had him pegged as Thierry Mulch, which meant that once again, he had to speed things up.

It was time to cut his losses, time to move on, he decided, squatting down to grab Acadia beneath the armpits. It was time to put an end to Marcus Sunday and all of his terrible obsessions.

CHAPTER

75

ACADIA STIRRED AT FLASHES of light, water spitting in her face, and wind howling all about her. She had a splitting headache and vaguely understood she was lying on her back in something chill and slimy.

When she forced open her eyes, she saw only shades of darkness. Then she tried to move, and panic flared in her gut. Her wrists were bound and pinned above her head somehow. Her ankles were tied down as well. She tried to yell, but cloth had been stuffed in her mouth.

Where am I? How did I get here?

Then, despite the pounding in her skull, Acadia remembered her mother's terror and Sunday telling her about the gun with the hair trigger.

Where is he? Where am I?

Thunder cracked. Lightning scarred the sky. The wind reversed direction and gusted up a sickening stench, and Acadia knew exactly where she was.

Closing her eyes, she screamed, and screamed again.

But the sounds that made it through the gag, though tortured and shrill, were muffled by the wind, no more than the noise of a teapot boiling in another part of the house or a train horn blowing in the distance, something easily dismissed on a dark and stormy night.

Acadia didn't care that no one could hear her. She screamed and yanked at her restraints until the skin at her wrist and ankles was raw, and her stomach seized up in knots. Flopping back in the mud on the bank above the backwater slough where her father's alligators fed, she started to sob.

There was a snapping noise, and a soft glowing light came over her from above and behind her head. It came closer, grew stronger. Acadia strained against her bindings, arched her head to look backward, and saw Marcus Sunday holding two of the Coleman lanterns her mother kept around for hurricanes.

Sunday hung them on barbed wire strung between fence posts driven into the ground. Her wrists were bound to the bottom of those same posts. She looked down at her feet, saw her ankles tied to two other posts closer to the water.

"Your mother told me the light brings them," Sunday said, appearing at Acadia's right side. "Light and blood."

He got out a pocketknife, locked the blade open, and crouched beside her. As he ran the dull blade up one side of her rib cage and across her breast, Acadia shook like someone lost in a snowstorm.

"Your mother likes to talk," Sunday went on. "Funny how some people are like that when they meet a published writer, just willing to open up and tell you all sorts of crazy things about themselves."

"Please, don't hurt her," Acadia tried to say through the gag.

"What's that?" Sunday said. "I can't get what you're trying to say there."

She screamed at him so hard, her face flamed red and veins bulged at her pounding temples.

"I didn't understand that one either," Sunday said, amused. "But I got the subtext, and honestly, lover, I don't give a shit about you begging for yourself or your mother. I don't even care to hear your flimsy excuses or pleas for mercy. I just need you both out of the way so I can move on."

He gestured at the slough and then up the bank to her. "And this little tableau? A gift of serendipity, an irony for me to treasure to the end of my days."

Acadia panted in the mud, and then screamed and writhed in agony when Sunday pressed the blade to her navel and sliced shallowly, down a good six inches. Blood poured from the wound.

"You can imagine now, can't you?" Sunday asked. "How they'll come for the place that's bleeding first?"

Acadia lost all control then, screaming and weeping in convulsions of fear that went on for a full minute and left her spent and almost catatonic.

"We could have gone farther, you and I," Sunday said, pocketing the knife. "A lot farther. But you pressed the issue, lover, so here you are, and here come your dead daddy's pets. I'm betting they'll make you sing before they're done."

"No, Marcus," Acadia tried to say through the gag. "Please?"

But Sunday snorted, walked away, and didn't look back.

For several long minutes there was only the howling of the wind and the rain. Then, as if the eye of the storm was passing overhead, the rain slowed to a drizzle, the wind died, and the moon peeked out through a vent in the clouds.

"Help!" Acadia screamed through her gag, managing to make a long, insistent whine of it. "Mom!"

She stopped, breathed in through her nose in short bursts, trying to listen.

Swish.

Plop.

Blip.

Swish.

Acadia had known those sounds her whole life: the *swish* of an armored tail against cattails, the *plop* of a ten-foot body submerging, and the *blip* of a creature coming to the surface. Each noise cut deeper than Sunday's blade.

Swish.

Swish.

Swish, plop.

That last noise felt like a hot sword jabbed in her back.

Acadia strained against her lashings, looking down at the bank and the clouded water of the back channel, seeing it swirl like cream in coffee.

Blip.

The prehistoric head breached first.

CHAPTER

76

SHORTLY AFTER ELEVEN, TESS AALIYAH and I raced out of Jennings on the Evangeline Highway heading north behind the flashing lights of the cruiser Sheriff Paul Gauvin was driving. Behind us roared three more cruisers, each with two deputies and one with a police dog too. None of the cars had sirens on.

We had ample reason for our urgency and our stealth. I had kept Sunday on the phone long enough for the triangulation to work, and it put the man within a five-mile radius of the cabin where Acadia Le Duc's mother lived. Not a hint of doubt now. Sunday was Mulch and was the man responsible for multiple murders, not to mention my torture and my family's peril. And Acadia Le Duc was definitely in the area as well. Hertz had run the GPS locator and put her rental car within three miles of the cabin.

It seemed logical to us that if Sunday and Le Duc were coming together at a remote cabin out on the Bayou des Cannes, there was a good chance that was where Bree, Damon, Jannie, Ali, and Nana Mama were being held.

"You okay, Alex?" Aaliyah asked.

I shook my head, said, "If I'd known he was here before I called, I never would have mentioned Acadia. I may have played my hand too hard."

"You needed to keep him on as long as possible," she said. "It was the right thing to do. We know he's there."

"But what's he doing?" I asked. "What are he and Acadia doing?"

Before Aaliyah could answer, Sheriff Gauvin shut down his lights and tapped his brakes and then turned onto a slick clay road that led off into forest. Two miles on, he pulled in behind a late-model Ford pickup and unfolded himself from the driver's seat. A long, ropy man in his midfifties with jug ears and a straw cowboy hat, the sheriff looked like a Hollywood version of a cracker cop.

But Gauvin had exhibited no prejudice toward me, and from our short, succinct conversations, I could tell he was certainly nobody's fool. He was smart, well trained, and uninterested in turf wars. If he could help save my family and take down Acadia Le Duc in the process, he and his department were more than happy to oblige.

Aaliyah and I climbed out and went to the sheriff, who was talking with the undercover deputy in the pickup.

"Tony says no one's been in or out since he got here," Gauvin said.

"Real quiet," the deputy agreed. "Except for the wind and all."

"So they came in expecting that the road might be watched," Aaliyah said.

"Looks that way," the sheriff said. "From where Acadia left her rental to here is all wild swamp. No easy thing to get in that way."

"But we have no idea how Sunday got in here," I said.

"Could have done it by shallow-draft boat," Gauvin said. "There's an arm of the bayou comes right past the cabin, but you'd have to know what you were doing to get there in the dark on a night like this."

Five other deputies, all young, fresh-faced kids, came up wearing body armor and carrying shotguns. I wondered how much training they'd had and said, "No one gets trigger-happy unless it's warranted. My family could be in there, and I don't want any of them shot by accident."

Several of the deputies looked insulted, but I didn't care. I needed to make the point in spite of bruising their egos. The sixth deputy walked up, a woman named Shields, and she had a muscular German shepherd named Maxwell on a tight leash. I liked police dogs. They'd saved me on more than one occasion.

"The two-track that leads into Le Duc's is about a hundred yards up the road," Gauvin said. "I figure it's better we walk in a piece, spread out, and surround the place."

It seemed smart, so I nodded and accepted a radio from the sheriff. We moved silently up the road, Deputy Shields and Maxwell leading the way to a narrow, muddy two-track. The trees and vines rustled in the stiff breeze and spit rainwater at us as we trudged single file and without lights toward Le Duc's cabin. At the first sight of lights ahead through the forest, we stopped, and Gauvin instructed four of his men to stay at this distance from the house and loop around it to the north. Then one pair would peel off and approach from directly behind the cabin, and the other would go to the opposite side of the yard.

"You're just looking, for now," the sheriff said quietly.

"That's it. Looking, and then calling in what you see to me. We clear?"

The four deputies nodded as if this were the most exciting thing they'd ever done on their job. As they set off, Maxwell perked up and whined softly.

"What is it, boy?" Deputy Shields said.

Maxwell panted and then whined again.

"He doesn't like something," the handler said.

"Then I don't like it either," Gauvin said, and he turned and headed straight for the lights with Maxwell and Shields right on his heels.

He slowed to a stop when the cabin and the yard were visible. Nothing moved in the soaked yard, which smelled of mud and decay. From inside the cabin, maybe on the radio, came the voice of a preacher of some sort ranting about salvation and damnation. The door to the house was ajar. There were several outbuildings, sheds mostly, that looked about as sturdy as toddlers. But they could hold kidnap victims, couldn't they? I supposed, but I figured the cabin to be the most likely place.

Guns drawn, the sheriff and I stood just outside the screened-in porch. Several reports came in over his radio. From what the deputies could see through the windows that weren't curtained, there was no movement inside.

"Marcus Sunday and Acadia Le Duc!" I roared. "You are surrounded! Lay down whatever weapon you have and surrender!"

We heard nothing but the radio.

Gauvin and I watched Deputy Shields open the porch's screen door and send Maxwell inside. He hesitated on the porch, and then bounded into the house. Ten seconds later, he barked furiously.

"He's got someone at bay in there," Shields said.

Gauvin, Aaliyah, and I went in first, the deputy trailing.

There was a comatose pit bull in the corner of the porch. We walked through the cabin's open door and entered a pack rat's den where the halls were built of stacks of *People* magazines and piles of Diet Coke cans.

We followed the sounds of barking to a lit doorway and found Maxwell sitting at the foot of a blood-soaked bed. Acadia Le Duc's mother's throat had been slashed ear to ear, the same way Mulch had killed his own mother.

Shields quieted the dog with a sharp command.

Then, over the radio's din, came a woman's ungodly screaming.

CHAPTER

77

IN SITUATIONS WHERE THE sane flee from danger, law enforcement officers sprint to engage it. That night was no different.

But I had more skin in the game than anyone else there, and I almost ran over Aaliyah and Shields trying to get outside, every cell in my body bellowing, *Bree, Jannie, Nana, Damon, Ali!* I rocketed off the porch and into the clearing and sprinted toward the bayou. The screams stopped sharply and then rose again in a wail of agony.

Pounding past the deputies, who were advancing more cautiously, I rounded a clump of trees and found a hidden part of the yard that slanted to an old wooden dock. Two cones of light came into view off to my right toward a backwater slough.

As if running into an invisible brick wall, I slammed to a staggering halt when I saw unfolding in those cones of light the most disturbing scene I'd ever witnessed, so shocking that for a beat, I was frozen in place, slack-jawed, unable to process or act.

In the soft light thrown by gas lanterns, an alligator crouched over Acadia Le Duc, who writhed, screamed, and shuddered as if she'd been plugged into something electric. The beast had bitten out a significant chunk of her right thigh.

A second creature circled the one feeding, looking for its own angle of attack. A third was scrambling up the bank toward her feet.

Maxwell came flying down the hill, barking, and went straight at the alligator closest to Le Duc. The reptile had been about to take another bite, but instead it turned its head to the dog, opened its bloody mouth, and let go with a hiss that sounded like a dozen alarmed snakes.

Maxwell did not hesitate but continued his charge, snapping his teeth and letting loose with savage growls and barking. For a second there, I thought the alligator would abandon its position.

Instead, when the police dog got within range and darted in from the flank, the alligator snapped its long armored tail like a two-hundred-pound whip and lashed Maxwell across his right shoulder and the side of his head.

It was like seeing a boxer knocked out. One second the dog was distracting the alligator, looking sure to drive it off, and the next he had been pummeled into the mud, where he lay twitching and senseless.

What happened next will forever be burned in my mind.

Sheriff Gauvin, his deputies, Shields, and Aaliyah all showed up at the same time. There were gasps and frozen expressions of horror on everyone.

"Max!" Shields said, and she made to go forward.

But Sheriff Gauvin was quicker. He ripped a pump-action

shotgun from one of his deputy's hands and charged the alligators, shouting, "Stay back, and no one shoots unless I say so."

The sheriff of Jefferson Davis Parish slowed to a march, shotgun up, its butt welded to his cheek. Without pause, he advanced on the second alligator; it had been scuttling around Acadia, but now it was bearing down on Maxwell. Angling, cutting the beast off, Gauvin let go of the twelve-gauge with his left hand. With his right, he reached out and stuck the barrel in the gator's eye before pulling the trigger and blowing a fist-size hole in its head with double-aught buckshot.

Driven by some primitive nervous system, the creature's entire body whipped side to side, and I thought for certain the sheriff was going to get his legs broken or worse.

But for a man in his midfifties, Gauvin moved with quickness and agility, leaping high over the dead gator, pumping a new shell into the chamber, and landing in a crouch two feet from the first one, now straddling Acadia Le Duc.

As it had with the police dog, the bigger, feeding alligator reacted with blinding speed, twisting its head toward the threat to its meal and making a loud, serpentine cough and hiss before lashing back at Gauvin with its tail.

The sheriff jumped again and landed right next to the six-hundred-pound reptile, which threw open its mouth and struck sideways with his upper body and head. The violent move knocked Gauvin over on his back, but not before he shoved the shotgun barrel deep into the creature's throat.

The alligator's jaws clamped down on the gun's steel receiver, leaving the trigger guard right up against its bloody teeth. The beast shook its head, yanking the pistol grip out of the sheriff's hand.

The butt of the shotgun waved in the air as the alligator

scrambled forward, front claws tearing at Gauvin's legs once and then twice, leaving deep gashes, before both of the sheriff's hands shot up and grabbed the exposed part of the gun. He got his thumb on the trigger and slammed it backward.

The buckshot blew out the reptile's spine. It collapsed on top of Gauvin and made a sound like a tire losing air.

CHAPTER 78

IN ALL MY YEARS of policing, I have seen few wounds as gruesome as that one. The alligator's serrated teeth had torn into Acadia Le Duc's thigh, ripped out several chunks, and snapped her femur. The splintered bone was visible, and blood fountained with every heartbeat.

"That's arterial blood!" I shouted, going to Sunday's woman. I grabbed a piece of rag lying near her and pressed it hard against the wound as she wailed, shook, and shivered and her eyes bugged out from her head.

"An ambulance is on its way, Acadia," I said. "You'll live." Out of the corner of my eye, I saw the third gator slip back into the water and disappear.

Acadia looked at me like I was the man on the moon, choked out, "After everything, you're trying to save me?"

"Where's Sunday?" I asked. "Where's my family?"

Her eyes started to glaze over, and I shook her. "Stay with me, Acadia. Where's my family?"

She had managed to free one of her wrists, and she must have been racked with unspeakable pain, because she grabbed my forearm with surprising strength, which made the panther tattoo on her arm coil up. I looked at her and said gently, "Tell me where Sunday has my family. Are they here?"

She said nothing.

"Tell me where they are," I insisted.

She remained mute but now locked on my gaze.

"Acadia," I said, unable to control the tremor in my voice. "You can redeem yourself here. You can show some goodness."

Acadia blinked slowly, and then her eyes softened, and for a moment I thought she was going to tell me.

Then she whispered, "Marcus says there is no redemption, Cross. No God. No absolute morality. Marcus is a universe unto himself. Am I a universe unto my—"

She tried to stay focused on me; her chin moved in small, ragged circles. "Kill me," she whispered. "I can't live in a prison, Cross. Kill me. Get your revenge. Be a universe unto yourself."

I stared in disbelief and horror at what Sunday had done to his accomplice in this whole mad scheme. He'd fed her to the alligators, and yet she defended his philosophy. And now she was asking me to end her life.

"Not a chance," I said. "You're paying for your crimes. But if you tell me where my—"

She gritted her teeth, closed her eyes, and the wounded leg began to spasm electrically. She screamed and screamed until the pain knocked her into unconsciousness. Her head lolled to the side.

I shook her again.

"Where's my family?" I yelled. "Tell me where he's got my family!"

I wanted to release the pressure on her wound and let her bleed out, make the world a better place by her absence. Instead, I slapped her, and slapped her again, trying to get her to wake up.

I felt a hand on my shoulder and looked up in confusion to find Aaliyah standing there. "That won't help us when she gets to court," she said.

A minute or so later, from the direction of the cabin, firemen and paramedics rushed onto the scene and started working on Acadia and Sheriff Gauvin. The second I saw the needle and the morphine go into her arm, I knew it would be hours if not days before we could question Sunday's woman.

I felt dazed and looked around as if none of it were real.

Deputy Shields knelt by Maxwell, stroking the dog's head; he had regained consciousness but looked incapable of getting to his feet.

"You're such a brave boy," Shields said in a baby-talk voice. "Such a brave, brave boy."

The dog slapped its tail as EMTs rolled the alligator off Sheriff Gauvin, who was conscious but in considerable pain. I wanted to go to him, lend him my support, but I simply couldn't because a thought had penetrated my brain and paralyzed me.

"Sunday was here to tie up loose ends," I said. "He may have already done the same to my family. He may have already fed them to alligators or pigs somewhere else."

I saw my despair mirrored in Aaliyah's face when she said, "We don't know that, Alex. We don't even know if they're here or not."

We checked all the outbuildings then and found a lifetime

of hoarded worthless junk but no evidence my family had ever been there.

The EMTs rushed a gurney bearing Acadia Le Duc up the hill, and I did hate her purely then, wished nothing but ill on her soul. I went to the second stretcher, to Sheriff Gauvin.

"Bunch of ribs broken," he said to me hoarsely. "I felt them go when he came down on me."

"That may have been the bravest thing I've ever seen," I said. And everyone else there, Aaliyah included, muttered or nodded agreement.

"I'm just a stupid old boy got lucky," Gauvin said. "Plus we used to hunt gators when I was a kid. You get to know their weak spots."

I checked my watch as they hurried him toward an ambulance. It was past midnight, and I'd been up since Aaliyah woke me too early the previous morning. I wanted to be angry and use that anger to push on, but I couldn't. Emotional and physical exhaustion crept up and strangled me.

"I'm no good right now," I told Aaliyah. "I need to sleep."

"I'm sure we can get a deputy to take you to a motel," she said, looking concerned. "But someone should stay to make sure the crime scene work will be admissible in DC."

"You're up," I said.

"Dr. Cross, we're not done with this case," the detective said, trying to sound encouraging. "Not by a long shot. One call, and the FBI puts out all points bulletins on Sunday. He'll be seen eventually."

"Eventually might not be soon enough," I said, feeling leaden. "Like I said, Mulch is cleaning up. If he hasn't already killed them, he's probably on his way to do it."

"Don't give up hope," Aaliyah said. "And text me where we're staying."

I promised to get her a room and then trudged back toward the rental car, not caring that it was raining again. Mulch had been here, done his dirty business, and fled, probably by skiff, and probably heading to wherever he was keeping Bree, Damon, Jannie, Ali, and Nana Mama.

For the first time since I'd left Damon's room at Kraft, fear got hold of me, captured me, entombed me, and I felt like dying would be better than once again facing the dark depths of Sunday's imagination.

CHAPTER

79

MARCUS SUNDAY WATCHED MUCH of it through high-power binoculars from across the bayou. He'd relished that swirl in the chocolate water, and he'd held his breath when the first alligator prowled up the bank toward Acadia.

The expression on Acadia's face before the attack was worth the price of admission. He didn't think it could ever get better than that. But then she'd gotten her gag spit out a few seconds before the alligator tore into her thigh.

As Sunday heard her shrieks, saw her writhe, his fascination had soared exponentially. In an instant, he understood why ancient Romans had flocked to the Circus Maximus when the gladiators were fighting animals.

Keeping the binoculars glued to the bloody drama, Sunday thought that he'd been born in the wrong time, that being here, watching this, was, well, exceptional, a peak experience if there ever was one.

Then Cross, the police dog, and a small army of cops had

appeared out of nowhere, which shocked Sunday, made him realize just how close he'd come to being surrounded and caught before he could bring his entertaining little experiment to an end.

Then the dog attacked the alligator, got hit by the tail, and was thrown to the ground. And the older cop had acted like a ninja or something, going in to save the dog and Acadia. Sunday had admired his bold moves, his élan, and his resolve, but he believed that it was too late. Bitten through the thigh like that, his lover almost certainly wouldn't survive. Right?

Sunday's confidence eroded, however, when Cross pressed a rag against the wound and appeared to be talking to her. The longer Dr. Alex stayed by her side, the more paranoia tried to worm its way into Sunday's brain.

What was Acadia saying to him?

Could she say anything?

Sunday watched Acadia's head loll to one side. Was she dead? He couldn't tell. He lowered the binoculars. Cross had been with her thirty, maybe forty seconds. Was it enough time for her to spill her guts and reveal where Cross's family was being held?

It was enough time, he decided. But had she? Could she even talk?

Sunday raised the binoculars again and kept them trained on Cross, anticipating some kind of hurry-up reaction, a sign that he had more desperate places to be. Instead, a woman came up behind Dr. Alex, and he just stayed there, looking at Acadia, hunched over in defeat.

Sunday allowed himself a thin smile.

Okay, then, he doesn't know. We move to the endgame.

But how best to do it?

A cautionary voice in his head told him that, Cross's defeated posture or not, he should assume that Acadia had confirmed that Marcus Sunday was Thierry Mulch. But honestly, that didn't really bother Sunday much.

As a writer, he knew that names were just names. You could change them anytime you wanted because it's the actions that really define characters, not what you call them. His dear departed mother had demonstrated that.

That same cautionary voice then told Sunday to cut his losses and slip away into a new identity. Forget the grand endgame. Let the Cross family be found, or die. It really didn't matter in the greater scheme of things.

But it did matter in Sunday's scheme of things. It mattered very much. He'd thought up the premise of the game. He'd looked at it from every angle; well, almost. Sure, there had been a few bumps in the road, but otherwise he was roughly where he'd hoped he'd be at this point, give or take a few days.

But how do I bring it to a satisfying end?

Flashing on the image of the container barge rolling on the high water coming fast toward New Orleans, Sunday played with the idea of meeting the barge, getting inside the container, and shooting air bubbles into the IV lines. Kill them all and let them rot, let Dr. Alex suffer the loss completely and permanently. And then slip away into a new identity. He had the money and the necessary documents already. Why take a bigger risk? He'd had his fun, and now it was time to move on.

Sunday had just about decided to let it end like that. He would get out his phone and punch in the GPS coordinates he'd taken on the way in, get to the skiff he'd stolen, take that to his rental truck, and then drive to New Orleans.

But then flashing lights across the bayou stopped him from

leaving. An ambulance pulled into the yard, and it rapidly became a chaotic scene with more and more people. EMTs went quickly to Acadia's side and began working on her. So she was alive.

And now Cross and Aaliyah were searching the outbuildings.

Sunday's grin returned. That confirmed it.

Dr. Cross doesn't know where his wife, kids, and granny are because Acadia did not *tell him. You watch: He's going to get chewed up now investigating the crime scene. He's going to be neutered, a cog disjointed and spinning with nowhere to go.*

Another sheriff's cruiser came into the yard, followed by a Louisiana state trooper's car and then another. In minutes, it would be a carnival. The investigation was moving out of Cross's control. Mentally, spiritually, and emotionally, the detective would be wandering now. Isolated. Lost. Just as he had been the night before Easter.

A zombie.

Sunday checked his watch. It was past midnight. He thought again of that barge swinging south on swollen spring currents. He put the binoculars back on Cross, watched him talking to Aaliyah and looking like a man at the end of a long, weak rope, already fearing his loss, already willing to grasp at the last strand.

Strand of what?

Hope?

The last strand of hope?

Like a pile driver, it hit Sunday then.

In a single, blinding instant of insight, he finally understood how he would end the game and the story of Dr. Alex Cross.

CHAPTER

80

AS I WALKED BACK along the two-track toward the dirt road that accessed the Bayou des Cannes, the breeze was stiffening again, and with it the rain, and there were rumblings of new storms to the west. By the time I got to the Jeep and started driving toward Jennings, jagged lightning tormented the night sky.

Each crack of thunder made my head feel as if it were coming apart. I needed water. I needed Tylenol. I needed—

The disposable cell phone buzzed, alerting me to a text, as I approached the Jefferson Davis Parish seat along a westward curve in the Evangeline Highway. At a stop sign, I picked the phone up and read it.

Go to New Orleans, it said. *Alone. You have until 4:30 a.m. to reach the Big Easy. Announce your arrival in the Casual Encounters section of Craigslist, women looking for men. Do as I say, and you will see your family alive. Try to be clever and involve any kind of law enforcement, and you will see your family dead. This is your last hope, Cross. Don't blow it now, when you're so close to your goal. By the way, the phone that sent this text will be destroyed upon your response.*

In all honesty, I wanted to smash my own phone to smithereens. I was exhausted. I was sick of being played. I didn't know if I had it in me to go on much longer, if at all.

When I read the message a second and a third time, however, I kept pausing on that phrase *your last hope.* It was like Sunday was dangling a strip of meat over a caged and starving dog that had had enough of cruelty. I didn't want to lunge at the offer just out of reach but knew I would.

Despite the anger, the fatigue, and the resentment, I could not help but grasp at the final straw. I simply could not leave hope to die.

I'm coming, Sunday, I texted back. *Alone.*

CHAPTER 81

I BOUGHT TWO HAM and cheese sandwiches and three cups of French roast coffee at an all-night gas station near the on-ramp to the I-10.

The sandwiches tasted like they'd been made days ago, and the coffee was stale and bitter, but I forced it all down as I sped east in a driving rain. Were Bree, the kids, and my grandmother in New Orleans? Was that where Sunday had taken them? Why there?

Some of Mulch's actions seemed as random as they were brutal. Or maybe that was simply a lack of information on my part. What drove a guy to do these things? He'd escaped his childhood with millions of dollars and then had indulged his desire for an education with a doctorate from Harvard. Marcus Sunday could have lived a comfortable life of the mind.

Instead, he'd viciously slain his mother for escaping her past, and Alice Monahan and her entire family for reasons I still couldn't fathom. Then he had the gall to write an entire book about the mass killings, extolling the murderer as a perfect killer who had left no trace and would never be identified.

The crazy thing was that Sunday might have been right if he hadn't decided, for whatever disturbed reason, to make me and my family the target of his ongoing homicidal vengeance. I still didn't get that, and it gnawed at me as I passed Lafayette and drove on toward Baton Rouge.

Other than the phone interviews and my giving Sunday a mediocre review in the *Post*—okay, a thumbs-down review in the *Post*—I'd had no contact with the man that I knew of. So why me?

Perhaps because of my reputation, he saw me as some kind of threat. Maybe he feared I was going to eventually uncover his role in the Omaha and Fort Worth killings. Or maybe this entire cruelty had grown out of something I hadn't seen or heard yet.

Had Bree done something to him at some time in her past? I couldn't see it. No, this was about me. It had always been about me.

But what if I was just an arbitrary object? What if some chemical in his dysfunctional brain had dripped at just the right time, and he'd obsessed on me like Mark David Chapman keyed in on John Lennon, deciding to punish me for no particular reason at all?

I think the idea that it might have been utterly random upset me the most. In spite of everything that had happened to me in the past twelve days, I still believed in my Lord and God and in the idea that He had a plan for us all. But as I drove through the night toward a showdown or an ambush, Sunday was testing the limits of my faith.

It occurred to me that he hadn't said anything about the

video of the double homicide I was supposed to send him later today. Seemed that wasn't important to him anymore—he just wanted me in New Orleans.

Crossing the Atchafalaya River, I was hit with waves of doubt and surges of raw emotion that brought tears to my eyes. What if, after enduring it all, I simply found them dead? What if it was as random as that?

I swiped at the tears with my sleeve and prayed, "Please don't let that happen. Take me if You want, but dear God, let them live."

The rain slowed, and I sped up toward the national wildlife refuge and the elevated highway that separates Lafayette from Baton Rouge. For several miles, there was a strange dead calm when the wind and rain stopped altogether. I sped up even more, going sixty-eight now.

Then, out of nowhere, gusts of wind rose up, turned gale force, buffeted the car, and sent leaves ripped from trees down in the refuge windmilling across the already slick surface of the highway. A small sedan in front and to the right of me fishtailed on the wet leaves, corrected, and almost straightened out.

Then it swung violently sideways into my lane, and I had to swerve, throwing my car hard to the right.

I'd taken all sorts of defensive-driving classes in the course of my career, but nothing I knew could save me from smashing my right front fender into the guardrail.

Going better than sixty when it hit, the car upended, spiraled up, and cleared the guardrail before plunging into darkness.

CHAPTER 82

METEOROLOGICAL DATA WOULD LATER conclude that four different tornadoes hit southern Louisiana that night. The third, an EF2-level twister, formed near Ville Platte around 1:35 a.m. and wreaked destruction all the way to Opelousas. The vortex lost shape there, but the forces of it continued on in spiraling powerful gusts that swept down over the wildlife refuge and the highway, causing the sedan in front of me to skid and making me swerve, which sent the rented Jeep Cherokee into the guardrail and then over the side of the elevated interstate.

I remember feeling outside myself as I fell, as if this were happening to someone else entirely. The single remaining headlight beam gave me a split-second view of a dense forest canopy before the driver's side of the car smashed into it. The window next to me shattered, and then everything went kaleidoscopic and herky-jerky as branches snapped beneath the car, interrupting but not stopping the fall.

The nose of the car smashed into an ancient cedar tree,

snuffing out the remaining headlight and causing the trajectory of my descent to change. The Jeep whipsawed rearward in one last, long drop, at least ten or fifteen feet.

The back of the car's impact with the ground should have been colossal, bone-breaking certainly, perhaps neck-snapping and fatal. And the sound should have been deafening.

Instead, the swamp seemed to open up and swallow the speed and mass of the car with a noise that was a bizarre cross between the thwacking of a tennis racket hitting a ball and the splash of a kid doing a cannonball into a pool. Reeds, swamp water, and oozing black mud blew out the rear window and sucked up half the car before it stopped.

For several long moments in the pitch-black, I sat there in the astronaut's position, rocked back in total shock. Finally I moved, shaky with adrenaline.

Nuggets of shatterproof glass spilled away from my arms, which, other than suffering from a funny-bone sensation, were working. So were my legs, and so was my neck, which, like my head and face, was splattered with the muck that had saved my life.

I pushed at buttons to get one of the interior lights to go on, but the electrical system had died. I dug in my pants pocket, found the mini-Maglite I always carry, and shone it about, trying to get a full sense of my predicament.

The swamp had swallowed the back half of the Jeep and pinned my door shut. The hood jutted above me, free of the mud. Broken branches and limbs stuck up from the grille like a bizarre floral arrangement.

I got my cell out and saw it had died. There was no calling until I could recharge it. The driver of the car that had swerved in front of me had to have seen me go over the guardrail, right?

The police had probably been alerted, or would be in minutes. Had there been any other cars or trucks close enough behind me to see the crash?

I couldn't remember. At that late hour, in the bad weather, traffic had been exceedingly light.

What if no one came?

Then it dawned on me that time was ticking away. Sunday had given me a deadline. I had to be in New Orleans by 4:30 a.m. That was two hours and forty minutes from now. I couldn't afford to wait for rescue. In fact, I couldn't afford to *be* rescued. There would be police and ambulances and questions that I had no time to answer.

After unbuckling my seat belt, I had to do several contortionist moves to get my head and shoulders across the front passenger seat and my feet and legs up onto the driver's seat. At some point during the car's fall, the passenger-side window had been blown out too. I punched out the remaining glass, pushed aside the vegetation, and looked out, happy to see that the muck was a good eight inches below me.

Shining the flashlight around, I saw a stand of cedar and cypress trees on a bank of sorts about five feet off the nose of the car. My beam picked up scars and broken branches on the tree closest to a twenty-five-foot cement stanchion that supported that section of the highway.

Overhead, a truck roared by and disappeared in a hiss. It was raining again, and if there were sirens coming, I couldn't hear them. I flashed the light back at the stanchion and up its side a solid ten feet, and I found what I was looking for. *Okay,* I thought. *I have a chance.*

Looking around, I smiled, dug in my pocket, and came up with my jackknife. With several quick cuts, I removed the driver's-side and passenger's-side seat belts and tied and snapped them together to form a makeshift rope about four feet long with a closed buckle at one end from which a two-foot piece of strap hung. I tied that around my waist.

After taking several deep breaths, I put the flashlight between my teeth and squirmed my head, shoulders, body, and hips out the car's window. At that point, I was sitting in an awkward position, gripping the windshield frame.

I needed another handhold and grasped the butt end of the windshield wiper and used it as leverage to hoist myself out and onto the hood of the car, which was canted left and rose steeply. I got my right shoe braced against the windshield frame and my left against the wiper base, and I was able to reach up and grab some of the tree limbs sticking up from the front grille.

It wasn't pretty, but I managed to pull myself up onto the nose of the car, which was rock solid. It took me three attempts to get into a crouch, left knee down in the branches, right foot up on the grille.

Gripping two other limbs, I took several deep breaths, said a prayer, and then sprang out into space.

CHAPTER 83

I ALMOST MADE THE bank. My right foot actually reached firmer ground, but my left leg plunged into mud up to my thigh. For three to four minutes, I couldn't move at all. But when I resigned myself to the fact that I was going to lose my left shoe and probably my right, I grabbed at the exposed root of the tree I'd crashed through and hauled myself out and up, left shoe gone, but right still in place.

Panting, I again listened for sirens but still heard none. I found the ground like a saturated sponge that demanded the gingerly placement of my bare left foot. Twice in the ten feet or so to the stanchion, I broke through the spongy earth into the mud. The second time, my right shoe disappeared.

I didn't bother trying to dig in the muck; I crept to the side of the cement upright. Shining my flashlight, I saw that the lower flank of the stanchion was smooth and uninterrupted cement. But ten feet up, a rung of bent steel rebar stuck out. I'd seen it from the car.

There were other rungs above it every two feet or so, climbing toward the underside of the highway and the guardrail. When road crews put up these kinds of giant engineered supports, they need a way up and down them during the installation process. The rungs are set in the cement to form a ladder.

When the work is done, however, they cut off the first four or so rungs to make it impossible for kids or thrill seekers to climb them. The rest are left in place in case the stanchion ever needs to be inspected from above.

Now, I'm six foot two and have a thirty-inch reach, but I'd known just looking at it from the car that I had no chance of snagging the lowest rung on my own. I untied the strap I'd made with the pieces of the seat belts and held it with the buckle and loose strap away from me. Then I began to spin it slowly, checking for any give in the knots and testing the weight of the buckle.

When I thought I had it right, I sort of underhand-lobbed the buckle up there. It clanged off the rung and rebounded back to me so hard, I had to duck. The second time and the third time were not much better. On my fourth attempt, however, I changed tactics, going back to basics, taking the buckle in my right hand and holding the end of the strap in my left.

I crouched, leaped up, and released the buckle as if I were making an outside jump shot. It went over the rung and swung there. I undid my leather belt and used the knife to slice a hole about three inches from the end of the strap. I fitted my belt buckle through the hole and then passed the leather through the buckle and drew it all tight.

My belt added thirty-six inches to the overall length of the strap, and I was able to jiggle and then snag the loose piece hanging off the seat-belt buckle. I tied a loop in that part of the webbing and passed my belt and the rest of the improvised rope through it. When I pulled on the slack, my lifeline was anchored tight to the rung.

I tested it, holding tight to the webbing and lifting my feet off the ground. There were *tut-tut-tut* noises as the knots tightened, but they held.

Understanding that in my weakened, exhausted condition, I was probably going to have one shot at this, I stood there for several moments listening to the swamp waking up from the storm, the thumping of frogs, and the first whine of insects.

I figured the slime on my socks would work against me, so I stripped them off and stood more firmly on the ground. Then I put the Maglite back in my pocket. There was no way I could hold it in my mouth during a climb. I was going to have to do this by Braille. Not necessarily a bad thing. The darkness would make me concentrate all the more.

I held the strap with my right hand, lowered my head, thought of my family, and then got the bottom of my left foot against the stanchion and reached high overhead, finding the strap again with my left hand. It was going to tear up my hands. I could already feel it.

But I grabbed hold as tight as I could and then exploded into a blind, frenzied scramble of bare feet up the wall, hand over hand up the rope, past my belt buckle and on. My left hand slipped on the fourth grab. The seat-belt webbing ripped a bloody groove, and I almost let go.

But Mulch's face appeared in my mind and triggered a rampage within me. My right hand stabbed up, slapped steel, but I couldn't hold on. I grabbed the strap again, took one breath, and then furiously threw my bloody left hand up and caught the rung.

Once upon a time, I might have had the upper-body strength to crawl up the ladder from there with little or no problem. But now it took a rage-fueled, all-out effort to get to the second and then the third rung before my right knee found the bottom one. I hung there like a two-hundred-and-fifteen-pound moth, panting and doing my best to forget the popping sound my shoulder had made and ignore the pain as the rebar dug into my patella.

When I couldn't stand it any longer, I reached up, wincing at a crunching noise in my right shoulder, and got my bare feet onto the lower rung. The adrenaline rush left me weaker than I could have imagined, and I spent several more minutes clinging to the side of the stanchion, waiting until my strength returned.

A truck passed on the highway above me. I felt the vibration of it ripple down through the cement and that was enough to get me climbing again. When I reached the guardrail and got over it, I almost cried.

Another truck was coming from the west, and a car behind it. I grabbed the Maglite, turned it on, and began waving it at the approaching headlights.

I must have been a sight. My clothes were torn and muddy. My hair was muddy. So was my face. And I was barefoot, wild-eyed, and bleeding from my hands. So in retrospect, it doesn't surprise me that the truck didn't stop.

The car that followed didn't stop either.

Nor did the next three vehicles that passed me.

I stood there dazed and frustrated as all those taillights receded east. I'd lost nearly forty minutes to the crash.

Overhead, the clouds broke and scudded across the sky, revealing the moon and stars. I stared up into them, my bloody hands hanging, and begged God for help, for someone to stop before it was too late.

For ten, maybe fifteen minutes, there was only the darkness. No trucks and no cars passed on either side of the interstate. Then a set of headlights appeared, low and wide, from the west, back toward Lafayette.

A few seconds later, the roar of the big block engine came to me and I realized the car wasn't just speeding. It was hurtling toward me, going a hundred miles an hour, maybe more.

CHAPTER 84

I STOOD IN THE near lane and slashed my light twice but then thought it unlikely the driver was going to slow, let alone stop, for some swamp creature, so I retreated to the guardrail and stood there. The headlights swept over me, and the car, an old Pontiac GTO with a chrome blower sticking out of the hood, roared past me. I didn't bother to look after it until I heard the engine die off into a fluttering chug.

A solid six hundred yards beyond me, the car's brake lights beamed. The reverse lights came on, and the car came swerving back my way. A truck went by, blew its horn, and veered into the passing lane, but the GTO kept coming.

The muscle car stopped beside me, rumbling and vibrating. The passenger window rolled down and I peered inside and saw a good old boy in his thirties with a blond buzz cut, wearing a white V-neck T-shirt over a tattooed and steroidal body.

A woman's frail voice said, "You look like you're having a bad day, pilgrim."

I noticed her then, sitting in the backseat, a tiny, older woman huddled under a blanket and wearing sunglasses. Her face was horribly scarred from some long ago trauma.

"You want us to call an ambulance? The cops?" the driver asked.

"I am a cop," I said. "My name is Alex Cross, I'm a detective with the Washington, DC, Metropolitan Police, and I have to get to New Orleans. It's a matter of life and death."

"See, Lester?" the woman said. "I told you."

"I don't care about your notions right now, Ma," Lester replied, looking over his shoulder. "He's not getting in here with all that mud on him. We'll call someone."

"Nonsense," she snapped. "Life and death."

"It's gonna take me a week to clean my Goat." Lester groaned.

"Then it takes a week," she said. "Here, have him sit on this."

She handed him the blanket. Lester scowled but spread it over the leather bucket seat. Apologizing and trying not to smear mud on anything, I climbed in, held out my hand, and said, "My family is at stake. I can't thank you enough for stopping."

Lester looked at the blood and dirt on my hand and sniffed. "That was Ma's notion, not mine. I barely saw you."

I shut the door and was trying to put on the seat belt when he punched the gas. The Goat bellowed out the mouth of its chrome blower. The back end of the muscle car sank, and the front rose almost like a boat's does when it's accelerating.

But this was no ordinary boat. Lester's car was "souped up to the max," as he put it. More than four hundred horsepower pinned me to the seat as he banged through gears and took us up to ninety miles an hour.

The suspension wasn't like what you'd find in a modern sports car. There was play in it, and we seemed to drift slightly left and then right down the interstate, with Lester lightly counter-steering back and forth. The swaying increased when he took us up past a hundred miles an hour.

"You're gonna get pulled over or flip this car," I said.

"Nah," Lester said. "We do this all the time. Three to four a.m. is the last hour of the shift for the state police; hardly any troopers on the road. And the scanner says most of them are at some murder scene north of Jennings. Far as me flipping us? The Goat and I are one, pilgrim. We've never once come close to a wreck."

"Lester *is* gifted behind the wheel, Detective," his mother said. "What's your name again?"

Though a part of me was desperate to keep looking out the windshield as we hurtled toward New Orleans, I twisted in my seat to see the shadow of Lester's disfigured mother. It was only then that I saw the white cane across her lap and realized she was blind.

I told her my name, and got hers. Minerva Frost and her son were from Galveston. Lester was taking her to work.

Before I could ask what kind of work she did, she asked about my family, and I saw no reason to withhold any of it. I gave her a thumbnail sketch of what had happened and where I was going and why.

Lester seemed impressed. "I heard something about this on the news the other night. Lord Almighty, that's tough."

I suppose I expected some kind of sympathetic response from Minerva Frost, but she stayed silent.

Her son, however, was glancing over at me, and then in the rearview mirror, getting agitated. Lester finally said, “Ma, you have to work today, you know. You promised.”

Minerva Frost stayed silent.

“Ma, there are people with appointments. People counting on you.”

Still, his mother remained silent, and I couldn’t figure out what was going on.

“Ma,” Lester said. “Did you hear what I—”

“I’m not deaf, Lester,” she replied at last. “And work will have to wait.”

“Am I missing something here?” I asked, confused.

“You need us, I think, Mr. Cross,” Minerva Frost replied.

“No. I’ll be fine. Just get me to New Orleans.”

“You have a car, Detective Cross? Shoes?”

That surprised me. How did she know I didn’t have shoes on?

“No shoes, but I’ll get them,” I said. “Really, there’s no need for you to miss work on my account, Mrs. Frost.”

“I disagree,” she said sharply. “And that is that.”

“Fuck,” Lester said under his breath.

“What was that, son?” his mother demanded.

“Truck ahead, Ma,” Lester said, and changed lanes to blow by an eighteen-wheeler as if it were standing still.

“What do you do for work, Mrs. Frost?” I asked.

“Never you mind about that,” she said. “Glad to help.”

“What, are you ashamed or something?” Lester asked his mother.

“No, I am not,” Minerva Frost retorted. “Just don’t know where Mr. Cross stands, and I don’t want to make it an issue.”

“Make what an issue?” I said, twisting around in my seat

again and wincing at the soreness that went from the tips of my fingers to my arms and up into my shoulders.

She didn't reply, and I looked at Lester, who eased off the gas, causing rumbling backfire, before he said, "She's my mom and all, Detective Cross, and you may believe in this kind of thing or not, but that little old lady behind you has got the gift, man, like for real."

CHAPTER 85

MINERVA FROST GOT HER gift the summer after her ninth birthday, eighteen months after she was splashed with battery acid and lost her eyesight in a terrible accident in the automotive repair shop her father ran in Galveston.

"She started seeing things, hearing things," Lester said, downshifting as we approached Baton Rouge. "We call 'em her notions."

Over the years I'd heard of police working with psychics, of course, and I'd heard of some of them having success, but I'd never worked with one personally.

I said, "Is that right, Mrs. Frost?"

"Kind of," she said softly. "I just spent so much time alone that year. I mean, what child wanted to be friends with someone who looked like this? And in that loneliness, I just started to hear voices and see things in my mind. I used to brush them off as my imagination going crazy because of the blindness, but then some of the things I saw seemed to come true."

Mrs. Frost claimed that she hadn't told anyone about the voices or the visions for nearly twenty years. But then the economy went bust in the late seventies, and her parents needed money, so she had gone to New Orleans and set herself up as "Madame Minerva, Palm Reader."

"She don't read palms, by the way," Lester said. "Just makes it look that way. People like it, for some reason, and they pay a lot of money to see her. One long day a month in the Big Easy, and the rest of them folks on the phone, and we got all we need."

My skepticism must have shown, because Lester said, "Hey, man, her gift is real. Like I said, I barely saw you standing there, but she did, and she told me you were in trouble and to stop."

"That true?" I asked her. "You *saw* me?"

"An image of someone in need," Minerva Frost said.

"How did you *see* me?" I asked.

"You mean the mechanics of it? The physics of it? I don't rightly know, pilgrim. It's like I've got this antenna, you could say, and every once in a while I'll hear or see things, like they're beamed in from outer space or something, and there you were, barefoot and covered in filth. I could tell you were a desperate man in need of help."

Now, I have a PhD in psychology from Johns Hopkins and my life's work has made me skeptical about everything I'm told. But I didn't want to question Minerva Frost. For too many reasons to count, I wanted to believe her.

"You see or hear anything about my family?" I asked. "Or Marcus Sunday?"

"I do not," she said sadly. "But if and when I do, you will most assuredly be the first to know."

We spoke little during the rest of the white-knuckle ride Lester Frost took us on from Baton Rouge to the western outskirts of New Orleans. At 4:22 a.m., we pulled off the I-10 and into a twenty-four-hour Phillips 66 truck stop.

"Do me a favor, and I'll pay for your gas," I told Lester, who looked suspicious.

"What favor?"

I handed him my cell phone and two twenties. "I can't go in there looking like this, but I bought this phone at one of these truck stops, and I remember they sell a backup battery that you stick in the charge port. Can you get it for me?"

Lester looked ready to refuse, but his mother said, "Course he will."

Scowling, Lester started the gas pump and then stomped off toward the truck-stop store. A few minutes later, he exited carrying the backup battery. It wasn't fully charged as advertised, but to my relief, it started the phone, and I was able to call up Craigslist New Orleans on the browser. As Sunday had instructed me, in the Casual Encounters section, women looking for men, I posted under the headline "Waiting for Sunday."

My message read, *I'm here, Mulch. Your move.*

I sat there while Lester topped off the tank and cleaned the windshield of bugs and leaves. It was still pitch-dark outside. Not even a hint of dawn.

"There now," Minerva Frost said out of the blue.

I kid you not, a split second later, before I could even look over at her, my phone buzzed with a text.

I thought you'd given up, it read. *Come alone. Or I end the game, and you lose absolutely everything.*

Following that was an address on Esteban Street, in Arabi,

just south of New Orleans on the east bank of the Mississippi River.

Lester Frost climbed in, said, “Give this to my mom?”

I took the coffee. Her hand came up but went far wide of the cup when I reached over the backseat with it. I had to guide her fingers to it. Her skin was as soft as a baby’s bottom, and for reasons I can’t explain, I felt calmer for touching it.

Lester reacted sourly when I gave him the address.

“Most of that area’s toast ’cause of Katrina,” he said, starting up the GTO, which rumbled so loud he had to almost shout at me. “Fifteen feet of water rolled through there when the levee broke. They found corpses in the attics. Place is haunted. I bet we get to that address and all we see is a cement pad, or sea grass, or at best a skeleton of a house.”

In the backseat, Madame Minerva said, “Arabi *is* a place for ghosts, Detective Cross, but the man you’re after, he’s waiting for you near there. And your family is close by, rocking in cradles.”

CHAPTER 86

THE ROCKING ROUSED NANA MAMA from a deep, dark, and puzzling place.

At first, Cross's grandmother felt only that she was shifting side to side, as if she were floating in water, and nothing more. For a very long time, she didn't know who or what she was.

But then she heard the pump and flush of her heartbeat in her temples, and something more high-pitched and infrequent. She smelled something sharp and medicinal. She tried to open her eyes to find the source of that tinny noise and that antiseptic odor but couldn't.

True consciousness came maddeningly slowly, one step forward and two steps back. Her mind wavered there in a pulsing zone of gradually building sensations—touch, mouth dryness, and that smell—and then retreated to that deep, dark, and puzzling place.

Was it death?

That was her first real thought: *Is it death?*

Am I dying? Am I dead?

But what was *death?*

It took forever before she could define the word. When she did, other things came back to her. She was Regina Hope. She was Nana Mama. And she was very old. She was lying on her back. She was sore everywhere, and she was rocking ever so slightly side to side and up and down.

What's causing that rocking? Nana Mama thought before the darkness took her once more.

CHAPTER

87

AT A QUARTER TO FIVE that morning, Tess Aaliyah watched the coroner seal the corpse of Acadia Le Duc's mother inside a black bag and then remove it from the house. She flashed on the image of her own mother being taken from her deathbed, and she wondered what would be worse, to die a lingering death from cancer or to feel the life cut out of you all at once.

Blinding fatigue hit Aaliyah then, and she asked one of the deputies still on the scene, a fresh-faced kid named Earl Muntz, if she could get a lift into town.

"Absolutely," Deputy Muntz said. "But I have to do something quick first, won't take but five minutes. Is that okay, or can I find you someone who'll get you there sooner?"

"No," Aaliyah said. "It's fine."

She walked with Deputy Muntz up the two-track from the Le Duc place wondering if she'd ever forget the gruesome things she'd seen there, and she decided she would not, and could not. That glimpse into the nightmare that was Marcus Sunday was so vivid and lurid, it would be impossible to erase.

How far would he go? she wondered. *How far will he go?*

These were the questions she wanted to ask Acadia Le Duc when she stabilized. The same questions had to be eating at Alex Cross, she thought, as they reached Muntz's patrol car. She got in, and for the first time in hours, she dug out her phone, looking for a text message about her hotel room.

There was nothing from Cross or anyone else. That was odd. Cross clearly said he'd book her a room, and that had been when? Around one?

The deputy put the cruiser in gear, turned north away from town. Aaliyah punched in the number of Cross's disposable cell. It rang several times and then went to a recording that said, "This message box has not been opened."

"Shit," she said.

"What's that?" Muntz said, driving on in the first pale light of dawn.

"I can't find Cross," she said. "He never texted me about my hotel room, and he's not answering his phone."

"Hotel room's not a problem," Muntz said. "My sister-in-law's parents own the Budget. I'll call and get you one."

"Thanks," Aaliyah said.

"Don't mention it," Muntz said, and punched a number on his speed-dial.

Aaliyah barely listened to him getting her a room. She felt drained to the point of dizziness, and her eyes got heavy and drifted shut. She was aware that the cruiser was slowing and turning. Muntz had hung up the phone. She dozed deeper on the whine of the tires and then bounced awake when the cruiser hit a rut.

Her head snapped forward. Her chin hit her chest, and her eyes flew open.

"Ouch," the deputy said, stopping the cruiser. "I was afraid that was going to happen. I'm sorry for waking you. You just sit here and crash, and I'll go ahead on foot to make sure the car is secure. Shouldn't take more than ten minutes."

"What car?" Aaliyah asked, yawning.

"That rental Acadia Le Duc was driving," he said.

"You have the keys?" she asked, coming fully alert.

"The forensics guys have them," he said. "They'll be here to process it after they finish with the cabin. I'm just supposed to check it, make sure the car's locked up tight."

"You have a slim jim?" Aaliyah asked. "Some latex gloves?"

Muntz's face lost color. "We're not messing with evidence."

"I'm not planning to mess with any evidence," she said. "I just want to see it first. So do you have a slim jim or am I going to have to use a rock?"

The deputy looked like he wanted to argue, but then he sighed. "I've got a slim jim and gloves."

Using Muntz's big Maglite, they walked across a dike above rice fields and found the blue Dodge Avenger parked in the weeds where the farmland gave way to dense woods and swamp. The doors were locked. The deputy proved handy with the slim jim and opened the door, which triggered the car alarm.

"Shit," Muntz said. "Now everyone's gonna know we broke in and tampered with—"

"Grow a set, Deputy," Aaliyah said. She pushed by him and reached under the dashboard, felt around until her fingers found a cluster of plastic electrical connectors. She yanked at wires that fed into them, felt them budge, and then one tore free, and then another. The third shut off the alarm.

Straightening up, she peered around inside the car, scanning, trying to catalog everything in plain sight. There were Diet Coke cans in the cup holders. On the passenger seat, there was a bulging white bag with its mouth rolled shut and grease bleeding through its bottom.

Aaliyah unlocked the other doors, went around to the passenger side, and opened it. The bag smelled of hamburger and fries, and when she unrolled the top, she saw the remnants of the meal and several smashed coffee cups. The glove compartment held nothing more than the rental agreement. And the storage in the central console was empty.

"Can we button this up now?" Muntz asked. "There's nothing in there or in the backseat. I looked through the window."

Aaliyah was about to tell the deputy to pop the trunk when she noticed something stuck down between the console and the driver's seat.

"Gimme your flashlight please, Deputy," she said.

Muntz reluctantly handed it to her. She shone it into the crack and saw several papers stapled together and folded. She got hold of them and exited the car before opening them up.

Aaliyah scanned the papers, seeing a smudged receipt for a $2,129 payment in cash and a two-page disclaimer of liability. The fourth and last page stopped her cold, and she didn't know why at first.

"What is it?" Muntz asked.

"A bill," she said. "For lading…"

Something clicked, and her hand shot to her mouth before she barked at the deputy, "Close it. Lock it. We've got to get out of here and find Cross. He needs to see these papers right now!"

Part Five

CHAPTER

88

I CLIMBED FROM THE GTO amid the ruins of Arabi.

Lester Frost was pissed off because his mother had insisted he give me his brand-new red high-top Converse sneakers, which fit surprisingly well. In the backseat, Madame Minerva had her chin up and was slowly drifting back and forth as if divining.

"You swim?" she asked.

"Why'd you say that?" I asked.

"The cradle is water," she said. "And this is just the first step in your water journey."

I had no time to ask her what that meant; I just nodded and shut the door. The address Sunday had sent me was down a block to the west. In the first light of day I walked past city lots bulldozed clean, others grown over with weeds, and still others haunted by the crippled skeletons of low-income houses.

Madame Minerva and Lester were right. Though there were new mobile homes here and there, Arabi did feel like a place for ghosts, and memories.

As I walked on, specters of my own memories flew before me. Nana Mama was in the kitchen, making pancakes and laughing at a joke Damon had told. Jannie and Ali were in the front room watching *The Walking Dead* and trying to convince me it was the greatest show ever. Bree and I were dancing at a club shortly after we met, and my heart was just beginning to melt for her.

I got closer to the address on Pontalba Street and forced the ghosts of those precious memories back into my mental cabinet and locked it. This could easily be an ambush. This could easily be Sunday's endgame.

I slowed and scanned the area around me in the gathering light. Did Sunday have my family in one of these condemned buildings? Or in one of the double-wide trailers? Were they here at all?

When I was able to see the actual wreckage of the house at the correct address, I stopped and watched and listened. Even in the gray light, I could see that the front wall of the baby-blue bungalow had buckled inward and was twisted like an old man suffering hip pain. The windows were boarded up. And I could make out a sign of some kind on the door, probably the condemnation notice.

Nothing moved.

In the distance I heard the tuba-deep braying of a ship's horn. But nothing moved.

When I moved, I did it quickly, dropping into an active combat position, the gun and the Maglite up before me, and running right at the house. I was alert to any threat; my eyes darted to every shadow, and my hands and gun followed, ready.

But nothing moved.

I jumped over a low, rusted chain-link fence and into the

yard, my attention and weapon now focused on the darkest places there: the windows, the door, that gap between the broken front wall and the cinder-block foundation.

But still nothing moved. No muzzle flashes. No shotgun blasts. If Sunday were inside, he'd have shot at me by now.

So why bring me here?

I began wondering how I was going to get inside. The windows were covered with sheets of plywood. And the door was sealed with two-by-fours and screws.

Then I put the flashlight beam on the condemnation notice inside a plastic sleeve that dangled from a screw in the center of the door. I could see the perimeters of the notice, but not the center of the document. A standard envelope blocked my view of that, and it stopped me cold.

On the envelope, scrawled in green crayon, were the words *Go to the river, Cross, and find the mythological box before it floats out to sea.*

Below that was a crude drawing of a boat with six crosses rising off the deck and six stick figures crucified upon them.

CHAPTER 89

A DEEP HORN WOKE Nana Mama, and she came around more fully than before. Her eyelids fluttered open into almost complete darkness save for tiny, soft green lights blinking above her and softly glowing red numbers changing above them: 71, 71, 72, 71 ...

What did they mean?

Regina Hope rolled her head to the left and saw nothing but pitch-darkness. When she looked lazily right, however, and up, she saw the edge of something long and silhouetted by the barest glow from other blinking green and red lights.

Where am I?

What is this place?

How did I get here?

Cross's grandmother strained for memories and saw herself in the front seat of a van of some sort. It was lightly raining out, and the van pulled away from the house. She remembered saying something to the driver about St. Anthony's being in the other direction, and then sharp pain.

Nana Mama saw it then in her mind's eye: a hypodermic needle driven into her leg, and then nothing after that. Fear rippled through her, roused her even more. She tried to sit up, but something was holding her snugly across her chest and legs.

Where am *I?*

The panic set in then. She knew she'd been taken. She knew she'd been drugged and brought to this place.

But where is this place?

And how long have I been asleep?

She squirmed and found she could move her body slightly beneath the restraints, especially her legs. When she tried to part them, she felt the catheter line and realized that she wore no underwear, and her fear turned to anger.

Who did this to me? Why?

"Hello? Who are you?" she demanded. "Why are you doing this to me?"

But she heard nothing, and she wondered if she *had* died and if this was her particular purgatory or hell.

Then the voice of her great-grandchild Jannie came to her weakly, said, "Nana? Is that you?"

CHAPTER 90

ON THE OTHER SIDE of the levee at the foot of Friscoville Avenue, the Mississippi River was the color of clay and smelled of spent fuel and something rotten.

Lester Frost's muscle car chugged behind me as I frantically scanned the surface of the water, hearing Sunday's words clang around in my head.

Go to the river, Cross, and find the mythological box before it floats out to sea.

Mythological box? All I could see were massive ocean-going cargo vessels, some heading to the port and others south toward the Gulf of Mexico. I strained to see the names of the ships but could make out only a few, and none of them suggested mythology or a box.

Before it floats out to sea.

I turned my attention south about a quarter mile to a small pier where a boom crane was loading pallets of supplies onto a flat-deck boat. Then I saw what bobbed in the water on the north side of the pier.

I sprinted down the embankment, opened the car door, climbed in, and said, "Take me down to that pier."

Lester Frost didn't like it, but he threw the GTO in gear and blazed down North Peters Street until he reached a ramp that led onto the small pier, which was owned by a service that ferried supplies out to the ocean-goers. As I was about to climb out, Madame Minerva said, "He means the box to be your tomb, pilgrim."

"Not today," I said, and jumped out and ran up the ramp to a small parking lot and the office.

"You rent boats?" I asked the woman behind the counter.

"Sometimes," she said, squinting one eye at me.

"I'm a Washington, DC, police detective," I said. "I need to rent that launch down there."

"The Whaler's not for rent," she said flatly.

"Please," I said, painfully aware of the desperation in my voice. "I'm trying to save my family. They were kidnapped almost two weeks ago, and I believe they're being held on a boat heading downriver."

She looked at me hard. "This is straight?"

"As an arrow. Please. I'm begging for their lives here."

She hesitated, and then she reached under the counter, came up with a set of keys. "It's my husband's new toy. Whatever you do, don't put a scratch on it. And give me a credit card to hold."

I started to tear up, blessed her, gave her a Visa card, and took the keys. As I was pivoting to leave, I spotted the binoculars on the ledge of the window, facing the river.

"I could use those binoculars too," I said.

She rolled her eyes and then got them for me.

"What's your name?"

"Sally Hitchcock."

"Sally Hitchcock, I will never forget your kindness."

Sally Hitchcock actually smiled.

I ran out and looked back toward the road, wanting to wave in thanks to Frost and his mother. But the GTO was gone.

Five minutes later, I was pulling away from the dock in a Whaler 240 Dauntless with a three-hundred-horsepower engine that frankly scared the hell out of me when I pushed down on the throttle.

In the next half hour, I went thirty miles downriver toward the wetlands that stretched to the Gulf of Mexico, checking out every ship and boat that I passed and scanning the water for a floating box of some sort. In all, I saw thirty-nine vessels, and not one of them had a mythological name.

For several miles there were no boats at all save barges docked at the refineries and coal-transfer stations. Around nine thirty that morning I reached the Pointe-a-la-Hache Waterworks where the car ferry was crossing from the east to the west bank of the river.

To say I was shocked to see Lester Frost looking at me from the ferry would be an understatement. I waved. He waved back, with little enthusiasm. Beyond him on the deck, I could see the muscle car with the windows rolled down, and I had no doubt that Madame Minerva was still in the backseat calling the cosmic shots.

They're following me, I thought. But how? They'd had no idea where I was on the river, right? In any case, the blind psychic seemed to think I needed her help. Part of me wanted to follow the ferry to the western shore, to ask Madame Minerva what she'd intuited in the past few hours.

But when the ferry passed, I happened to look downriver,

and I saw the blue-and-white tower of a river barge about a mile ahead. A feeling came over me then, like I was being pulled by forces beyond myself, and I sped after the barge until I was within four hundred yards of it.

Backing off on the throttle, I raised the binoculars and saw a Zodiac-style raft tied to the stern of the *Pandora,* and scores of colorful container cars stacked on her deck, and I understood immediately that I had found the mythological box, my family, and Marcus Sunday.

Sure that this was the endgame, I lowered the binoculars and closed my eyes to summon all my smarts, strength, and determination.

But then my phone buzzed, alerting me to a text: *You are tenacious, Cross, but far too slow for your own good. I couldn't wait any longer. Your family? They're all d…*

CHAPTER 91

SUNDAY WAS PLAYING ME yet again.

I knew it in my gut, but the last sentence and the way it trailed away after the letter *d* still threatened to suck the resolve right out of me.

Then I realized the maniacal sonofabitch had made a mistake sending the text, a big mistake; my attention shot to the barge, and I scanned its stern and wheelhouse. I saw no one on deck and nothing through the tinted windows on the tower and wheelhouse. But I knew he was right there somewhere, watching me, probably through his own set of binoculars.

That thought went beyond bolstering me. It turned me to ice and steel.

Drawing my pistol, I ducked down behind the windshield and hammered the throttle. The Whaler reared up like a warhorse. The four hundred yards that separated me from the *Pandora* were covered in seconds.

We were passing mile marker forty-six when I cut the engine and brought the Whaler in at a forty-five-degree angle to the starboard rear corner of the barge, hoping I'd present such a poor target from the windows of the tower that Sunday would hesitate to shoot and reveal his position.

In any case, I hauled back on the throttle and threw the engine in reverse for less than a second and then cut it again. The Whaler's bow came up within feet of the rubberized bumpers on the barge's stern. Pocketing the ignition key, I ran forward, grabbed a rope tied to the bow, stepped up onto the padded sitting area, and jumped.

I landed on a narrow aft deck thirty feet below the wheelhouse and tied the Whaler to a cleat. Years of police training suggested that I clear the working and living areas of the barge before I went searching for my family.

Moving with my gun drawn, I saw no one on the way to a narrow metal stairway that climbed the tower. Behind it was a door with a sign that read *Engine Room.*

Taking a long breath, I put the Maglite between my teeth and yanked open the hatch. The heat came out like a blast furnace, and the throbbing of the engines boomed up out of the hold below an interior staircase.

The engine room was reasonably well lit, and I stepped inside onto a steel grate landing. I scanned the place, alert for movement, and spotted a crumpled figure lying between the two huge diesel engines that powered the river barge.

Male. Late thirties. In a greasy wife-beater and equally greasy shorts. That was definitely a close-range gunshot to the side of his head. When I was certain there was no one else in the engine room, I eased back out into the sunshine and shut the door quietly before stalking up the side of the tower to an unmarked hatch door.

I smelled bacon when I opened it. Looking down a short passage, I could see a stove and part of a countertop. Country music was playing from the galley: Miranda Lambert singing about hiding her crazy and acting like a lady.

Beyond the galley was another passage, and I figured it led to the berths. How many people were in a barge crew? I wondered. Two? Three?

When I stepped into the galley, I looked to my right, saw a booth, and understood the *Pandora* carried a crew of at least two. Sprawled sideways onto the table in a puddle of spilled coffee was a man in his late twenties, sandy-haired and bare-chested. He had a tattoo of a bleeding heart over his own heart and a bullet hole just above the bridge of his nose.

Creeping up the exterior staircase toward the wheelhouse a minute later, I could hear radio chatter and a woman's insistent voice. I slid up beside the slightly open door and took a quick peek inside.

A thick-necked bull of a man in a Chicago Bears T-shirt sat in a high-backed padded chair mounted on a pedestal bolted into the forward deck of the wheelhouse. A horseshoe-shaped console surrounded the chair, with controls, computers, and screens around the pilot. One screen clearly showed the barge's position on the river.

Below that screen, there was a steaming mug of coffee on a narrow workspace. The rest of the wheelhouse looked empty, so with my pistol leading, I opened the door and stepped softly inside.

"*Pandora?* Scotty Creel? You answer me now, you hear?" the woman's voice squawked over a shortwave radio mounted on a shelf above him.

"Shirley, do you ever shut the fuck up?" the pilot grumbled as he reached up and turned off the volume.

"Sir?" I said.

He startled, swiveled in the chair; his eyes went wide, and his head retreated sharply. I suppose turning to see a six-foot-two-inch strange man in filthy clothes and bright red high-tops holding a pistol might make a man do that, as well as raise his hands, which he did.

"What the fuck is this?" he said, looking terrified. "Who the fuck are you? Some kind of pirate?"

CHAPTER

92

I TOOK IN THE rest of the room at a glance, seeing closed compartments and charts, a coffeemaker, and little else. "My name is Alex Cross. I'm a Washington, DC, homicide detective. You?"

"Creel," he choked, staring incredulously at me. "Scotty Creel. I'm the captain."

"Are you aware that your crew is dead?" I asked.

He stared at my gun now, looking shocked and almost frantic with fear. "Why'd you kill them?"

"No, I found them dead just now," I said. "One in the engine room. One in the galley."

"Hawkes?" Creel said in dismay. "Timbo?"

"Where's Sunday?"

He recognized that name right away, and he looked stunned. "No—you think that guy—"

I cut him off. "Where is he?"

The captain's hands were still raised as he gestured behind

him, through the window. "Out there, checking up on his research project. What in God's name is he—"

"Show me," I ordered, and crossed the room.

Creel turned the chair halfway and stood uncertainly before pointing out the window and saying in a wavering voice: "See the one there with the solar panels? The single one forward on the main deck? It's supposed to be some kind of refrigeration experiment."

"Can you put the barge on autopilot?" I asked.

"On this stretch?" the captain said, incredulous. "No way. The river's heavily silted, and sandbars are always changing. It's a sight job the next twenty miles to Port Sulphur."

"You have a gun aboard?"

"A real gun?" he said. "No. A flare gun? Yes. You want it?"

Shaking my head, I said, "What I want you to do is get on that shortwave of yours and call in the nearest law enforcement agency. Tell them to send a medevac unit."

"Medevac?" Creel said, confused.

"There are people being held hostage in that refrigeration unit," I said. "My family."

"What?" he said, his expression twisting to disbelief as he looked from me to the window and then back. "No, I never heard…all this time he…"

Looking frightened again, he said in an almost tearful voice, "Look, Detective, I had absolutely no idea that anyone was holding anyone hostage on my boat. I swear to God, Sunday said it was a test trial, see if his solar—"

"Make the call and we'll talk later," I said, turning away from him.

"I'll call the Coast Guard," he said, sounding calmer. "They have a search-and-rescue unit out of New Orleans."

"Perfect," I said as I went out the door. "Tell them to bring an armed escort and to notify the FBI that this entire vessel is a crime scene."

I could hear Creel calling behind me as I pounded down the staircase. "U.S. Coast Guard, this is the river barge *Pandora,* I have a medical and law enforcement emergency south of mile forty-six. Repeat, I have a—"

The door slammed shut, and I was left with deadly purpose that carried me down the staircase to the deck. I circled to the starboard side, jogged forward in a crouch tight to the stacks of containers. When I reached the corner nearest the bow, I took a quick look around, saw that the container car with the solar panels and the forward reefer unit was not fifteen yards away.

There was a hatchlike door below the reefer. It hung loose on its hinges.

Seeing a light glowing through the opening, I was almost paralyzed with dread. Sunday was in there with my family. And he was waiting for me to arrive.

I knew how potentially suicidal my next move was, but I made it anyway, advancing fast and quiet across the deck and up beside the loose hatch. I reached over and tried to open the door as silently as I could.

"Just come on in, Dr. Cross," Sunday called from inside. "We've been waiting for you for the longest time."

"Dad?" Jannie cried softly.

"Alex?" Nana Mama choked. "No. Go away. He's going to—"

I heard a slapping sound, and my grandmother groaned. Embracing death, I threw the hatch door open. Pistol up, finger on the trigger, I stepped into a clear line of fire and then ducked inside, hearing my grandmother sobbing quietly.

The smell was nasty: sweat, shit, and stale ammonia. It shocked me, made me suffer my family's mistreatment even before my eyes adjusted. Six bunks bolted into the walls.

All but one held a member of my family. There was hospital apparatus around every one of them. On the near right wall, Jannie was twisting against her restraints to look back at me.

"Daddy?"

"Right here, little girl," I said, my voice quivering.

Just seeing her alive and hearing her voice after all that I'd been through, I almost lost control and wanted to go straight to hold and comfort her.

But I couldn't go to her, or to Ali, who seemed to be out cold below her, or to my grandmother, who was breathing shakily on the bunk under Damon's, or to Bree, who was opposite him on top of the second set of bunks on the right.

Sunday had taken cover between the two right-hand sets of bunks and was aiming a nickel-plated Colt .357 Magnum at Jannie and a smaller Ruger nine-millimeter at my grandmother. His face was only partially showing behind a pair of medical monitors, but he appeared very different from his author's photo and from his fake driver's license as the red-bearded Thierry Mulch.

Sunday's face was shaven, and his salt-and-pepper hair close cropped. Gaunt, maybe late thirties, but what struck me most were his gray soulless eyes that danced with excitement.

"Put the gun down, Cross," Sunday ordered. "Or I shoot the both of them."

Sunday was twenty-five, maybe thirty feet from me, and my instincts screamed, *Head-shoot him! Head-shoot the bastard like he did the crew!*

"Daddy!" Jannie said again.

"Quick, Cross," Sunday said. "Or that will be the last word of hers you ever hear."

If I hit him in the perfect spot, which was anywhere above his eyes and below his hairline, he would go lights-out, lose all muscle control, and collapse, the guns with him. But if I was just the slightest bit off, he'd tense before he dropped, the guns would fire, and Jannie and Nana would die.

"It's over," I said, pressuring the trigger and trying to keep the sights on the center of his forehead. "The Coast Guard's on the way."

"Are they, now?" Sunday said, amused.

I heard feet scrape behind me, and Captain Creel said, "Not a chance, Marcus. And Detective? I've got a twelve-gauge pointed at your spine. You might want to drop that."

CHAPTER 93

SUNDAY GLOATED. "I'VE NEVER had problems getting followers, especially those people needing money and a whole new life. The way the captain tells it, his wife, Shirley, is a nominee for bitch of the century, and he just can't take it anymore. So, one last time, drop your weapon, Cross."

"Don't, Alex," Nana Mama said.

I lowered the gun.

"On the floor, and kick it to me," Sunday ordered. "Then on your knees, hands behind your head."

I did as I was told. What else could I do?

Creel came up behind me and used duct tape to bind my wrists and strap them tight to the back of my head. As he did, I said, "Captain, has Sunday told you what he did to his last accomplice?"

"Shut up," Sunday said.

"He fed her to alligators," I said.

"Sounds like a hell of an idea," Creel said. "I'd love to do the same to Shirley, but a new life in Colombia will have to do."

"How much time now, Captain?" Sunday asked, tossing him my pistol.

Creel caught it, said, "Seventy minutes."

"Back to your controls, then. I'll take it from here."

"You want the hatch closed?"

"Please," Sunday said, and when the door shut behind me, he took a long deep breath and let it out in a sigh. "Game over, Dr. Alex. I win."

"The game's not over, Mulch, and you will lose no matter what you do to me or my family," I said. "The FBI is hunting for you now. So is every cop in the country. As we speak, your face is all over the news and the Internet. Not even the perfect criminal could get away. No matter what you do to us, you *will* be caught, and you *will* be judged and punished in the harshest manner. High-profile guy like you? Harvard PhD intellectual gone mad? Prosecutors absolutely love to see guys like you face justice and fry."

In a voice rich with mirth and disdain, Sunday said, "Let them hunt me, Cross. Let them bring dogs and agents. I don't care. I'll relish showing them how quickly and permanently I can disappear. It's all been arranged. A long time ago. I'm a planner."

"And I used to be FBI. And I'm a cop. They won't quit looking. Ever."

"Tell it to Whitey Bulger," he shot back. Then he licked his lips and smiled. "You fulfilled one of my fantasies, Cross. Did you know that?"

"What fantasy?" I asked, content to keep him talking.

"Shooting Atticus Jones in cold blood," he said, his eyes dancing again. "How did it feel?"

"It felt like nothing because it never happened," I said. "He's dying but by no means dead."

"Bullshit. I saw you take the shot."

"You saw what a Hollywood A-list CGI specialist can do," I said. "Friend of Jones's daughter, Gloria, an NBC news producer."

This seemed to upset Sunday a great deal, because he stood there fuming for almost a minute before he looked up with a cruel smile on his face.

"There's still time," Sunday said.

"For what?"

"Lessons," he said. "In the meaninglessness of life."

"Life is full of meaning."

"I'm going to rid you of that ridiculous idea forever," Sunday said, his cruel smile curling toward pleasure. "One by one, Cross, I am now going to kill your family in front of you. By the time I'm done, we'll be out in the Gulf. I'll make my escape to Mexico with the good Captain Creel in the Zodiac and leave you locked in here with the corpses, adrift. And I guarantee, in your last hours, you *will* come to see the world my way."

CHAPTER

94

MY FEAR AND BEWILDERMENT must have shown, because Sunday began to crow, "That will break you, won't it? That will be the proof!"

Jannie said, "Is he for real?"

"Oh, I am real, young lady," Sunday said. "In the end, I'm the only real that will matter."

I saw the mad conviction in his expression and was so shaken by the possibility of seeing my family murdered before me that I didn't know what to say and almost didn't catch the movement behind him.

Bree's arm was out from under one of the straps, and with her hand she was making a circular motion toward the rear wall. I tried not to look, but then I saw Damon doing the same thing. Ali seemed to be moving too. *They're awake, playing possum, and—what? Telling me to keep him talking? Telling me to get him closer?*

But would either of those things help the situation? He had

the guns, and as far as I knew, there was no one looking for us here.

Or was there? Lester Frost and Madame Minerva seemed to have been following me back there at the ferry. Maybe they had already called the police, and help was on the way. Maybe hope had not really died.

"So who should enjoy my skills first?" Sunday asked. "Your awake, nubile, and athletic daughter? Or your comatose, ripe, and buxom wife?"

I said nothing as he reached around and tucked the Ruger in his waistband. Then he switched the .357 to his left hand and moved it toward Jannie.

"Don't!" she yelled. "You frickin' creep!"

Sunday laughed. "Feisty, aren't you?"

I said, "He's not a creep, Jannie. He's a wallowing pig."

You'd have thought I'd slapped him, the way his face turned red and his expression hardened. "You have no idea who I am or what I am capable of," he said in the coldest voice I'd ever heard. "I am limitless."

"I know who you are and I know your limitations," I shot back. "When it comes down to it, Mulch, you're just the kid who smelled like pig shit in school. It was why you killed Alice Littlefield, right? Because she commented on your piggish odor in class?"

Sunday took two long strides and kicked me hard in the stomach. It blew the wind out of me, and I fell to my side, gasping for air.

"You shut up and watch now," he said calmly, but in a West Virginia accent, before turning and walking past Jannie. "I'm gonna tear your heart right out of your chest, Alex Cross."

He went toward my wife then, pressed the pistol muzzle to the side of her head, and looked back at me.

My stomach turned inside out, but I tried to show Sunday no reaction.

Bree's hand was still free—he hadn't seemed to notice—but the gun against her skull effectively neutralized her threat. My mind flashed on the corpse of the woman at the construction site who'd looked like Bree. I felt the bottomless grief of that moment again and wondered if I could bear seeing her actually die right in front of me. No fake photos. No look-alike. For real.

I had to act. I had to do something.

Do I continue to attack him?

Or plead for Bree's life?

CHAPTER

95

SUNDAY MADE UP MY mind for me. With his free hand, he drew down the sheet covering her breasts, glanced at them, and then winked at me.

"My, oh my, Alex Cross," he said, and whistled. "Must have been something to have this fine woman in your bed every night. Yes, sir. Yes siree."

"Leave her alone, asshole!" Jannie cried. "She's drugged, defenseless."

"Oooh, that helps," Sunday said, nodding. "Keep it up there, girlie-girl. Stir that pot!"

He lazily traced his index finger around my wife's nipples, watching me and smacking his lips as if he were savoring a meal of my misery and a wine of my hatred.

"Shall we see more?" Sunday asked, teasing the sheet down over her belly. "If I remember, no Brazilian-wax fan down there. Uh-uh, Bree's got the prettiest little trim job. I like that, fits perfectly with a man in your line of work. Leave a little mystery, right?"

Remembering how he'd lost it when I brought up his life as Thierry Mulch, I attacked there again.

"Baby Boar," I shot back. "That's what they called you, right? At home, anyway. But at school? I heard it was just Pig Boy and Little Piggy-Shit Boy."

His shoulders hunched. For a second, I thought he was going to come for me again. Instead, he watched the action of his fingers on Bree's breast, saying in that Thierry Mulch accent, "You best hush, you know what's good for you, Alex Cross."

Sunday's fingers traveled toward my wife's throat as if he might choke her or hold her down when he sent the bullet into her brain.

"Soooweee!" I called to him in a high, thin tone. "Isn't that how they taunted you, Thierry? Soooweee! Here, piggy, piggy, piggy that smells like shit!"

Sunday flushed purple and began softly smearing his free hand over Bree's face as he hissed, "You keep it up now, Cross. Just makes my job easier."

"And your mom? Did she abandon you because of your stench?"

Sunday laughed acidly. "That traitorous bitch sure knew who she was when she died. She went out squealing and choking."

"And Alice Monahan?"

"And all their young'ns," he said. "Same way before they got the knife."

Then his nostrils flared in deep amusement. He studied me while twiddling three of his fingers just above Bree's slack jaw and open mouth.

"Listen for it, you hear, Cross?" Sunday said. "Even out cold, this sow of yours is gonna squeal 'fore she dies."

CHAPTER

96

A LOW, THROBBING NOISE grew outside the container car.

Sunday looked to the roof in alarm.

And then the sonofabitch let loose with an absolutely bloodcurdling scream.

Sunday struggled and screeched trying to get his fingers out of Bree's mouth. But she'd bitten into him hard and she held on like a crazed terrier until he pistol-whipped the side of her head.

He staggered back against Damon's bunk, staring in shock at his wounds. The pinkie and ring fingers were almost completely severed above the second knuckle. His middle finger was spurting blood and was bent grotesquely.

For me, the next few moments unfolded in slow motion. I just couldn't get there fast enough, but I saw every second of it with a weird clarity.

As I lurched to my feet, Sunday's pain and disbelief turned to rage. He screamed something incomprehensible at Bree, who was dazed and smiling weakly, his blood trickling from her mouth.

He aimed the gun at her point-blank and screeched, “Die, you fucking—”

Damon’s elbow smashed the back of Sunday’s neck and unbalanced him. He lurched to his left. Damon’s second swing at him just missed.

“Get him, Dad!” Ali yelled as I barreled past with my hands still duct-taped behind my head.

Sunday seemed not to hear me coming; he shook off Damon’s blow and made a bizarre clacking sound with his teeth before trying to aim at Bree again.

Out of his peripheral vision, he caught me charging and tried to swing the gun my way. But I dropped my shoulder under his line of fire, exploded from my knees, and smashed all my weight and momentum into his rib cage.

The impact knocked Sunday off his feet.

He hit the container floor so hard, the .357 flew from his hand, ricocheted off the rear wall, and went skittering under Nana Mama’s bunk.

The force knocked me down at an odd, twisting angle, and I hit the container floor hard, face-first and then left shoulder. I saw stars and felt bones break.

“Kill him, Dad!” Ali yelled. “Kill him!”

Pain pulsed like fire and radiated in my shoulder and face. But the hit must also have triggered some kind of full-on adrenaline response, because instead of lying there in shock, I went insane with fury.

Sunday’s back was to me. He was hurt but trying to get to his feet.

I kicked him high in the hamstring, just below his ass

cheeks. He stumbled and hit his head against the container wall. Ignoring the agony of my blown shoulder and fractured face, I squirmed forward and lashed out with my foot, trying to kick him in the back of his knee, his calf, his ankle, anything.

I missed.

"Dad, watch out!" Damon yelled.

In a single motion, Sunday pushed away from the wall, pivoted, and hauled off and kicked me in the ribs just below my bad arm, blowing the air out of me and making me curl up like a whipped dog. He jumped over me, spun, and kicked me even harder in the kidney.

Sunday might as well have hit me with a Taser because it felt like a lightning bolt passed through me, and I puked. Then he looped his belt around my neck and cinched it tight.

"No!" Ali yelled. "Don't!"

"You just don't learn, do you, Cross?" Sunday snarled, and he wrenched me up off the ground by my neck, the belt right up under my jaw. "You'll never learn, will you?"

"Never," I choked, fighting not to pass out.

He dragged me against him and pulled even tighter on the belt, cutting off my air and the blood supply to my brain.

"Incorrigible, I can see that, and I admit defeat with you." He grunted. "But let's see if your family learns better. Let's let them see what life's all about."

Sunday yanked again, and I strained against the strangler, whipping my head side to side.

"It's meaningless!" he crowed. "It's all so meaningless!"

I stopped struggling, and my eyes sought my family.

Bree watched me, blinking slowly, blood from the head wound streaking her cheeks. Damon and Jannie were almost free of their restraints but frozen on their bunks, watching me die. Ali hung off his bunk, screaming and reaching for me.

Spots were becoming blotches in front of my eyes, and all I could hear was my heart pounding like so many anvil strikes when I looked to my last hope on earth.

CHAPTER

97

"LET HIM GO, OR I'll shoot you!"

Sunday wasn't sure who'd shouted the order at first. He'd been staring at the top of Cross's head, waiting for the big collapse, the pissing and shitting in the pants that always seemed to mark a death by strangulation.

But then he glanced up and saw Nana Mama.

The old woman was lying on her bunk with her knees drawn up under the sheets. Her bony hands held his .357.

She was aiming at him from ten, maybe fifteen feet away, and the nickel-plated barrel of the gun rested in a cradle of sheet fabric stretched between her knees.

"Do it!" Nana Mama shouted.

Sunday grinned lazily at her and eased up slightly on the belt. Cross started coughing and hacking.

"Watch yourself there," he said to the detective's grandmother. "Bullet gets to ricocheting around here, who knows who it will kill."

"Shoot him, Nana!" Ali said. "In the head. Like he's a zombie!"

Sunday considered himself a brilliant interpreter of body language, and he saw in the old lady's face and trembling upper body that she did not want to kill him and that she was afraid of even trying.

"You won't kill me, now," he drawled. "Catholic, southern lady and all. Thou shalt not kill. Thou shalt not."

Every inch of Nana Mama was shaking now.

"See there?" Sunday said, as soft and sincere as a funeral director. "You can't even aim, you old bitch. You shoot, you'll kill your grandson."

"No," she said. "I *will* shoot *you!*"

"No, you won't," Sunday said with a knowing grin as he leaned back and pulled on the belt with all his might. "Not in my universe. No—"

The flash, the explosion, and the impact seemed to happen all at once.

It felt like some invisible force had swatted Sunday, backhanded him as if he were no more than a fly. The bullet caught him square in the chest and flung him against the rear wall of the container car.

Looking down, Sunday saw the bright red color expand on his shirt like a rose unfolding, and he felt sick and began to slide down the wall, all too aware that he had lost his grip on the belt around Cross's neck.

"No," Sunday rasped, already tasting blood in his throat. "There's no meaning…no point if he doesn't…"

The hatch door at the far end of the container opened as the blood poured from him, and his breath got labored and raspy, and Sunday's life began to ebb away. But not before one last image registered in his brain, a final vision that filled him with acute terror as he died.

A sunbeam had come in through the open hatch door, run across the container floor, and lit up Cross, who was not two feet away, fighting for air.

CHAPTER

98

I CAN'T SAY THAT I remember everything that happened in the moments after Sunday began to strangle me again, only that Nana Mama was yelling and then she shot. And for what seemed an eternity after that shot, there was nothing but the ringing in my ears, blood rushing to my head, and me wanting air.

Then someone was cutting the duct tape that bound my wrists and hands to my head. Flames shot through my shoulder, and I gagged against the dry, bruised sensation in my throat as someone turned me over. It was Tess Aaliyah. She was grinning through her tears.

"They're all safe!" she said. "They're all alive!"

I looked beyond and around her, seeing Damon sitting on the edge of his bunk, and Bree smiling sleepily, and Jannie and Ali being freed by Louisiana state troopers. A U.S. Coast Guard medic was already working on my grandmother.

All alive.

All safe.

Never abandoned.

"Help me up," I said to Aaliyah in a harsh whisper.

"Let's get you—"

"Help me up," I demanded. "I want to hold them."

The detective hesitated, but then she got me under my good arm and lifted me to my feet. The container car swam, and then steadied.

I went to Bree first, put my hand on her bare shoulder and my forehead against hers, and the dam burst, and I broke down weeping.

"There were times when I thought I might never…" I choked.

"Shhh, now, sugar," my wife said with a slight slur, stroking my cheek. "We're good now. It's all good and good."

Through my tears, I could see her pupils were constricted and her gaze was drifting. I drew my head back, saw a tiny trickle of blood in her ear, and panicked. "She's got a closed-head injury," I shouted.

Another Coast Guard medic who'd just come into the container rushed to her side, did a quick exam, and said, "Okay, her vitals are good, but she's on the first flight out."

"And great-grandma," said the other medic. "She's having trouble breathing and I don't like the sound of her heart."

I turned from Bree and crouched by Nana Mama, whose breathing was labored. She looked at me sideways, and then her hand shot out and grabbed mine tight.

"I did the right thing, didn't I?" She gasped. "You have to put mad dogs down, don't you?"

I started to break down again as I nodded. "I'm sorry."

"For what?"

"For all of this. Because of me you had to—"

"Sir," the medic said. "We really need to get her to a hospital."

"I'm going with them," I said.

The two medics exchanged glances, and then the one working on Nana Mama said, "We'll make room."

Louisiana state troopers and coastguardsmen brought stretchers. I went to my children, and as I held each of them, I broke down, thanking God they were alive.

"Do people at school think I'm dead?" Damon asked.

"They held a memorial service for you. I was there."

He frowned at that. "What'd they say?"

"That you were the very best kind of person. You have made a big impression on the Kraft School. You have many friends and admirers. And I am very proud of you."

"I screwed up," he said, blinking back tears. "That woman. Karla Mepps."

"It doesn't matter now," I said. "We caught her."

After a pause, he said, "It was Bree's idea for some of us to act like we were still out and then follow her lead."

"You did good, son," I said, stroking his hair. "Real good."

He whispered, "She almost bit his fingers off, Dad!"

"I saw that. Well, almost."

"I would never, ever mess with her," he said. "Or Nana Mama either."

I smiled and laughed softly. "I learned a long, long time ago never to mess with the women in this family."

CHAPTER 99

JANNIE AND ALI WERE sitting up on their bunks as medics removed their IV lines.

"I knew you were looking for us," Jannie said, breaking into tears that wrecked me all over again. "That was the first thing I thought when I woke up. *Dad's looking.*"

"From the moment you were taken," I said. "And I never gave up hope that I'd find you and that one day you'd run again."

"Will I?"

"Of course," I said firmly. "You will not let this stop you in any way."

Jannie nodded and kissed me. "I love you, Daddy."

"I love you too," I choked.

"What about me?" Ali asked.

"You!" I said, kneeling to hug him with my good arm. "You are my best little boy. My..." I stopped and couldn't say anything while they were moving Bree onto the stretcher.

Ali said, "He was that guy who wore the red beard and came to school, wasn't he, Dad? The one who smelled like a zombie?"

"He was," I said. "And I should have listened to you about that, because you, Ali Cross, are an expert in all things zombie."

He beamed and said, "My friends say that too."

"Smart kids, your friends."

They took Nana Mama out first. "I'm fine," she said weakly as she went past me. "I'll see you all soon."

"Nana Mama, zombie killer," Ali said in awe as she was carried through the hatch door.

Troopers picked up the stretcher my wife was on and took her out next.

"I'm going with Bree and Nana," I said to the others. "But you'll be right behind us."

"In a helicopter?" Ali asked.

"I think so."

"Oh, this is so cool."

"I know," Jannie said. "No one at school's going to believe it."

"No one," Damon agreed.

Aaliyah helped me to the hatch. I refused to look back at the sheet that covered the doomed, soulless creature that had been Thierry Mulch and Marcus Sunday.

Instead, I stepped out into the heat and the humidity of a late Louisiana morning and squinted at the sun, feeling like I'd been in that claustrophobic box for days, not less than an hour.

The sky was this incredible blue, and the vegetation the deepest of greens. There were birds diving and arcing, hunting an insect hatch. I took deep breaths through my nose and smelled the salt marsh and the river and thought there had never been a better smell or a better day, ever.

Two helicopters had landed on the stacks of container cars. One bore the logo of the Louisiana State Police, and the other, larger, one, that of the U.S. Coast Guard.

Airmen in the federal chopper were working a winch to lower a rescue basket to the deck for Bree and Nana Mama. Behind them, a Coast Guard officer stood next to Captain Creel, who was in plastic cuffs, despondent.

I looked at Detective Aaliyah as if she were some kind of miracle worker and asked, “How in God’s name did you ever find us?”

CHAPTER

100

AS THE COAST GUARD rescue specialists winched up the baskets containing Bree and Nana Mama, Aaliyah explained how she'd discovered lading documents inside Acadia Le Duc's rental car and how she'd come to realize that my family was probably being held in a container on a Mississippi River barge called the *Pandora.*

Paul Gauvin, the Jefferson County sheriff, was in the hospital on heavy doses of painkillers, and his deputies were highly skeptical of her theory. The Louisiana police investigators had been too until she'd finally reached a woman who worked at the shipping and barge service listed on the documents.

Her name was Shirley Creel.

Aaliyah learned that the container car was supposed to be offloaded at a multimodal transfer station in New Orleans. The barge captain's wife tried to call her husband on his cell phone and via shortwave radio and got no answer.

"She promised to keep calling, but I badgered the state police guys into getting me a helicopter," she said. "First, we flew to the pier in New Orleans where the barge was supposed to have offloaded the container. It had never docked. That's when we started downriver and called the Coast Guard. Luckily, they had a search-and-rescue helicopter doing training about twenty-five miles from here, at their Venice station. It started upriver soon afterward. We both found you at almost the same time."

I threw my good arm around her shoulder and kissed the top of her head. She drew back, surprised.

"Thank you, Detective," I said. "You've been like my guardian angel in this whole sordid mess."

Aaliyah didn't seem to know what to say at first, but then she smiled and said, "Glad to help."

"You've done your dad prouder than proud."

Blushing, she looked down and said, "Well, thank you, Alex. That means a whole lot."

A Coast Guard airman signaled me to the basket. I told Aaliyah about the Whaler. She promised to have it returned and to bring my kids to me. When I got in the helicopter, a medic was working on Bree's scalp wound. My wife was conscious, but confused.

My grandmother's eyes were closed. They had hooked her up to a new set of IV lines and monitors, and the ninety-something-year-old David who'd slain Goliath looked as tiny and fragile as a newborn bird.

I wanted to sit between the two of them, but an airman told me I had to harness myself into one of the jump seats. I took one where I could see out a window in the side door.

The chopper began to vibrate, and we got airborne, leaving several state police officers and coastguardsmen to control the crime scene and keep the barge from floating out to sea.

As we rose, the chopper slowly rotated, revealing the mighty Mississippi and the vast deltas that surrounded it. We cleared a low line of trees to the west, and I was surprised to see how close State Route 23 was to the riverbanks and positively amazed to see Lester Frost's GTO parked on the narrow shoulder.

I saw Madame Minerva standing next to the open passenger door of the muscle car and gesturing frantically with her white cane before we turned and flew upriver.

"Did you see that crazy old lady down there?" one of the airmen said.

Before I could nod, an alarm sounded inside the hold.

And the medic tending to my grandmother shouted, "Code blue! She's in cardiac arrest!"

CHAPTER

101

WHEN THE FUNERAL ENDED, pallbearers lifted the casket, which was draped in forest-green cloth and an American flag. They carried it solemnly down the church's central aisle.

The pews were packed, and people were still dabbing at their eyes as the casket of Atticus Jones passed by. Standing there with Bree beside me, I dealt with the tremendous sense of loss by dwelling on the number of people who had cared enough about the old detective to attend the service. There were at least eighty of them in the church, maybe more.

There goes a life chock-full of meaning, I thought, and I felt tears well up in my eyes.

I watched the casket leave; it was followed by the priest, the deacon, and the altar boys. Jones's family came next, and I nodded to each of them as they passed. Gloria Jones and Ava exited last, both of them in black dresses.

We followed the procession out of the church and into a warm, dry June day almost six weeks after we'd flown off the *Pandora.*

Atticus Jones's daughter came over to hug me.

"You gave my dad peace, Alex," she said. "He was ready to let go after he knew Mulch was finished and your family was safe and sound."

"We never would have found Sunday without your dad."

"And you wouldn't have lived without Nana Mama," Ava said.

"Not a chance," Bree agreed.

"How is she doing?" Gloria Jones asked.

I shook my head. "She's one tough, tough old lady, and the meds they've got her on for her heart seem to be working."

"I meant with the shooting and all," Gloria said. "My dad was really worried how it would affect her."

"Other than to say it was a terrible thing that had to be done, she doesn't talk about it," I replied. "But even though her dream kitchen is done and she loves it, there are times when we catch her staring off and worrying her apron strings or her rosary beads."

Bree said, "And I've heard her crying more than a few times at night."

"Oh, the poor old doll," Gloria said. "You tell her from me that she should be up for sainthood for wiping that scumbag off the face of the earth."

"I'll do that," I said, and fought a laugh.

"Well," Jones's daughter said, "I have one more service to attend, family only. I'll see you at the reception?"

"We actually have to leave," I said. "My daughter's running in a big meet and we want to watch her."

Gloria hugged Bree, said, "It was so nice of you to come too."

"Alex adored your dad," Bree said. "So of course I came."

Then Gloria made me promise once more not to talk to the media until her full report on the case ran on *Dateline* later in the week. She nodded supportively to Ava and walked off toward the black limo that would carry her to Atticus Jones's gravesite.

Ava looked nervous and asked Bree, "How're you feeling?"

"I get agitated and irritable," my wife said. "But it's all part of the recovery."

"Your shoulder?" she asked me.

"Held together with screws, pins, and Teflon wire," I replied. "Next week I start physical therapy for it, which I am not looking forward to."

She kept toeing the grass.

"You good?" Bree asked.

She looked up at my wife and nodded as she pushed back a lock of her hair. "I'm real good, actually."

"That's excellent to hear," Bree said.

"It is," Ava said. "And I don't want to sound like I'm ungrateful or anything, because I'm more grateful to you two and to Nana Mama than you could ever understand."

I got where she was heading and said, "But you want to stay with Gloria, live in Pittsburgh?"

She smiled and nodded. "A new start. Somewhere different. Finish high school, go to college, and learn more about the news business."

"Sounds like a plan," Bree said, though she had tears running down her cheeks. "But I am going to miss you, young lady, and you have to promise to come visit."

"Got to see the new showplace, don't I?" Ava asked as she went into Bree's arms.

They held each other for several long moments, and I

knew how hard it was going to be for my wife to let her go. Even when Ava was at her lowest, Bree had refused to give up on her. Bree had been the one who kept pushing to find her and get her off the streets again.

"I love you both," Ava said when they separated.

"We love you too," I said, and I held out my good arm to embrace her. "Without you, we might never have caught Mulch."

"You said that about Detective Jones."

"I did. It was a team effort."

Ava beamed. "I'll call you to hear how Jannie did in her race."

"You better," Bree said, and we watched Ava run off to catch up with Gloria Jones and her new family.

"This is hard," my wife said, wiping away tears.

"It is," I said, putting my good arm around her shoulder and then kissing her. "I love you, you know?"

"I know," she said quietly. "It's what keeps me going."

"Ditto."

"Ditto?"

"What do you want me to say? You are my sunshine, my only sunshine?"

"That would be a good start," she said, and poked me.

I laughed, said, "We better get going or we'll miss the race."

CHAPTER

102

TWO AND A HALF hours later, we hurried from our car into the stadium at the University of Maryland in College Park. The stands were crowded for the special meet, which had brought in the top under-eighteen track stars from Virginia, Maryland, the District, Delaware, and Pennsylvania.

It took us a few moments to locate the official Jannie Cross cheering section. John Sampson and his wife, Billie, were already on hand. So was Damon and his new girlfriend, Sylvia Mathers, the student at the Kraft School who had first told me about Acadia Le Duc. A row in front of them, Ali was standing on a riser next to Nana Mama, who looked annoyed.

"We didn't miss it, did we?" I asked when I realized she was annoyed with me.

"Jannie's been looking for you," my grandmother said. "She's over there, warming up by the long-jump pit. You better make sure she knows you're here."

I left Bree and climbed back down the bleachers. When I reached the fence that surrounded the track, I called, "Hey, you!"

Jannie smiled, ran over to me. "I was afraid you weren't going to make it."

"Nothing was getting in the way of our being here."

She toed the grass. "I'm nervous."

"Don't be," I said. "Your coach says you were born to be here. You have to believe that."

Her eyes got glassy and she nodded. "I do. Even after everything, I do."

"Especially because of everything," I insisted. "You survived for a reason. *This* is the reason."

Jannie knitted her brow, said, "I'll see you after?"

"You will, and I'll love you truly, madly, and deeply no matter what happens. But before the gun goes off?"

"Yes?"

"I want you to believe in yourself, and I want you to have faith in the gift God gave you."

"Okay," she said, then she smiled and trotted away.

"She got the jitters?" Bree asked when I'd climbed back up into the bleachers.

"A little."

"This is for, like, five states, right?" Ali asked, fidgeting.

"It's big," Damon said. "There are all sorts of college coaches here to recruit."

They called for the finalists in the women's 400-meter race, and Jannie got off her warm-ups, walked into her starting lane, and then danced toward her mark on the stagger, looking like a strong girl among powerful women. She was the only fifteen-year-old in the field.

I helped Nana Mama to her feet and glanced at Bree, who was hugging herself.

"You good?" I asked.

"I am," she said. "You?"

We'd all been asking each other that question multiple times a day since our rescue. For a brief period, two weeks, I'd been consumed with guilt that Sunday had done all those heinous things—murder, kidnapping, and the persecution of my family—because of me. I mourned the fact that so many innocent people hadn't survived Marcus Sunday, including Bernice Smith, the Pennsylvania woman who had been murdered and mutilated simply because she looked like Bree, and Raphael Larkin, a Baltimore teen lanky and tall enough to have resembled Damon.

It had all happened because of me. But beyond knowing that Sunday was an obsessive, homicidal narcissist, I did not fully understand his actions.

Acadia Le Duc had been interviewed about it, and she said she'd asked Sunday the same thing on repeated occasions. Some of the time he'd replied that he was using me as living proof of his philosophical theories, and other times he'd told her he was doing it to me simply because he could.

Both reasons upset me. They still do.

But I'd been talking with Dr. Adele Finaly, an old and dear friend as well as a shrink of the highest caliber. It helped. And Bree had also found someone to talk to. So had the kids. And my grandmother had her priest.

For the most part, we *were* good. In ways, we'd never been closer, and as the starter called the athletes to their marks, I chose to embrace the good in my life and push all thoughts of Marcus Sunday aside.

All our focus went to Jannie when he called, “Set.”

The gun cracked, and they took off.

We screamed and cheered, and it was as if all the terrible things that had happened to my family no longer existed, because when the other girls on the track ran like the wind, our Jannie believed and came on like a hurricane.

ABOUT THE AUTHOR

JAMES PATTERSON has created more enduring fictional characters than any other novelist writing today. He is the author of the Alex Cross novels, the most popular detective series of the past twenty-five years. His other bestselling novels feature the Women's Murder Club, Michael Bennett, Private, and NYPD Red. Since his first novel won the Edgar Award in 1977, James Patterson's books have sold more than 300 million copies.

James Patterson has also written numerous #1 bestsellers for young readers, including the Maximum Ride, Witch & Wizard, Middle School, and Treasure Hunters series. In total, these books have spent more than 330 weeks on national bestseller lists. In 2010, James Patterson was named Author of the Year at the Children's Choice Book Awards.

His lifelong passion for books and reading led James Patterson to create the innovative website ReadKiddoRead.com, giving adults an invaluable tool to find the books that get kids reading for life. He writes full-time and lives in Florida with his family.

BOOKS BY JAMES PATTERSON
FEATURING ALEX CROSS

Hope to Die
Cross My Heart
Alex Cross, Run
Merry Christmas, Alex Cross
Kill Alex Cross
Cross Fire
I, Alex Cross
Alex Cross's Trial (with Richard DiLallo)
Cross Country
Double Cross
Cross (also published as *Alex Cross*)
Mary, Mary
London Bridges
The Big Bad Wolf
Four Blind Mice
Violets Are Blue
Roses Are Red
Pop Goes the Weasel
Cat & Mouse
Jack & Jill
Kiss the Girls
Along Came a Spider

THE WOMEN'S MURDER CLUB

14th Deadly Sin (with Maxine Paetro)
Unlucky 13 (with Maxine Paetro)
12th of Never (with Maxine Paetro)
11th Hour (with Maxine Paetro)
10th Anniversary (with Maxine Paetro)
The 9th Judgment (with Maxine Paetro)
The 8th Confession (with Maxine Paetro)
7th Heaven (with Maxine Paetro)
The 6th Target (with Maxine Paetro)
The 5th Horseman (with Maxine Paetro)
4th of July (with Maxine Paetro)
3rd Degree (with Andrew Gross)
2nd Chance (with Andrew Gross)
1st to Die

FEATURING MICHAEL BENNETT

Burn (with Michael Ledwidge)
Gone (with Michael Ledwidge)
I, Michael Bennett (with Michael Ledwidge)
Tick Tock (with Michael Ledwidge)
Worst Case (with Michael Ledwidge)
Run for Your Life (with Michael Ledwidge)
Step on a Crack (with Michael Ledwidge)

THE PRIVATE NOVELS

Private Vegas (with Maxine Paetro)
Private India: City on Fire (with Ashwin Sanghi)
Private Down Under (with Michael White)
Private L.A. (with Mark Sullivan)
Private Berlin (with Mark Sullivan)
Private London (with Mark Pearson)
Private Games (with Mark Sullivan)
Private: #1 Suspect (with Maxine Paetro)
Private (with Maxine Paetro)

THE NYPD RED NOVELS

NYPD Red 3 (with Marshall Karp)
NYPD Red 2 (with Marshall Karp)
NYPD Red (with Marshall Karp)

STANDALONE BOOKS

Miracle at Augusta (with Peter de Jonge)
Invisible (with David Ellis)
Mistress (with David Ellis)

Second Honeymoon (with Howard Roughan)
Zoo (with Michael Ledwidge)
Guilty Wives (with David Ellis)
The Christmas Wedding (with Richard DiLallo)
Kill Me If You Can (with Marshall Karp)
Now You See Her (with Michael Ledwidge)
Toys (with Neil McMahon)
Don't Blink (with Howard Roughan)
The Postcard Killers (with Liza Marklund)
The Murder of King Tut (with Martin Dugard)
Swimsuit (with Maxine Paetro)
Against Medical Advice (with Hal Friedman)
Sail (with Howard Roughan)
Sundays at Tiffany's (with Gabrielle Charbonnet)
You've Been Warned (with Howard Roughan)
The Quickie (with Michael Ledwidge)
Judge & Jury (with Andrew Gross)
Beach Road (with Peter de Jonge)
Lifeguard (with Andrew Gross)
Honeymoon (with Howard Roughan)
Sam's Letters to Jennifer
The Lake House
The Jester (with Andrew Gross)
The Beach House (with Peter de Jonge)
Suzanne's Diary for Nicholas
Cradle and All
When the Wind Blows
Miracle on the 17th Green (with Peter de Jonge)
Hide & Seek
The Midnight Club
Black Friday (originally published as *Black Market*)
See How They Run (originally published as *The Jericho Commandment*)
Season of the Machete
The Thomas Berryman Number

FOR ADULTS AND TEENS

Maximum Ride Forever
Witch & Wizard: The Lost (with Emily Raymond)
Confessions: The Paris Mysteries (with Maxine Paetro)
Homeroom Diaries (with Lisa Papademetriou, illustrated by Keino)
First Love (with Emily Raymond)
Confessions: The Private School Murders (with Maxine Paetro)
Witch & Wizard: The Kiss (with Jill Dembowski)
Confessions of a Murder Suspect (with Maxine Paetro)
Nevermore: A Maximum Ride Novel
Witch & Wizard: The Fire (with Jill Dembowski)
Angel: A Maximum Ride Novel
Witch & Wizard: The Gift (with Ned Rust)
Med Head (with Hal Friedman)
FANG: A Maximum Ride Novel
Witch & Wizard (with Gabrielle Charbonnet)
MAX: A Maximum Ride Novel
The Final Warning: A Maximum Ride Novel
Saving the World and Other Extreme Sports: A Maximum Ride Novel
School's Out—Forever: A Maximum Ride Novel
Maximum Ride: The Angel Experiment

FOR YOUNGER READERS

Public School Superhero (with Chris Tebbetts, illustrated by Cory Thomas)
I Totally Funniest (with Chris Grabenstein, illustrated by Laura Park)
House of Robots (with Chris Grabenstein, illustrated by Juliana Neufeld)
Treasure Hunters: Danger Down the Nile (with Chris Grabenstein, illustrated by Juliana Neufeld)
Middle School, Save Rafe! (with Chris Tebbetts, illustrated by Laura Park)
Middle School, Ultimate Showdown (with Julia Bergen, illustrated by Alec Longstreth)

I Even Funnier (with Chris Grabenstein, illustrated by Laura Park)
Treasure Hunters (with Chris Grabenstein and Mark Shulman, illustrated by Juliana Neufeld)
Middle School, How I Survived Bullies, Broccoli, and Snake Hill (with Chris Tebbetts, illustrated by Laura Park)
Middle School, My Brother Is a Big, Fat Liar (with Lisa Papademetriou, illustrated by Neil Swaab)
I Funny (with Chris Grabenstein)
Daniel X: Armageddon (with Chris Grabenstein)
Middle School, Get Me out of Here! (with Chris Tebbetts, illustrated by Laura Park)
Daniel X: Game Over (with Ned Rust)
Middle School, The Worst Years of My Life (with Chris Tebbetts, illustrated by Laura Park)
Daniel X: Demons and Druids (with Adam Sadler)
Daniel X: Watch the Skies (with Ned Rust)
The Dangerous Days of Daniel X (with Michael Ledwidge)
santaKid

MANGA AND GRAPHIC NOVELS

Daniel X: The Manga 1–3 (with SeungHui Kye)
Daniel X: Alien Hunter (with Leopoldo Gout)
Maximum Ride: The Manga 1–8 (with NaRae Lee)
Witch & Wizard: The Manga 1–3 (with Svetlana Chmakova)
Zoo: The Graphic Novel (with Andy MacDonald)

For previews of upcoming books and more information about James Patterson, please visit JamesPatterson.com or find him on Facebook or at your app store.

THE TRUTH WILL SET YOU FREE—IF IT DOESN'T KILL YOU FIRST...

“WHERE EXACTLY did it happen?” I asked.

“West End Avenue at Seventy-Third. The taxi was stopped at a red light,” said Lamont. “The assailant smashed the driver’s side window, pistol-whipped the driver until he was knocked out cold, and grabbed his money bag. He then robbed Ms. Parker at gunpoint.”

“Claire,” I said.

“Excuse me?”

“Please call her Claire.”

I knew it was a weird thing for me to say, but weirder still was hearing Lamont refer to Claire as Ms. Parker, not that I blamed him. Victims are always Mr., Mrs., or Ms. for a detective. He was supposed to call her that. I just wasn’t ready to hear it.

“I apologize,” I said. “It’s just that— ”

“Don’t worry about it,” he said with a raised palm. He understood. He got it.

"So what happened next?" I asked. "What went wrong?"

"We're not sure, exactly. Best we can tell, she fully cooperated, didn't put up a fight."

That made sense. Claire might have been your prototypical "tough" New Yorker, but she was also no fool. She didn't own anything she'd risk her life to keep. *Does anyone?*

No, she definitely knew the drill. Never be a statistic. If your taxi gets jacked, you do exactly as told.

"And you said the driver was knocked out, right? He didn't hear anything?" I asked.

"Not even the gunshots," said Lamont. "In fact, he didn't actually regain consciousness until after the first two officers arrived at the scene."

"Who called it in?"

"An older couple walking nearby."

"What did they see?"

"The shooter running back to his car, which was behind the taxi. They were thirty or forty yards away; they didn't get a good look."

"Any other witnesses?"

"You'd think, but no. Then again, residential block…after midnight," he said. "We'll obviously follow up in the area tomorrow. Talk to the driver, too. He was taken to St. Luke's before we arrived."

I leaned back in my chair, a metal hinge somewhere below the seat creaking its age. I must have had a dozen more questions for Lamont, each one trying to get me that much closer to being in the taxi with Claire, to knowing what had really happened.

To knowing whether or not it truly was…*fuckin' random.*

But I wasn't fooling anyone. Not Lamont, and especially

not myself. All I was doing was procrastinating, trying hopelessly to avoid asking the one question I was truly dreading.

I couldn't avoid it any longer.

"FOR THE record, you were never in here," said Lamont, pausing at a closed door toward the back corner of the precinct house.

I stared at him blankly as if I were some chronic sufferer of short-term memory loss. *"In where?"* I asked.

He smirked. Then he opened the door.

The windowless room I followed him into was only slightly bigger than claustrophobic. After closing the door behind us, Lamont introduced me to his partner, Detective Mike McGeary, who was at the helm of what looked like one of those video arcade games where you sit in a captain's chair shooting at alien spaceships on a large screen. He was even holding what looked like a joystick.

McGeary, square-jawed and bald, gave Lamont a sideways glance that all but screamed, *What the hell is he doing in here?*

"Mr. Mann was a close acquaintance of the victim," said Lamont. He added a slight emphasis on my last name, as if to jog his partner's memory.

McGeary studied me in the dim light of the room until he put my face and name together. Perhaps he was remembering the cover of the *New York Post* a couple of years back. *An Honest Mann,* read the headline.

"Yeah, fine," McGeary said finally.

It wasn't exactly a ringing endorsement, but it was enough to consider the issue of my being there resolved. I could stay. I could see the recording.

I could watch, frame by frame, the murder of the woman I loved.

Lamont hadn't had to tell me there was a surveillance camera in the taxi. I'd known right away, given how he'd described the shooting over the phone, some of the details he had. There were little things no eyewitnesses could ever provide. Had there been any eyewitnesses, that is.

Lamont removed his glasses, wearily pinching the bridge of his nose. No one ever truly gets used to the graveyard shift. "Any matches so far?" he asked his partner.

McGeary shook his head.

I glanced at the large monitor, which had shifted into screen saver mode, an NYPD logo floating about. Lamont, I could tell, was waiting for me to ask him about the space-age console, the reason I wasn't supposed to be in the room. The machine obviously did a little more than just digital playback.

But I didn't ask. I already knew.

I'm sure the thing had an official name, something ultra-high-tech sounding, but back when I was in the DA's office I'd only ever heard it referred to by its nickname, CrackerJack. What it did was combine every known recognition software program into one giant cross-referencing "decoder" that was linked to practically every criminal database in the country, as well as those from twenty-three other countries, or basically all of our official allies in the "war on terror."

In short, given any image at any angle of any suspected terrorist, CrackerJack could source a litany of identifying characteristics, be it an exposed mole or tattoo; the exact measurements between the suspect's eyes, ears, nose, and mouth; or even a piece of jewelry. Clothing, too. Apparently, for all the precautions terrorists take in their planning, it rarely occurs to them that wearing the same polyester shirt in London, Cairo, and Islamabad might be a bad idea.

Of course, it didn't take long for law enforcement in major cities—where CrackerJacks were heavily deployed by the Department of Homeland Security—to realize that these machines didn't have to identify just terrorists. Anyone with a criminal record was fair game.

So here was McGeary going through the recording sent over by the New York Taxi & Limousine Commission to see if any image of the shooter triggered a match. And here was me, having asked if I could watch it, too.

"Mike, cue it up from the beginning, will you?" said Lamont.

McGeary punched a button and then another until the screen lit up with the first frame, the taxi having pulled over to pick Claire up. The image was grainy, black-and-white, like on an old tube television with a set of rabbit ears. But what little I could see was still way too much.

It was exactly as Lamont had described it. The shooter smashes the driver's side window, beating the driver senseless with the butt of his gun. He's wearing a dark turtleneck and a ski mask with holes for the eyes, nose, and mouth. His gloves are tight, like those Isotoners that O. J. Simpson pretended didn't fit.

So far, Claire is barely visible. Not once can I see her face. Then I do.

It's right after the shooter snatches the driver's money bag. He swings his gun, aiming it at Claire in the backseat. She jolts. There's no Plexiglas divider. There's nothing but air.

Presumably, he says something to her, but the back of his head is toward the camera. Claire offers up her purse. He takes it and she says something. I was never any good at reading lips.

He should be leaving. Running away. Instead, he swings out and around, opening the rear door. He's out of frame for no more than three seconds. Then all I see is his outstretched arm. And the fear in her eyes.

He fires two shots at point-blank range. *Did he panic?* Not enough to flee right away. Quickly, he riffles through her pockets, and then tears off her earrings, followed by her watch, the Rolex Milgauss I gave her for her thirtieth birthday. He dumps everything in her purse and takes off.

"Wait a minute," I said suddenly. "Go back a little bit."

LAMONT AND McGeary both turned to me, their eyes asking if I was crazy. *You want to watch her being murdered a second time?*

No, I didn't. Not a chance.

Watching it the first time made me so nauseous I thought I'd throw up right there on the floor. I wanted that recording erased, deleted, destroyed for all eternity not two seconds after it was used to catch the goddamn son of a bitch who'd done this.

Then I wanted a long, dark alley in the dead of night where he and I could have a little time alone together. Yeah. *That's* what I wanted.

But I thought I saw something.

Up until that moment, I hadn't known what I was looking for in the recording, if anything. If Claire had been standing next to me, she, with her love of landmark Supreme Court cases, would've described it as the definition of pornography according to Justice Potter Stewart in *Jacobellis v. Ohio.*

I know it when I see it.

She'd always admired the simplicity of that. Not everything that's true has to be proven, she used to say.

"Where to?" asked McGeary, his hand hovering over a knob that could rewind frame by frame, if need be.

"Just after he beats the driver," I said.

He nodded. "Say when."

I watched the sped-up images, everything happening in reverse. If only I could reverse it all for real. I was waiting for the part when the gun was turned on Claire. A few moments before that, actually.

"Stop," I said. "Right there."

McGeary hit Play again and I leaned in, my eyes glued to the screen. Meanwhile, I could feel Lamont's eyes glued to my profile, as if he could somehow better see what I was looking for by watching me.

"What is it?" he eventually asked.

I stepped back, shaking my head as if disappointed. "Nothing," I said. "It wasn't anything."

Because that's exactly what Claire would've wanted me to say. A little white lie for the greater good, she would've called it.

She was always a quick thinker, right up until the end.

NO WAY in hell did I feel like taking a taxi home.

In fact, I didn't feel like going home at all. In my mind, I'd already put my apartment on the market, packed up all my belongings, and moved to another neighborhood, maybe even out of Manhattan altogether. Claire *was* the city to me. Bright. Vibrant.

Alive.

And now she wasn't.

I passed a bar, looking through the window at the smattering of "patrons," to put it politely, who were still drinking at three in the morning. I could see an empty stool and it was calling my name. More like shouting it, really.

Don't, I told myself. *When you sober up, she'll still be gone.*

I kept walking in the direction of my apartment, but with every step it became clear where I truly wanted to go. It was wherever Claire had been going.

Who was she meeting?

Suddenly, I was channeling Oliver Stone, somehow trying to link her murder to the story she'd been chasing. But that was crazy. I saw her murder in black and white. It was a robbery. She was in the wrong place at the wrong time, and as much as that was a cliché, so, too, was her death. She'd be the first to admit it.

"Imagine that," I could hear her saying. "A victim of violent crime in New York City. *How original.*"

Still, I'd become fixated on wanting to know where she'd been heading when she left my apartment. A two-hundred-dollar-an-hour shrink would probably call that sublimated grief, while the four-hundred-dollar-an-hour shrink would probably counter with sublimated anger. I was sticking with overwhelming curiosity.

I put myself in her shoes, mentally tracing her steps through the lobby of my building and out to the sidewalk. As soon as I pictured her raising her arm for a taxi, it occurred to me. *The driver.* He at least knew the address. For sure, Claire gave it to him when he picked her up.

Almost on cue, a taxi slowed down next to me at the curb, the driver wondering if I needed a ride. That was a common occurrence late at night when supply far outweighed demand.

As I shook him off, I began thinking of what else Claire's driver might remember when Lamont interviewed him. Tough to say after the beating he took. Maybe the shooter had said something that would key his identity, or at least thin out the suspects. Did he speak with any kind of accent?

Or maybe the driver had seen something that wasn't visible to that surveillance camera. Eye color? An odd-shaped mole? A chipped tooth?

Unfortunately, the list of possibilities didn't go on and on.

The ski mask, turtleneck, and gloves made sure of that. Clearly, the bastard knew that practically every taxi in the city was its own little recording studio. So much for cameras being a deterrent.

As the old expression goes, show me a ten-foot wall and I'll show you an eleven-foot ladder.

The twenty blocks separating me from my apartment were a daze. I was on autopilot, one foot in front of the other. Only at the sound of the keys as I dropped them on my kitchen counter did I snap out of it, realizing I was actually home.

Fully dressed, I fell into my bed, shoes and all. I didn't even bother turning off the lights. But my eyes were closed for only a few seconds before they popped open. *Damn.* All it took was one breath, one exchange of the air around me, and I was lying there feeling more alone than I ever had in my entire life.

The sheets still smelled of her.

I sat up, looking over at the other side of the bed…the pillow. I could still make out the impression of Claire's head. That was the word, wasn't it? *Impression.* Hers was everywhere, most of all on me.

I was about to make a beeline to my guest room, which, if anything, would smell of dust or staleness or whatever other odor is given off by a room that's rarely, if ever, used. I didn't care. So long as it wasn't her.

Suddenly, though, I froze. Something had caught my eye. It was the yellow legal pad on the end of the bed, the one Claire had used when she took the phone call. She'd ripped off the top sheet she'd written on.

But the one beneath it…